DEFENDING SARINA (SPECIAL FORCES: OPERATION ALPHA)

MORGAN THOMPSON SECURITY, BOOK 1

DANIELLE PAYS

This book is a work of fiction. Names, characters, places, and incidents are products of the author's imagination or used fictitiously. Any resemblance to actual events or locales or persons living or dead is entirely coincidental.

Cover Photography: Furious Fotog/Golden Czermak
Cover Designer: Maria @ Steamy Designs
Editing: April Bennett, The Editing Soprano
Proofreading: ReGina Raham

Dear Readers,

Welcome to the Special Forces: Operation Alpha Fan-Fiction world!

If you are new to this amazing world, in a nutshell the author wrote a story using one or more of my characters in it. Sometimes that character has a major role in the story, and other times they are only mentioned briefly. This is perfectly legal and allowable because they are going through Aces Press to publish the story.

This book is entirely the work of the author who wrote it. While I might have assisted with brainstorming and other ideas about which of my characters to use, I didn't have any part in the process or writing or editing the story.

I'm proud and excited that so many authors loved my characters enough that they wanted to write them into their own story. Thank you for supporting them, and me!

READ ON!

Xoxo

Susan Stoker

CHAPTER 1

DONNY "MAVERICK" REIS

"SHIT, MAVERICK! THAT HURT." Rover aka Dax Adams, my friend and coworker, rubs the side of his head where the paintball hit.

"You're supposed to stay below the neck!" Rover complains.

I chuckle. "I would have if you hadn't ducked at the last minute."

"Maverick, Rover, CT, I need you to come to my office."

Stormy, my boss, stands in the back doorway of Morgan Thompson Security.

"Break's over," Stormy says.

It might look like a break to some, but we all know this is part of our regular training and I'm thankful Stormy has agreed to let us play paintball in the woods on the back half of the property.

"Looks like you got in a cheap shot, Maverick," Stormy says with a grin.

"He ducked!" I defend.

"Clean up and get in here. I don't want any of that shit in my office." Stormy shakes his head and goes back into the building.

Stormy may have sounded pissed but we know better. He's the reason we use the wooded area behind the office building for paintball and other tactical training.

"Hey, you guys quit and didn't tell me?" CT says as he steps out from the trees with not one drop of paint on him.

"Stormy wants to see us," I tell him.

"Okay, let's go." CT walks toward the door.

"Hey, we have to clean up first," I say as I motion to the paint smeared on my leg.

CT smirks. "I'll meet you in there."

Before he can get a foot in the doorway, Rover aims and fires.

"Fuck!" CT jumps, rubbing his ass.

"Hang out with us. It's so much more fun," Rover says.

I laugh so hard I have to lean against the wall.

"You're supposed to have my six, asshole," CT says.

"Not in paintball."

I peel off the coveralls that provide some protection from the paint as CT and Rover do the same. The chill of the November air hits me as I deposit the paint-stained clothes into a bin kept by the door. Rover is rubbing his head with the coveralls trying to get off some of the offending paint. I snort and head inside to Stormy's office.

He has the largest office in the building even though he co-owns the company with Josh Morgan, or Cowboy, as Stormy calls him. Cowboy is rarely around and leaves all the day-to-day operations to Stormy.

"CT, can you close the door behind you?"

He closes the door then takes a seat. "Instead of CT, I'd like to be called Dozer now. Short for Bulldozer."

Rover and I laugh. Stormy shakes his head. At least once a week, CT tries to convince us to change his call sign. A call sign he got after a night of drinking and one unfortunate decision."

The name stuck.

"Dozer? Not a chance. Besides, it's too close to mine," Rover says.

"Rover. Dozer. Not really." CT grins.

"Sit your ass down, CT," Stormy says.

I bite back my laugh.

"This is serious. This assignment is local but it's a matter of national security," Stormy says.

National security? That has my attention.

CT sits in the chair next to me.

"I was contacted by Chief Petty Officer Cramer. This morning a truck that was carrying a very important piece of equipment for the Navy was run off the road. It is imperative we get this equipment back before it finds its way out of the United States."

Cramer had been our superior when CT, Rover, and I served together. What a small world he's here in Washington now too.

"I didn't see any headline about that," CT says glancing at his phone.

"And you won't. Not if we can help it. Cramer believes an insider tipped someone off because few people knew what was on the transport."

"Inside the Navy?" Rover asks.

"Yes, or Asher Vaughn Enterprises."

"Asher Vaughn? Shit. Did they take a missile?" I ask.

Asher Vaughn is the main manufacturer of military defense equipment and the largest supplier to the Navy.

"Technically not. It's worse," Stormy says.

Stormy flips his laptop around, revealing something much worse indeed.

"The PV Transport truck was transporting a Laser Weapon System called Peggy to the Naval Base on Whidbey Island for training. It's one of the newer systems manufactured by Asher Vaughn. While en route, they entered a two-lane highway. A truck turned onto the highway from a side road in front of the lead truck. The driver then slammed on his brakes. The driver of the transport veered to his right to avoid a collision. Four men then exited the front truck and commandeered the other vehicles."

Stormy turns his laptop back around and clasps his hands.

"Six of PV Transport's men were killed at the scene. The driver of the front truck was shot and is in surgery now. Another man had been shot and was conscious when aid arrived. He's the one that stated they had four men. He has since passed."

"Whoever's behind this knows the drivers are trained to avoid collisions. That person also knew the route the transport was taking and when it would be vulnerable."

"You said they had four men? Then they also must've been well-trained," Rover says. "After I got out of the service, I looked into getting a contract job with a transport company and they had high standards."

"This place was your second choice?" CT asks, feigning shock.

"No, dipshit. This was before I talked to you and found out there was an opening here. Morgan Thompson Security is my first choice."

Knowing that these two could bicker all day, I redirect the conversation. "Where did the transport originate?"

Stormy frowns at the other two men in the room before turning his attention to me.

"And who all knew about the transport?" I ask.

"According to Cramer, only a handful of people should have known. But since he can't rule out it was someone on the inside, he's hired us. As of now, only seven people know what happened to this transport."

"Seven plus the men who stole it."

Stormy nodded.

"You said it could be someone at Asher Vaughn. Why would they know the transport route?" I ask.

"I don't know if they do. It's just a possibility. They certainly knew it was on its way to the Navy base. Sadly, we don't know anything more about it."

The idea that someone from inside the Navy could've been involved in the theft of this weapon makes me sick.

"Maverick, I'd like you to go to Asher Vaughn. The VP of weapons systems is expecting you. Her name is Sarina McIntyre. CT, I need you to meet with Cramer on base. Rover, I want you to talk to the driver when he comes out of surgery. And dig into the other drivers. How long had they been working for PV Transport?"

I glance at the other guys and I'm sure they're thinking the same thing.

Please don't let this be a Navy leak.

"Report everything back to me," Stormy says. "Now go."

"I don't like this," CT says as we walk out to the parking lot.

"I don't either," Rover agrees.

None of us do. To steal a few military guns was one thing, but this?

"What are you thinking? A foreign government?" I ask.

I'd been chewing on the idea since Stormy first told us what happened.

"Could be. Or terrorists." CT pulls a fob out of his pocket and unlocks his car.

Car being an understatement. The man had recently purchased a red Audi sports car.

"You know you stand out in that thing," Rover says as he throws a leg over his motorcycle.

"Stand out to all the ladies, you mean." CT winks. "I'll check in as soon as I know something."

"Sounds good." I hop in my Yukon and I follow them out of the lot and head to Asher Vaughn.

CHAPTER 2

DONNY

THE SECURITY at Asher Vaughn is impressive for a commercial enterprise. Although, this location houses the manufacturing of the defense equipment sold directly to the United States military.

As I drive toward the guard gate, I take note of the tall fence surrounding the entire company. At the top is what appears to be barbed wire. Off to my left is a guard tower. Due to the tinted glass, I can't see if anyone is in there. And I've already spotted three cameras aimed at the road leading toward the complex.

I pull up to the guard at the gate.

"What is your business here?" he asks.

"I'm Donny Reis, here to see Sarina McIntyre. She's expecting me."

I shoot him a smile, but he doesn't smile back.

"Just a minute." The guard returns to his booth and makes a phone call. I scan what I can of the fenced-in area while he talks. Through the gate is a large warehouse to the left and a five-story office building set towards the rear of the property.

"Yes, Mr. Reis, Ms. McIntyre is expecting you in 10-05."

The man holds up a map of the premises. "Follow this road around to your right." He marks a building with an X. "There is visitor parking on the ground level. Then go to the second-floor reception and let them know you're there."

I take the map and visitor pass from him.

"Thank you."

The man nods and then the secured gate in front of me opens. I drive slowly inside and follow his directions.

Once I'm parked in the ground level garage, I grab the visitor badge and note that it has today's date on it.

Despite only needing to go up one floor, I opt for the elevator. When the doors open, there is a large waiting area filled with expensive-looking furniture and to the left is a rather large, impressive indoor fountain surrounded by several tropical plants. Natural daylight streams in from the windows on that side of the building.

A handful of people in the waiting area are typing on their laptops.

I make my way to the reception desk and am greeted by a young brunette woman who smiles brightly.

"Welcome to Asher Vaughn. How can I help you today?"

No reason for her not to be happy. With the security they have around this place, it isn't like she's dealing with the regular public.

"I'm here to see Sarina McIntyre."

"Is she expecting you?" she asks.

"She is."

"Great. Have a seat and I'll let her know you're here."

I give her a nod and then walk to a chair next to the window where I can scan everyone here. That's when I notice that this part of the lobby opens up to a skylight four floors above.

I check my phone to see if Stormy or the guys have sent any more information. I've just confirmed they have not when I sense someone walking toward me.

I glance up and lock eyes with her. Her dark hair is pulled back at the nape of her neck and she's wearing a gray suit that, while looking professional, also looks sexy as hell. I imagine what she looks like with her hair down, her jacket cast off, her skirt—I shake my head then return my gaze to her. She arches a brow. I stand. I have to know her name. Fortunately, she walks directly to me. Maybe she feels this attraction as much as I do.

"Mr. Reis?"

Or maybe not.

"Yes."

She stretches her hand out. "I'm Sarina McIntyre, Executive Vice President of Weapons Systems."

I take her hand. She gives mine a firm shake and I hold on a beat longer than necessary. Her hand is small but feels so right in mine before I release it. She frowns but quickly catches herself as she pulls her hand back. Shit, now I probably look like a creeper.

"Follow me please," she says with no expression. I can't read her.

She turns and as I follow her out of the atrium and down a long hallway, my eyes can't help but zero in on her ass as it sways in her skirt. And her legs, they are long. She's wearing heels which puts her only a couple of inches shorter than my six foot two. That means she's a tall woman. I force my gaze up. Seriously, I need to focus on the task at hand. But something about this woman causes a strong reaction inside me.

"In here." She motions for me to enter a conference room.

The walls are all windows so anyone walking by can see what's going on.

"Let me guess. The fishbowl?"

She smiles. "Not very creative but yes."

If I had to guess, there's a video camera in here too. A company like this can never be too secure. Although maybe they weren't if someone here leaked information leading to the truck-jacking earlier.

"Please have a seat." She motions to the other side of the table as she sits down. But instead of sitting across from her, I pull out the chair next to her, subtly scooting back a little to give us more space. Then I sit down.

"Ms. McIntyre, are you aware of the situation that occurred this morning during the transport?"

She nods. "I've been briefed. I understand six men are dead." She swallows and I sense she's trying hard to remain calm. "And that your firm has been hired to investigate the situation."

"It's correct that six are dead but fortunately the driver that was cut off survived. My partner is questioning him now."

She nods again and sniffles.

"Did you know any of the men involved?"

She narrows her eyes as she stares at me.

"No. Why would I?"

"You seem very affected. I thought perhaps you did."

Her nose wiggles and she moves her arm and sneezes into it, then she sniffles again.

"I'm not crying if that is what you think. I'm allergic to cats and one of my coworkers has a lot of cats. Sadly, I often react after I've met with her."

"That's unfortunate."

"Yes, it is. Now, regarding why you're here, I'm not sure how I can help. I don't deal with the transport company."

I lean back and study her. She's sitting up straight and making eye contact, yet she is tapping her foot. Is it impatience or nerves?

"Can you give me the names of everyone here that knew the item was set to be delivered today?"

She reaches for a pad of paper and pen from the center of the table and proceeds to write. When she finishes, she hands it to me.

"Aside from me, there's the director of the program, Norah Jensen. She has several managers but only one who's involved in this program, Tim Maddow. I spoke to him, and he said he had one direct employee who was in contact with the Navy and the transport team."

I stared at the list. "Only four employees?"

She nodded.

"What about your boss?"

She reaches to her neck and touches the charm on her necklace. It's a gold four-leaf clover. "Sorry. You're right. I report directly to the CEO, Jim Albright."

Five potential suspects at Asher Vaughn.

"I'd like to meet the other four employees who knew about the delivery."

She frowns. "I can try but Jim usually won't take meetings off the fourth floor."

I flash her a smile. "I have no problem going up to the fourth floor."

Her cheeks flush pink.

"I'm sorry but you don't have permission."

I cock my head. "I'm a former SEAL. If this is about security, I have clearance at most levels."

She turns toward me crossing her legs. It takes all my strength to keep my eyes on hers.

"You have military clearance, not Asher Vaughn clearance."

I chuckle. It's the first time I don't have the clearance necessary. I'll find a way.

"Ms. McIntyre?"

I turn to see a young woman with red hair smiling at me.

"Your next appointment is waiting in your office."

"Thank you, Melanie. I'll be right there."

She leaves us alone.

"I'll ask Melanie to call the others in here for your questions, but I suspect only Tim will come down."

Is she stonewalling me? Is this coming from her? Or her boss?

I nod. "Thank you."

I stand as she stands, and I extend my hand again.

She shakes it and damn, I don't want to let go. But the last thing I need is to be attracted to a potential suspect. Especially one that appears to be difficult.

She glances down at her hands. I'm still holding hers. I release it and she backs up.

"It was nice to meet you, Mr. Reis."

"Please. Call me Donny."

"Donny." She smiles.

"Here," I say as I pull out my card. "If you think of anything more, please call me."

She takes it. "I will."

Before I could say anything else, she turns and walks out of the room.

CHAPTER 3

Sarina McIntyre

"Sorry to interrupt your meeting but Jim said he wanted to see you right away," my assistant says as we walked toward the elevators.

I hide my frustration. Jim always wants me at his beck and call. I'm a VP, not his personal assistant. But that's between me and Jim so I put on a smile.

"Oh, that's fine. I was just about done with Mr. Reis anyway."

Donny Reis. He's not what I'd expected. Not that I really knew what to expect.

Melanie laughed. "If I was in a room with a man like that, I'd sure as hell want more time."

I shook my head. I loved Melanie. She said things as they were and never held back. I'd heard about Morgan Thompson Security, but in my mind I pictured someone much older. Not the young hottie who walked in. Damn. I don't recall ever seeing someone that good looking in person before.

"He was pretty hot, wasn't he?"

As we reach the elevator, Melanie fans herself with the file in her hand. "So hot."

Someone coughs behind us. I spin around to see Donny standing only a few feet away wearing a smirk.

Oh, dear god, he heard every word. Thankfully it isn't a long wait and the doors open. I step in the elevator and turn to take one last look at him.

"For the record, I think you're hot too," he says just as the doors separate us.

"Holy shit! Should we go back down there?" Melanie asks.

I reach for the charm on my necklace. "No, that was highly inappropriate."

And why the hell was he behind us? He was supposed to wait in the conference room.

I didn't have long to ponder it because the moment I get off the elevator, Jim is waiting for me.

"Sarina, we need to talk privately."

"Melanie, can you ask Norah and Tim to speak with Mr. Reis?"

"Sure thing, boss. Then I'll go tell Mr. Reis when to expect them." Melanie grins as she walks off towards her desk.

I bite back my laugh. I bet she'd tell him in person.

"Actually, Melanie, please don't do that. It won't be necessary," Jim says.

Melanie frowns.

"It won't?" I ask.

"No, if we can go into your office, I'll explain."

I follow Jim into my office, turning to shrug at my assistant.

He leans against the wall and sighs. "I had hoped to catch

you before you met with that guy from the security firm. I plan to set up our own investigative team."

I sit down behind my desk. "Are you saying you don't want to cooperate with their investigation?"

Jim runs his hands through his hair.

"I'm not saying that."

Jim stares at me, clearly unwilling to say more.

"And how do you want to explain to Mr. Reis that while we are cooperating, he cannot speak to Norah or Tim?"

Jim smiles. "Tell him whatever you want."

"Are you concerned Norah or Tim might reveal classified information?"

He shakes his head. "I'm concerned that Chief Petty Officer Cramer hired this firm for the sole purpose of making sure we take the blame. The board is concerned too that the Navy is looking for someone with deep pockets to hold accountable. That's why we're setting up our own investigative team and I want you to be in charge of that."

Me? He has to be kidding.

"Jim, I can't just drop everything I'm doing for this. We are on the cusp of military approval for the Allen project. No one else can handle that."

There's a knock at my door and we both turn to see Norah standing in the doorway. Her eyes lock on Jim. She's wearing a new pin on her lapel. This one appears to be a white kitten. All her pins are of cats or kittens.

"Sorry to interrupt but I couldn't help overhear the last part. Sarina, I'd be happy to take over the investigation for you."

That's surprising since Norah expressed concern over her workload last week but I'll let it go. I'm happy to pass this off to anyone else.

Jim smiles. "That would be great. Thank you, Norah."

Then Jim shoves his hands into his pants pockets. "I have

a meeting to get to. I'm sure you two can discuss this without me."

He leaves before I can ask him any more questions. Why the hell would he think the Navy would try to frame our company? It doesn't make sense. We're their largest vendor in terms of weapons and supplies. Hurting us would only hurt them.

"Sorry, I really didn't mean to listen in," Norah says as she drops into a chair across from me. She begins tapping her fingers on the arm of the chair.

I bite back my smile. That's a sign she's nervous. It's also something I've seen her do on a few other occasions. The first time was when she was presenting a new idea to Jim at a meeting a few months ago.

"It's fine." Normally I'd be irritated but the fact she took this task off my plate alleviates that.

The light catches on her earrings. I've never seen Norah wearing diamonds before.

"I love your earrings. Are they new?"

Her hand goes to one ear. "Yes. A gift from my father."

"I didn't think you spoke with him."

Norah has been tight lipped about a lot of her life, but I do recall her mentioning this once at a happy hour.

"He got in contact last week. He's between jobs so he's in the area. I've spoken to him a few times. It's been nice. I even agreed to let him stay in my rental property since it was vacant."

That's very generous for a man who basically abandoned her. I've been to the house. She could probably get two thousand dollars a month for rent, easy.

"Jobs? What does he do?"

She smiles. "He's a food critic."

"That sounds fun."

Since we're the only two women in upper management,

we've grown close. Norah is older and has on more than one occasion told me I remind her of the daughter she never had.

"About the investigation—" she starts.

I hold up my hand. "I really don't have time to take that on, so if you're able to head it up, that would be great."

"Consider it done. Besides, it'll be fun making my managers sweat."

I frown, not following her line of thinking.

She leans forward. "I'll start by questioning them. Tim always assumes I'm mad at him about something." She rolls her eyes.

Melanie knocks on the open door as she walks in. "Sarina, Phillip from Prince's Parts is on the phone, and he isn't happy."

I close my eyes. "I need to take this."

Phillip Prince is the CEO of Prince Parts and if he's calling, something is wrong. I've been pushing him and his company to meet the deadline on the Allen project and hopefully I haven't pissed the man off with my demands. But he must understand, normally a VP wouldn't deal with issues of this nature. But this is important so here I am.

"Of course. I'll let you get back to work," Norah says.

"What about Mr. Reis? We can't just leave him down there."

"Melanie, can you tell him no one else will be coming down to speak with him?"

Melanie smiles brightly. "No problem." Then she bounces out of my office. Yes, bounces. Norah raises a brow at me, and I shrug.

As soon as Norah leaves, I pick up line two. "Mr. Prince, what a surprise to hear from you."

I grit my teeth and hope for the best.

"Ms. McIntyre, I wish I was calling under better circumstances but I'm afraid my company not only won't be able to meet your deadline, but we must terminate all of our contracts with you."

I lean back in my chair and take a deep breath. "Mr. Prince, what are you talking about? You can't terminate your contracts—"

"Look, Sarina, I'm only calling out of courtesy to you because I know you're working really hard over there. But your boss, Jim..." Phillip breathes heavily into the phone. "My wife is having an affair with him."

I clench my teeth. No. I refuse to clean up another one of Jim's messes. I don't know how he has held onto the CEO position this long. The man has been caught up in a number of scandals—all involving other men's wives.

"I realize you could sue us and probably ruin us but Sarina, I can't work with that man."

And we can't afford to have this go public. Not now when we have a missing weapon. I could just see the headline now. *Incompetent CEO leads company into the ground.*

How the hell am I going to find a replacement supplier on such short notice?

"Phillip, how about this. Instead of canceling, you fulfill our existing orders. You only deal with me."

"Sarina, I understand what you're saying but frankly none of my staff ever talks to Jim directly nor do I so dealing with only you won't solve the issue. The man has blown up my marriage, he is unethical, and I cannot in good conscience work for him in any way."

I sigh. I understand. Better than he realizes. But I'm not about to share the stories of my mom and how she ruined our family with this man. I just need the parts he promised to deliver.

"And before you try another line of argument, know that I walked in on them. In my bed. The only reason Jim is still alive is because he can run faster than me."

I suppress a laugh imagining Jim running naked down the street. He might have good business acumen but he's an idiot in every other way.

"Try Elroy's for your orders. I won over one of their bigger clients and I suspect they might be able to fulfill the orders for you."

The line clicked dead before I could thank him. Elroy's wasn't as fast as Prince's but what choice did I have?

I spoke to the manager at Elroy's and had everything set up by lunch. I was able to include Tim on the call since it really was his department. The only reason I had taken on this project directly was to fix one of Jim's messes. Not to mention, I knew I was being watched by the board. I'm still fairly new and while there technically isn't a probation period, I certainly felt like I was in one.

Speak of the devil. Jim appears in my doorway.

"We need to talk," I tell him.

"Did you find the missing equipment?"

I know he's talking about the laser weapon system but since it's a top level security item, he's not going to say anything more than equipment.

"No. But I did get a call from Phillip Prince."

Jim lets out a heavy sigh as he sinks into the chair across from me.

"I was afraid of that. He canceled, didn't he?"

I'm exhausted. Not just by the fact I have too much on my plate, but by this man.

"Jim, this is it. I'm done. I'll find a new supplier for the Allen project because I pushed so hard for it. But if you find yourself into another mess, I'm going to the board."

Jim glares at me. "Sarina, I'm sorry about this. It won't happen again. You know I don't mean for these things to happen. I seem to be a magnet for trouble."

I jump up. "Are you serious? You don't mean for these things to happen? Then stop sleeping with married women!"

I take a deep breath. "You know what, do what you have to do, and I'll do what I have to do."

Jim stood and leaned over my desk. "Don't go to the board. I can't lose this job. And if I do, it will only end badly for you." Then he stands up straight and walks to the door.

I bite my tongue to keep from saying anything more. If it weren't for our very competent CFO, this company wouldn't remain viable. Not that it's doing great. Six months with Jim at the helm has taken its toll.

I sit back down and spin my chair to the window. My view is of the warehouse, which I sometimes stare at when I need to think. I can't help but worry that someone here is involved in the theft. That kind of bad press could destroy this company. We've already been in the news a few times—well the tabloids—due to Jim and his life choices.

If it's someone here, I have to get ahead of it anyway I can. I'll have to make sure Norah reports anything she learns to me. I spin back to my laptop and my eyes catch on Donny's card. I'd tossed it on my desk when I arrived. Right now, he's likely talking to Melanie. His card includes an office number and a cell number.

Hmm.

I take a chance and pull out my cell phone and shoot off a text before I can think better of it.

Sarina: *This is Sarina McIntyre. We just met. I know it's early in the investigation but if it looks like the leak is someone at Asher Vaughn, can you give me a heads up? I want to get ahead of a potential PR nightmare.*

I hit send and toss the phone on my desk. A moment later it buzzes.

Donny: *I'm happy to hear from you. Let's meet and discuss why you think someone from your company might be responsible.*

What? No. I grab my phone and begin furiously typing.

Sarina: *You misunderstood. I didn't say that. I meant "if" you find evidence pointing to one of our employees, please let me know.*

Donny: *Are you familiar with the taco truck right off Meridian Drive?*

Is he asking me for food recommendations?

Sarina: *Yes. They have great tacos. I'm sure you'll like it.*

Donny: *I'll meet you there in one hour.*

I stare at the phone. He couldn't be serious.

Sarina: *Not necessary.*

Donny: *Actually, it is.*

I'm about to write him back and tell him no, but something stops me. The truth is I want to see him again. And if that helps get me some kind of in with knowing what is going on, well, I'm doing it for the good of the company. Only for the company. It has nothing to do with the man's thick dark hair, deep blue eyes or me wondering what he looks like without a shirt on. Good, based on how well he fills one out.

CHAPTER 4

DONNY

I CHECK the time on my phone. Fifteen minutes until I need to be at the taco truck. I glance back up at Tim Maddow who'd been blathering on since I ran into him. I asked direct questions and he some how managed to not once answer one but instead went off on tangents.

After Melanie informed me I wouldn't be able to interview Tim or Norah and that Asher Vaughn had their own investigative team, I was angry. Why wouldn't Sarina have told me that directly?

But running into Tim in the garage was a bonus. Gotta love those large photo IDs they have to wear.

I turn my attention back to Tim. I need to focus in case he says something useful.

"He actually complained to Norah saying I smelled like a cat litter box. Can you believe it? Anyway, if I were you, I'd question Scott."

Now that got my attention.

"Did you smell like a cat litter box?"

The man's mouth falls open. "No, of course not!"

"Do you own a cat?"

Tim frowns. "Yes, but that doesn't—"

"How many?"

"How many what?"

"How many cats do you own?"

Tim smiles. "Four but they're all very well groomed."

I run my hand through my hair. One thing I've learned about Tim Maddow is that he's clueless.

"Look," I say as he shifts, uncomfortable in his loafers. "If you own four cats, odds are you likely smell a little."

Tim's smile fell and I could see him gearing up to give his best defense. I put my hand up to stop him.

"Regardless of whether you smell or not—"

"I don't! Smell me!"

"Pass. Do you have any other reason we should question this other guy, Scott?"

Tim crosses his arms and frowns like a petulant child.

"Nothing I can put into words. It's just a gut feeling."

"Duly noted. If there's nothing else, I do need to get going."

I only make it a few steps away.

"There is one more thing," he says.

I turn back to face him.

"I love Sarina, don't get me wrong."

Hearing her name has my attention.

"But she's new and frankly I'm not sure how much we can trust her."

That reminds me, I have to send Stormy all the names I need background checks run for.

"How long has she worked here?"

Tim shrugs. "About eight months."

"Do you know where she worked prior?"

Might as well see if the employees are talking about her or if it's only Tim who's concerned.

"I don't know her entire history, but I do understand that she was in the service, got out and went to some private college, and then worked at her daddy's company for a while. Apparently, that gave her enough experience to become a VP here."

Tim does not hide his emotions well.

"You don't think she's qualified?"

Tim rolls his eyes. "That's not what I said. I don't understand why they didn't simply move someone else up."

Ah, Tim doesn't like being stuck in middle management.

"Thank you for your time, Tim. I appreciate your candor."

Tim frowns as I spin on my heel and walk to my car.

Tim didn't seem to have much knowledge about the actual shipment once it left these premises. And according to him and Sarina, only five employees knew anything about the date and time of the shipment. I've spoken to two of them. Once I have Norah's address, I'll try to accidentally run into her in her neighborhood. Hopefully she can provide more answers because I doubt I'll get to question the CEO, Jim Albright.

I shoot off a text to Rover and CT before I get in my car, letting them know I'm coming up empty. I hope they're having more luck.

The drive to the taco truck is short and I find I'm chuckling to myself as I replay the text exchange with Sarina. I shouldn't have wanted to see her so badly but then after what Tim told me, I do have a few more questions. This is definitely work-related, I tell myself.

I park a block away and walk until the truck is in view. Sarina is nowhere to be seen and it's been an hour. I can't ignore the disappointment I feel. Really though, what are the odds a VP of Asher Vaughn could drop everything to meet me for lunch? A man she just met. Yeah, it's under the guise of the investigation but that could as easily be handled with a phone call.

After another five minutes, I finally accept my fate and get in line. Lunch for one coming right up.

I check my phone, but she hasn't texted.

"Sorry I'm late," a familiar voice says from beside me.

I turn to find Sarina standing at my side.

She smiles and I'm struck again by how beautiful this woman is.

"You didn't think I was coming, did you?"

We take a step up as the line moves.

"No. But I'm glad you did."

Maybe a little too glad, based on my now-sunnier disposition.

We order our food and then stand to the side and wait as it's prepared.

"How did you get into investigative work?" she asks.

"I was in the Navy and after I got out a friend suggested I apply to Morgan Thompson Security. I did and here we are."

Her brows pull tight as she stares at me. Then she bursts out laughing.

Now, I'm not a self-conscious guy but I'm pretty sure she's laughing at me.

"What?" I ask.

"Sorry, I don't mean to laugh. Usually when you ask someone about themselves, they go on and on. But not you."

"Ah, let me guess, you work with a lot of guys like Tim."

Her lip curls up again. "You met Tim, did you? Funny, since my assistant told you he wasn't available for questioning."

I shake my head. "Hey, I ran into him in the garage. Total coincidence."

"Uh huh," she says.

I grin. "I was asking the man about a breach of security, which he never answered by the way. But now I know all about the fact he has four cats, and his coworker thinks he smells like a litter box. If that isn't an over-talker, I don't know what is."

"Number thirty-two."

That's us. I grab the bag of food and Sarina leads me to a picnic table further from the rest. I know I should sit across from her to gauge her reactions to my questions but the pull to be close to this woman is strong. When I sit beside her, her eyes widen. Only briefly. Then she glances away.

After I pull out our containers and hand her a fork, I hit her with what I really want to ask.

"You think someone at Asher Vaughn is behind this?"

She turns eyes back to me. "I never said that."

"Your text implied it."

She opens her to-go container and pulls out a taco, taking a bite and savoring it while staring out over the parking lot. She's taking her sweet time chewing, I wonder if I pissed her off. Finally, she sets her food down and directs her gaze to mine.

"I never implied anything. I simply want to know if you find something."

Two can play this game. I finish off my taco and watch her watching me. But she doesn't get uneasy like I'm expecting. Instead, she stares up at me with a glint in her brown eyes. The sun catches on highlights in her hair and the woman is positively radiant.

"Tell me about you," I finally say.

She frowns. "What about me?"

"Did you always want to become a VP at Asher Vaughn?" I ask.

This causes her to snort which is actually very cute. Everything about this woman is cute.

"Sorry. No. I enlisted right after high school."

"Which branch?"

"Army." She quirks a brow waiting for my challenge.

I shrug.

"I realized a military career wasn't for me so once I got out, I got my degree in business. I had some credits from when I was in high school which helped speed that up."

"Speed it up? You weren't into the college life."

She shakes her head. "No. I was older than most of them at that point and listening to their drama between classes was enough."

She takes another bite of her taco which gives me a chance to watch her without looking like a stalker. I know she has more to say.

She swallows. "After I graduated college, I went to work at my dad's company. That was great until it wasn't. Then I applied to Asher Vaughn and here I am."

I chuckle.

"What?"

"You thought my answer was short? There has to be a hell of a lot between working for your dad and finding yourself in upper management at one of the nation's major military equipment manufacturers. And at such a young age."

Her cheeks flush red. I might be fishing a little. I don't know why. Once I have her background report, I can simply look there.

"I'm older than I look."

Interesting. She's held her own for our entire conversation, but this is what embarrasses her?

"Your age bothers you?"

Her head jerks up. "No."

"How old are you?"

Her eyes widen. She's surprised I asked. I have to admit

this almost feels more like a date than me asking her more questions.

"Thirty-four."

I grin. "Just as I thought. Young for a VP."

I move my leg just a little and it accidentally bumps into hers. She doesn't move back and I feel tingles where we touch. Damn, I should move but I'm enjoying this too much.

"How old are you?" Her hand goes to her mouth. "I'm sorry. You don't have to answer that."

"Thirty-one."

She shifts away from me. The loss of her touch bothers me more than I want to admit. Then she gives me a tight smile as she closes up her to-go container.

"I need to get back. I have a meeting."

Before I can object, she's already halfway to her car.

What the hell just happened? I catch up and reach for her shoulder. Again the sparks are there just as they were when we first shook hands. She spins, her lips parting in surprise and I have a strong urge to lean down and kiss her. The way she's looking up at me, I'm thinking I'm not alone in my fantasy.

Instead, I step back. I need to keep things professional. At least until I know what's going on.

"Thank you for meeting with me. I'll be in touch if I have more questions."

She nods then leaves without another word. While I'm not sure what happened, I can't help but feel like it was my fault.

CHAPTER 5

SARINA

AS SOON AS I'm parked in the garage at Asher Vaughn, I bang my head against the steering wheel. "Stupid. Stupid."

A knock on my window causes me to jump. I glance up and see Norah. Great. I just keep embarrassing myself today.

It was bad enough to ask Donny his age. He's here to do an investigation. That was not a date. Then to find out he's younger. In my experience men always want younger women. Men hear my age and assume I want to settle down and immediately start having kids. That couldn't be further from the truth. No, I have plans that could take this company to another level. That's why this job is so important to me. At least I can climb the corporate ladder. Assuming I don't make an ass out of myself to my subordinates.

But who am I kidding? Norah is more of a friend than anything.

I step out of the car.

"Hi Norah."

She quirks a brow. "Why were you banging your head on the steering wheel?"

I grab my purse and lock my car.

"I just embarrassed myself in front of a guy."

"What happened?"

"I thought he was interested. He wasn't. That's all."

No need to give her any details. The man is investigating all of us, me included, for potential criminal activity. Actually, worse than that. This is a matter of national security and possible treason. He's the last man I should even consider flirting with. But when I'm around him, I feel a strong connection between us. I thought he must feel it too. But now I think it's all in my head.

Norah loops her arm in mine. "I'm sorry. That sucks. But I know there's a good man out there for you somewhere. You'll find him."

"I know you believe that but I'm not so sure. I haven't had the best luck with the men I've known."

Norah shakes her head. "That's because you have terrible taste in men. No offense, but you do."

I laugh. "No offense taken. You're right. But honestly, I don't have time right now. Jeffrey wasn't the first one to complain that I was too busy."

Norah pushes the button for the elevator. "That's the problem. You only seem to find needy men who need you at their beck and call. What you need is a real man who understands you have your own life. If only I had a son."

I grin. She's said this so many times before.

"What about you? Do you want to find someone?" I ask.

Norah grins. "I met someone. It's too soon but I think he could be the one."

"Oh Norah! I'm so happy for you. When do I get to meet him?"

Her face flushes. "I'm not sure about that. He doesn't

exactly know how I feel yet. But hopefully soon."

The elevator doors open and we step in, saving me from the need to respond. Norah has been known to get crushes on men she's never spoken to, nor will she speak to. She lives more in her head. Melanie and I have tried to set her up on dates but it never works out too well.

Norah swipes her key card in front of the keypad and hits the button for the third floor.

"Hold the door!" someone shouts.

Just before it closes, a hand stops the door. Once it opens, Tim is standing there smiling at us.

"Good afternoon, did you two enjoy lunch?"

I glance over at Norah, who's still blushing.

"Yes. Did you?" I ask Tim.

"I did. Oh Norah, I was going to tell you the pet store is now selling fresh wheat grass. My cats love it. I highly recommend it."

"Oh, thank you," she says.

The elevator reaches the third floor and both Norah and Tim exit. I swipe my key card and go to the fourth floor.

I'm almost to my office when Melanie stops me.

"Your brother has been calling for the past hour. Despite the fact I told him you were out, he left four messages. Still haven't given him your cell phone number yet, I see."

Melanie quirks a brow.

"No, I haven't, and I don't plan to. I'll call him so he stops harassing you."

"Thank you."

I close the door behind me as I enter my office. No one needs to hear my family drama. I take a deep breath before I return the call.

"Preston, I understand you called?"

"Dammit Sarina! I know you don't want to be dragged into the family business but tough shit. And not giving me your cell phone number isn't going stop me from showing up at your job if I have to."

"Good afternoon to you, too. And brother, you forget—you wouldn't make it past security at the front gate."

"Fuck. I'm sorry. I didn't mean to snap at you. It's just..."

"Dad. I know. That's why I left."

I hear the sound of glass clinking.

"A little early for scotch, isn't it?" I ask.

He laughs. "Not with the day I've had."

I sit and lean back in my chair. "What happened?"

Preston sighs. "Today Dad was going to announce his retirement. I was going to take over his role."

I roll my eyes. "Let me guess, he changed his mind?"

Dad swore to me when I joined his company that I would eventually take over. Then I overheard him talking to a friend and he said he'd never retire. After I confronted him, he made it quite clear I'd never be more than his assistant and couldn't understand why I would believe otherwise. He was actually upset I wasn't thankful for being given a Vice President level title.

Yes, my dad's an asshole. I quit that day and soon after came to work for Asher Vaughn.

Then my dad recruited my brother Preston.

"Yes. Sarina, he made me look like an asshole. I told my assistant and several managers I'd be taking over starting next month."

I cringe. I learned that lesson that hard way, too.

"Then Dad gets up in front of all the directors and instead of announcing his retirement, he tells them we're expanding! And he plans to stay at the helm for at least ten more years. Ten years!"

Yep, I know this story all too well.

"He lied to me," Preston says.

"Now you see why I left. You have to leave, Preston. Not

just for your future but for your sanity. I guarantee you in ten years he won't retire."

He groans. "I know. It's just now I look like either a power-grabbing asshole or an incompetent idiot Dad couldn't trust with the company. Neither look is good."

I can't help but laugh. "Sorry. I'm just so happy to be out of there and away from all of Dad's drama."

"I should leave, shouldn't I?"

"Yes, you should."

"Any chance you're willing to come back?"

"Never."

He sighs again. "At least Billy's too young to work here yet." He's referring to our half-brother who's three.

"Hopefully he'll never have to suffer that fate."

"True. Because I'm sure Dad still won't be retired by then. Oh, I have to go. Another meeting." I hear him swallow and set down the glass. "Thanks for the chat."

"Good luck."

I hope he does leave. Then I won't have to avoid his calls about Dad and that toxic place.

Leaving my dad's company was the best move I've ever made. My military experience is appreciated here at Asher Vaughn. I have no doubt I could be CEO someday. As long as I stay on the Board's good side.

There's a knock on my door.

"Come in."

Melanie walks in and closes the door. She's wearing a funny expression.

"What's wrong?"

She sits across from me and smiles.

"I want to know all about your lunch with a man."

How the hell? Oh wait.

"Norah?"

Melanie nods. "She said you met a man at lunch. Tell me

all about it."

Melanie loves to talk about men. All. The. Time. Even though she's my assistant, she's become a good friend. Both her and Norah. I probably shouldn't be doing that with my assistant but dammit, Melanie is fun. Unless she's grilling me. Then it's not so fun.

"It's nothing like that. Donny asked me to meet him for lunch to discuss a few things."

Melanie's eyes widened. "Is that code for sex?"

I bark out a laugh. "No, that's not code. And the lunch wasn't personal. It was business."

"Are you sure about that? I saw how that man checked you out when you left the room earlier."

Now that had my attention.

"He checked me out?"

"Well, his eyes were on your ass so I would say so."

Hmm. But I didn't get an interested vibe from him. I shake my head. Of course I didn't. I'm a suspect to him.

"No. It was just a business lunch. Nothing more."

"But you want more," she presses.

"Why won't you let this go?"

Melanie cocks her head. "Because you haven't shown interest in any man despite the fact someone hits on you every time we go out. But I saw the way you looked at Donny. You're interested. And I bet you'll use some excuse like you can't mix business and pleasure to avoid actually pursuing something with him."

"That's a very good reason."

Melanie rolls her eyes.

"Fine. But you're coming with me to happy hour later and we're finding you a man."

I laugh and shake my head. "No promises."

It's highly doubtful anyone will catch my interest when the only man on my mind is Donny Reis.

CHAPTER 6

Donny

I rub my eyes as I finally close my laptop. For the last two days I've been going over all the background reports and every bit of information Rover and CT found, which sadly isn't much. There's no point in reading Sarina's background check again. Damn, I have the thing memorized by now. And I find I'm trying to convince myself that she can't be involved. She can't. My gut tells me she isn't. I also have this strong urge to protect her that I can't seem to shake. I have to though, because until this investigation is complete, she is technically a suspect. Everyone I spoke to at Asher Vaughn is.

It's been two days since we parted ways after lunch. Two days that I haven't been able to get her out of my head. If I'm not thinking about her as part of the investigation, then I'm visualizing her at home—usually while holding myself in the shower.

"Damn it!"

"Haven't found anything either?" Rover is standing in the doorway to my office.

"No." I'm not going to admit the real source of my frustrations.

Rover steps into the office and flops down in a chair on the other side of my desk. "I've gone over the background report on every employee at PV Transport that knew about this delivery. There isn't anything suspicious in any of them."

Just as there shouldn't be. PV Transport mostly hires veterans and former police officers to drive their trucks. Everyone has to pass a rigorous background check and lie detector test to even qualify to touch a truck. For this delivery, they used only their top employees.

A notification comes up on my laptop.

"Stormy just sent us a video. From PV Transport. Apparently, the truck had a dash cam."

"What the hell?" Rover shouts, pulling his phone out of his pocket. "And why are we just now finding out about this?"

CT steps into my office. "Apparently they have their own investigative team, and they took their sweet time analyzing the video."

I hit play.

"Did they come up with anything?"

CT shoves his hands into his pockets. "The shooter was wearing a hoodie and he turns just enough at one point they were able to figure out his sweatshirt is from Dave's BBQ."

"Really?" I ask as I watch the video.

The quality is good. A truck pulls in front of the dash cam and slams on its brakes. The dash cam shows the PV Transport driver swerving and narrowly missing the truck in front of it. He curses and then gets out of the truck.

"He got out of the truck?"

CT sits in the chair next to Rover.

"Yeah, I thought that was odd, too," CT says.

"When I interviewed him, he said he got out of the truck because he smelled smoke. He thought the engine might be on fire," Rover says.

We stare at the video. If it was, we couldn't tell.

"I checked with the team that inspected the truck after the fact and they said there was some damage that could have caused some smoke."

CT nods in response. "So, the driver's been cleared then?"

Rover nods. "His record is spotless, and his story checks out. Plus, he got shot."

"But they're trained to not exit the truck until they've evaluated if there's a threat. And there clearly is a fucking threat," I say.

Rover runs his hand through his dark hair. "He claims the smoke was thick."

We can still hear the driver cursing. It sounds like he didn't close his door. Then he appears in front of the hood of the truck. A man exits the other truck and walks toward him. That man is wearing a hoodie and I can make out some writing on the back. It could be Dave's BBQ. But the man appears to be purposely looking away from the dash cam.

"He knows about the dash cams," I say.

The driver of the PV Transport is irate. "Mother fucker, what the hell—" He falls to the ground before he can finish his sentence.

"Shot in the stomach," Rover says. "Fortunately, the bullet missed any major organs."

The hoodie man then aims his gun at the camera and fires. The video ends.

"He definitely knew about the dash cam," I say.

I rewind the video to the point where the man is about to fire at the dash cam. His face is in shadows from the hoodie, and I can't make out any of his features.

"PV Transport has their best guys working on this video, but they can't get a usable photo of the guy," CT says.

"But they know his hoodie came from Dave's?"

Dave's BBQ is near the base. I've eaten there a time or two. It's pretty good.

"Dave's BBQ sells the hoodies both online and in their store," Stormy says as he enters my office.

I lean back. "How does the hoodie help us? Unless you're about to tell me they've only sold one."

Stormy leans on the door frame. "Well, Trip was able to pull up a list of everyone who's purchased that hoodie with a credit card in the last six months."

Damn, Trip amazed him. That man was able to find out nearly anything you asked him for.

"How the hell did he hack into a private business's records?" Rover asks.

Rover wasn't fully aware of Trip's capabilities. I was. After working with him on the last case, I was in awe of the man.

"He asked and Dave's gave him the information," Stormy says.

"Really? I'm surprised," I say.

And I am. Most people don't want to give anything for free.

"You'd have to ask Trip how he pulled it off."

"What if the guy purchased the hoodie with cash?" I ask.

Stormy smiles. "Then this list does you no good. I sent you all the list of customers. Go through it and see if anyone stands out."

Well, any bit of information is better than none.

Stormy's phone rings. "I have to take this."

He answers his phone as he steps out of the office.

I open the customer list and scan through it quickly. Two thirds down, my eyes catch on one name. Sarina McIntyre.

"Damn it."

CT and Rover look up. "You recognize a name?"

I nod. "Sarina McIntyre. She's the VP for the weapons systems at Asher Vaughn."

"Didn't you interview her?" Rover asks.

I nod. "My gut says she didn't do this."

I lean back. Is my judgment flawed because I find this woman attractive? Did I miss something? Could she be involved?

Pulling up her background report again, I shake my head.

"She's new to Asher Vaughn. She worked for her dad's company before that."

"What's his company do?"

"Manufactures and sells guns to retail stores."

Rover cocks his head. "Like Walmart?"

"Yes, exactly."

Rover crosses his arms. "How the hell did she go from manufacturing guns to becoming the VP of weapons systems at a company like Asher Vaughn?"

It was a good question and one I needed to ask the CEO. Unfortunately, he has been less than cooperative.

"VP of weapons systems? Well, she would likely have known about the scheduled delivery," CT says.

Yes, she would.

"I'll question her again," I volunteer.

Two sets of eyes glance up.

The corner of Rover's mouth turns up, but he quickly suppresses it.

"Want me to come with you?" he asks.

I shake my head. "No. I'm sure you have enough on your plate."

Rover stares at me for a minute then nods.

CT jumps up. "I'm due back at the base in a couple of hours. Stormy wants me to finish my interviews before the Navy's official investigative team arrives."

"I thought we were the official team," Rover says.

"We're the unofficial team until Cramer is convinced no one from base was involved," CT says. "In the meantime, they have some SEALS from San Diego coming up."

"San Diego? Do you know who?"

The three of us had a couple of missions with a team stationed in San Diego. I would love to see some of the guys I served with. But what were the odds?

"Let me see if Stormy sent their names," CT says as he scrolls through his messages.

The moment I see his smirk I know.

"You won't believe this. They're sending Rocco, Phantom, and Ace."

I can't help the grin. "No shit?"

My mood is immediately brightened. I've worked with all three of those guys on a few missions. I knew every time Rocco was in charge, things would go well. And they did. I bet they will get a kick out of seeing me, Rover, and CT again.

CT nods. "Damn, it's been a while since I've seen those guys."

"I'm glad we know it's a group we can trust," Rover says.

"When are they coming?" I ask.

"Sunday. That should give me plenty of time to finish up. I'll catch you guys later." He pats me on the shoulder as he leaves. "Hey, Maverick, good luck with the VP."

Once CT is out of earshot, Rover leans forward. "Is there something you want to tell me about this Ms. McIntyre?"

I turn my gaze to his. "What do you mean?"

Rover shrugs. "You were quick to say you didn't need help. Just thought I picked up on something."

"Nothing to pick up on."

He crossed his arms. "So, you can be objective then?"

Is he trying to offend me? "Do you think I'd let a woman manipulate me?"

Rover sighed. "No not at all. I'm just wondering if you might be a little blinded when it comes to her."

I'm about to launch into my defense when Rover raises his hand.

"Don't. I saw her photo. The woman looks like she should be a model, not working her way up the corporate ladder. Plus, I'm still a little curious how exactly she got the job given her employment history."

Now I'm offended on her behalf at his words. "You think she slept her way into her position?" I huff out.

Rover's brows shoot up. "I didn't say that. But I do wonder why you're so defensive.

Shit. I am. I rub my hand over my face.

"You're right. I am defensive. I don't know why. The moment I met her, something was different."

"Okay, you need to ignore that until this case is resolved. Then, if she isn't involved, you can pursue her. But Maverick, don't do anything stupid. You hear me?"

"I hear you."

I really did. Now I just hoped like hell she wasn't involved.

CHAPTER 7

SARINA

"WHAT ABOUT HIM?" Melanie asks pointing at a man sitting at the bar.

I take a sip of wine. "I didn't come to happy hour just for you to try to set me up with someone."

Melanie smiles. "You didn't. But I did. What about him?" she asks, pointing to yet another guy.

"No. And if you don't stop, I won't come out with you next week."

Every Friday we meet Norah here at The Barrel for happy hour. It's nicer than the name might sound. The lighting is dark and there are several tables scattered throughout so it can accommodate many but never feels too crowded. The selection of wine is fabulous and it's the only reason I'm suffering through this endless matchmaking that Melanie insists on doing.

"Sorry I'm late," Norah says as she takes a seat next to me. "I wrapped up the last of the investigation. I'll have the report to you by Monday, Sarina, but the short version is whoever leaked information on that delivery, it wasn't an Asher Vaughn employee."

I let out a breath. Deep down I figured the leak was more likely someone working for the transport company, but it's still a relief to hear it. I'd been worried about potential negative PR all week.

Melanie pours Norah a glass of wine from the bottle we ordered.

"Norah, any more developments with your man you can tell us about?" Melanie asks.

Norah takes a healthy drink of wine. "No. I've been too worried about my dad to do anything else."

"What's wrong with your dad?" I ask.

She shakes her head. "Nothing. But I couldn't reach him for a couple of days so I was worried."

"Didn't you go years without talking to him?" Melanie asks.

"I did. I guess that's why I thought his being closer meant I'd get to see him more. Unfortunately, that hasn't been true."

"I'm sorry," I say.

I do know what it is like to want time and attention from your dad but not receive it.

My phone buzzes and I check it. Jim has a habit of needing something over the weekend. But it isn't Jim's name lighting up my phone.

Donny.

"Oh! How is he?" Melanie asks.

I glance up. "What?"

"That smile. You just got a message from Donny Reis, didn't you? Now I know why you weren't interested in anyone here."

Yeah, that's the reason.

"It's actually work-related."

Donny: *I need to ask you a few more questions. Can you meet me tonight? Or tomorrow morning?*

Another man who works on the weekends.

Well, he can wait for the reply. She put her phone back in her purse.

"But I'm not going to answer it because I'm here having a good time with you two."

"Woohoo!" Melanie shouted, catching the attention of most of the other patrons.

I really lucked out getting Melanie as an assistant. If anyone had told me I'd be having drinks with her I would have laughed. At my dad's company, you did not socialize with those who weren't on your level. Since both Melanie and Norah technically work for me, I would have missed out on their friendships. At Asher Vaughn, it's encouraged for the women to bond together. There aren't many of us in the tech and engineering fields so I appreciate knowing I can trust these two.

"Norah, you are, too. Put your phone away," Melanie says.

I glance over and Norah is frowning at her phone.

"You're right. I'm sorry." Norah smiles as she sets her phone down. "I was hoping to hear from someone, but I haven't." She reaches for her glass of wine. "Let's toast to it being Friday and hoping we can relax this weekend."

For Norah, relaxing means making more cat outfits. I still don't understand how there is a demand for those but apparently there is.

"How is Kitten Kapers doing?" I ask.

Norah's face lights up. She loves talking about her online business. "Really good. I created kitty mood T-shirts and they're selling really well."

Melanie frowns. "What's a mood T-shirt?"

"It fits the cat like a T-shirt and has arm holes for its front legs. Then across the cat's back it says something to express its mood. My most popular one says, 'Wake me and die.'"

Melanie frowns and I bite back a laugh. I won't lie. I don't get this fascination with cats. But if it makes Norah happy then good for her.

Melanie asks Norah to tell her about the other T-shirts and that's when Norah pulls up her store front on her phone.

Three glasses of wine later, my phone is buzzing again. Melanie is at the bar ordering another bottle and Norah went to the bathroom. I decide to check it and discover another text from Donny.

Donny: Are *you ignoring me?*

I roll my eyes.

Sarina: *No, it's Friday night and I'm at happy hour, not work.*

Donny: *Where are you?*

Sarina: *The Barrel.*

Melanie returns to the table with two men.

"These men bought us a bottle of wine. Isn't that nice of them, Sarina?"

Melanie's grinning.

I glance at the men. They both appear to be in their fifties and are wearing suits.

"Hello Sarina, my name is Sam, and this is Fred. We're in town for a conference and thought we'd say hi." The man extends his hand to shake while his friend just grins at me.

"Thank you for the wine," I say shaking his hand.

I glare at Melanie. The last thing I wanted was to deal with a man tonight. I was enjoying our girl's night.

Norah returns to the table, frowning again.

"This is our friend Norah. Norah this is Sam and Fred."

"Hello." Norah glares at Melanie.

Yep. She knew who was behind this. Melanie once tried to set Norah up on a date when she found out she was single. I don't know what Norah said but she shut that down and

Melanie hasn't tried since. Which is probably why there are only two men now at our table and not three.

Fred grins at me. "Sarina, that's such a beautiful name."

He sits down in the chair next to me.

"Thank you." I pour myself more wine. Probably not the best choice but at least if I sip on a drink, I don't have to make conversation.

It turns out the drink isn't necessary. Fred proves he's able to do all the talking. I simply nod every now and again. Although I notice he keeps inching closer to me. Then I inch away. I'm practically climbing into Norah's lap at the present moment.

Fred touches my cheek and I flinch. What the hell is he doing?

He tilts his head while gazing into my eyes. "Sorry, I just had to know if it was as soft as it looked. Your skin is amazing."

His other hand is on the back of my chair. Not only did this man not pick up on the fact that I'm trying to get away from him, but now he's further crowding me.

"Sarina?"

That voice. I glance over. What the hell is Donny doing here?

"Got a moment?" he asks.

"No, she doesn't. She's with me," Fred says.

Before I can respond, Donny crosses his arms. His large, muscular arms. I can't take my eyes off of them.

"Let's let the lady speak for herself," Donny says.

"You have two men fighting over you? Ugh," Norah says under her breath.

"Mr. Reis, what a surprise seeing you here," Melanie says.

She turns to Fred. "He's a coworker of sorts, isn't that right?" She turns back to Donny who doesn't answer but is staring at Fred's hand on the back of my chair.

I should say something, but I can't. I'm sitting next to a man I don't want and staring at a man I want but can't have. The situation is ridiculous. But what I don't understand is why Donny is acting like a jealous boyfriend.

"Sarina." Donny's voice is firm. "A word. Please."

Norah arches a brow. I finally push back my chair and stand up.

"Excuse me," I say and grab my purse. If I'm lucky, I can use this as an excuse to leave. I should request an Uber now so it will be here by the time I'm done talking to Donny.

I walk past Donny to the door of the bar. Once I'm outside, I pull up the app.

He takes my phone out of my hands. "I'll drive you home."

Before I can object, he's walking toward his car. Did I mention he's still holding my phone?

"Wait," I say as I jog to catch up.

Mistake. Big mistake. I catch my toe on the uneven gravel and go barreling forward.

Donny moves fast and catches me before I fall. But now I'm pressed up against his chest and his arms are around me.

The man smells good. Too good.

And his lips. They are so kissable. I lick my lips, imagining what they'd feel like on mine. I glance up and his eyes are on my mouth.

Could it be possible he wants this too?

The grip he has on my back tightens. I decide to take a risk and lean forward.

The moment our lips meet, it's fireworks. All of a sudden, I can't get enough of this man.

My hand is in his hair and my leg is coming dangerously close to climbing him. Then suddenly he pulls back.

I open my eyes. He's staring at me with pure lust in his eyes. His lips are swollen and his hair is a mess from where I've pulled.

I sway and he steps forward, placing his hands on my shoulders, keeping me steady. I lean forward, ready to do that again when he stops me.

That's when it hits me. I just made a move on this man. And now he is turning me down. What the hell was I thinking?

I hiccup.

Oh yeah, I wasn't. I knew I shouldn't have had that last glass of wine.

"Can I have my phone back please? I'd like to call an Uber."

I hold my hand out. He doesn't give me the phone. He lets go of my shoulders and steps back. Then he steps forward back into my space.

"I'm sorry. I shouldn't have let that happen."

I hold my hand up. "Understood. I won't try to kiss you again. Sorry."

He growls in frustration. I glance up to see the heat is still in his eyes.

"I'm driving you home," he demands. "And for the record, the only reason I stopped the kiss is because you're still part of this investigation. Well, that and you've clearly had too much to drink."

I push past him and walk to the passenger side of the car. He follows me and is in my space again. This man is hot and cold. He's driving me insane. I can't think around him.

"What the hell was that you did in the bar? You might as well have pissed on me. And now you want to keep your distance?"

Although it doesn't feel like he wants to keep his distance right now. He's standing so close I can smell his cologne. Damn it smells nice.

I'm clearly drunk. I would never say these words otherwise. But I can't stop myself.

He quirks a brow. "I'm sorry. Did you want that man's attention? Because from the moment I walked into the bar I saw him scoot closer to you and you scoot away. Or is that some kind of game you like to play with men?"

His voice is harsh.

"I don't play with men."

I close my eyes as I realize how that sounds.

"Again, why are you here?" I ask.

He nods to the car. "Get in. We'll talk as I drive."

I reluctantly get in the car. Not that I have a choice. The man is still holding my phone. Part of me realizes this is stupid, getting in a car with a man I don't know. But deep down, I know I can trust him. I don't know why but I just do.

Once inside the car, he hands me my phone then turns to me.

"Did you buy a hoodie from Dave's BBQ last month?"

The question is so random that all I can do is laugh.

"You think that's funny?" he asks

"No, I think all of this is funny. Ridiculous actually. As for your investigation, Norah finished our internal investigation, and everyone was cleared. So, you're wasting your time here."

He turns to stare at the front window, and he grips the steering wheel tightly.

"Please just answer the question. Did you buy a hoodie from Dave's BBQ?"

"Mr. Reis, I don't even know what Dave's BBQ is."

He pins me with his gaze. "Call me Donny."

"Donny," I breathe out. His pupils dilate and I watch in fascination as his gaze becomes heated again.

"Are you sure about the hoodie? Because I have a receipt that says you bought it on October seventh at eleven forty-five."

My eyebrows shoot up. "Wow, that is very specific."

I pull up my work calendar on my phone and go to the date he mentioned.

"On October seventh I was in meetings all day. I remember because I didn't even have time to get my own lunch. My assistant ordered it for me and brought it to me."

"You're saying you didn't order the hoodie?"

I laugh again. "No, I didn't order a hoodie. Nor would I. It's not my style."

His eyes roam over my body and I can't help it but having his eyes on me turns me on. I squirm in my seat.

"Did you have your wallet with you?"

"At the meeting? No. I keep my purse in my desk when I'm at work."

He stares at me intently like he's analyzing me. It's unnerving.

"Do you lock your desk?"

I frown. "No. I work in one of the most secure buildings around. I have no need to lock my drawer. I trust my employees."

He nods. "But someone could have gone into your office, into your desk, and used your credit card."

"Well, yes, but Melanie sits right outside my office. She would see anyone going in."

"Unless she was away getting your lunch," he says.

I lean back. "Or if she was in the meeting too, which she was for part of the day."

"Have you noticed any unusual purchases on your credit card?"

"How would I know? Apparently, I didn't notice the charge for a hoodie. And why would someone steal my card and just buy a hoodie? Why not a diamond necklace or something expensive?"

I'm struggling to not slur my words. And I'm suddenly very sleepy.

He chuckles. "Okay. What's your address?"

I turn to him. It is then I realize we're still in the parking lot. I rattle off my address and ease the seat back.

"Please don't pass out," he says.

"I won't. I'm just going to rest."

This is why I don't like to drink too much wine. It makes me sleepy. I'm just going to close my eyes for a moment.

CHAPTER 8

Donny

Shit. She passed out. I pull into her driveway and study the house. It isn't what I expected. I expected her to have a condo in some fancy high-rise building. Not a house that she has to maintain. There are flowering bushes lining the walkway. It's a modest home. Not the home of someone who makes what she likely makes.

I can't shake the fact I want to get to know this woman. Why this house? Why here?

A quiet snore draws my attention to the beautiful woman passed out in my passenger seat. I nudge her.

"Sarina, you're home."

"Okay," she says then turns on her side and snores again.

I exit the car and walk around. When I open the passenger door, I stop. She's curled up and looks so cute.

"Sarina." I nudge her again.

Nothing. She's out cold. I grab her purse and find a set of keys. I unlock her front door then go back to the car.

Reaching a hand under her legs and another one behind her back, I lift her. Her arms go around my neck along with her hot breath.

Holding her feels right. I can't shake that feeling. Or the other feelings having her so close is bringing on. I close the car door with my foot and carry her inside.

I find a light switch and flip it on. I'm not sure what I expected, but this isn't quite it. The living room is sparsely decorated. There's a couch, television, and coffee table. I guess I envisioned more. Maybe pillows. Shaking my head, I walk down the hall and find what I believe is the master bedroom. Now this is more what I expected. The walls are painted a deep blue and her bedding is a light gray. The entire effect is soothing even if there are way too many pillows in here.

I set her on the bed and push most of the pillows off to the side. Then I grab the blanket folded at the base. I pull it up and over her. When I step back, her hand reaches out for my arm.

"Please stay. The room is spinning."

Ah shit. She's going to puke.

"Okay, just a minute." I rush to her bathroom and find a trash can. After I place it next to the bed, I bend down and remove her shoes. Then my fingers trace her jawline as I move some hair behind her ear.

"I'll be right back," I tell her.

I walk out to the living room and pace. What the fuck am I doing? I can't stay. But I can't bring myself to leave either.

Pulling out my phone, I call a friend I haven't talked to in a while. I know what Rover or CT would say. I need to talk to someone who's been in a situation like this.

"Maverick? Wow, it's been a while. How the hell are you?"

The familiar voice makes me smile. I haven't talked to

Rocco in a couple of years but that's the great thing about our friendship, we just pick up where we left off.

"Hey, Rocco. I've been good. I'm working for Morgan Thompson Security now."

"Really? That's great. They've got a great reputation."

I sit down on her couch and it's actually comfortable. I smile, realizing she didn't buy furniture and decor just for the sake of buying it. She has what she needs.

"What's wrong?" he asks.

I laugh. "How do you do that?"

"You sighed into the phone three times. Either something is wrong or you're about to ask me what I'm wearing."

I bark out a laugh. "Yeah, I have something I want to talk to you about."

"I'm all ears."

"When you first met Caite, did you know?"

Now he's the one laughing. "Maverick, are you saying you met the one?"

"I'm not sure. It's just she's different, you know?"

"I know. I knew Caite was different the moment I saw her. Everything with her felt different. It felt right."

I sigh again.

"You don't sound happy about it."

I rub my temples to stave off the tension headache threatening to come on.

"She's a suspect in one of our investigations."

"Oh shit. That's not good."

"No, it's not."

"What's your gut tell you? She guilty?"

I jump up and walk over to a bookcase studying the books lined up. "That's just it, my gut says she's innocent. But can I trust my gut right now?"

"Only you can answer that. You were always good at reading people, Maverick. Don't doubt that now. But if she's a suspect, I'd keep my distance until the investigation is over."

"Yeah, about that."

Rocco sighs. "You slept with her?"

"What? No! But I am at her house. I went to question her, and she was drunk. Now she's passed out in her bedroom, and I feel like I should stay in case she gets sick."

Rocco groans. "Maverick..."

"I know."

"Whatever you do, don't sleep with her."

"Fuck you. I wouldn't do that. She's drunk."

A photo next to the books catches my attention. It's Sarina with her assistant. They're both laughing as they stare into the camera. Sarina really is stunning.

"Good. Keep an eye on her but get out of there before she wakes in the morning."

"Thanks for the advice."

"Anytime. And you can tell me more about it next week."

I laugh. "I heard a rumor you might be coming up to this area."

"How the hell did you hear about that?" I sense the worry in his voice.

"Let's just say we might be working on the same thing."

"Got it. We'll talk more when I get up there."

"Sounds good. Thanks again."

"Anytime."

I end the call and turn my attention to the books lined up. *Crime and Punishment*. *Great Expectations*. More books by Steinbeck, Hemingway, and Mark Twain. Not what I would have imagined her taste to be. Although what was I expecting? Military books?

I laugh to myself as I go to the kitchen and get a glass of water. When I return to the bedroom, Sarina is asleep and hugging the blanket I'd covered her with. I set the water down on the nightstand.

Kicking off my shoes, I move to the other side of the bed and gently lay down on top of all the covers, making sure to keep distance between us.

Before I can stop her, Sarina turns over to face me and wraps her arm over my chest and tucks herself up against me.

I won't lie. It feels good. It feels right. And that right there is fucking with my head.

I wrap an arm around her and pull her closer. I've never had the desire to cuddle with someone all night. But with this woman, I do.

She had no idea what I was talking about with the hoodie. It does sound possible someone could have stolen her credit card. Tomorrow, I'll insist she go over all the transactions and find anything else suspicious. If someone used her card for this, then someone might be trying to frame her. I can't rule anything out.

CHAPTER 9

Sarina

My eyes pop open and I stare at the ceiling in my bedroom. Flashes of the night before hit me and I sit up. Donny put me to bed last night. Did he stay? I glance over and see a rumpled blanket as if someone slept on top. But no Donny.

Then I remember the kiss. I grab my pillow and scream into it. I kissed the man investigating my company for a stolen weapon that is a matter of national security. And he pushed me away. It was after kissing me first. I probably caught him off guard. Because he ended it and now I can never look him in the eyes again.

I crawl out of bed and realize I'm still in last night's clothes. That's a relief; I didn't do anything too stupid like strip in front of him and come onto him again. Slowly I make my way to the kitchen. No sign of the man.

Then I find his note.

Hope you don't feel too bad this morning. I made you an omelet. It's in the fridge. D.

My stomach flutters as I reread the note. The man made sure I got home all right and even fixed me breakfast. I close my eyes. No. It wasn't a date. He was simply making sure I was okay like any nice person would do. And I notice he didn't mention the kiss. Neither will I.

Pieces of our conversation came back to me. A hoodie. Someone had purchased a hoodie using my credit card.

I pull up my credit card history online as I eat the omelet. Damn, it's good.

Sure enough, there was a purchase from Dave's BBQ on October seventh. That must be it. I searched the month prior and the month after, but I found no other unaccounted for purchases. I would have just thought this was a lunch order if Donny had specifically asked about it.

Why would someone steal my credit card just to buy one thing? Certainly no one at the company. Everyone there went through extensive background checks.

I check my wallet and the card is in there.

After a call to my credit company, and their recommendation to cancel the card and get a new one, I decide to text Donny. I wasn't sure what to say. Frankly, I'm embarrassed. But the man deserved a thank you at least.

Sarina: *Thank you for the omelet. It was really good.*

His response was immediate.

Donny: *Glad you liked it.*

I stare at the phone, but he doesn't send anything else. I'm disappointed but that is ridiculous. What else do I expect?

My phone buzzes again, and I smile. I knew he'd say something more. But instead, it's a text from Jim with a link. I click it.

It takes me to a news site and the headline reads "Asher Vaughn blames Navy for theft of major weapon system upon transport."

What? We don't blame the Navy.

Then my phone rings. Jim.

"Jim, what the hell is this? Where did it come from?"

"I was going to ask you the same thing. It looks like we have a leak. I need you to resolve it. Now."

So much for a relaxing weekend.

"I'm on it."

* * *

THREE HOURS LATER, I am sitting at a conference table with Norah, Jim, and our PR representative, Gunnar Tomlinson. Gunnar works directly for Asher Vaughn and is subject to the same confidentiality rules as the rest of us. I still feel uncomfortable with a PR person having this much knowledge of the inner workings of the company. My dad always told me only those that need to know, need to know. Most of the things Gunnar knows, he doesn't need to know.

"Jim, I understand you're upset, and you want to find out who leaked that headline, but right now we need to get in front of it. You can investigate later," Gunnar says.

Jim is as red as a beet and he's about to break the pencil he's holding. I'd never seen him this angry. But then, this is the first time someone in our company has betrayed us.

"Gunnar's right. We need to focus on how to put this fire out," Norah says. "Besides, we don't know if there really is a source at Asher Vaughn. The reporter could be lying."

I hadn't thought of that. It's possible. But why would he? It would come out eventually he lied and that could end his career.

Jim stands up. "It's very unlikely the reporter is lying. And so few people in our company knew about this. How'd it get out?"

Norah coughs. "I'm afraid that may have been my fault."

All eyes turn to Norah.

"Last night, I was in the bathroom at the bar with Melanie. She was talking about that investigator who showed up and took Sarina home," she says while staring at me. "And then she asked me if I thought we'd ever find the missing weapon."

Norah shook her head. "I peeked under the doors of the stalls and swear no one was there. I told Melanie we only call it equipment. But now I'm thinking someone was there. I'm so sorry."

Jim turned his back to all of us and pressed his hand to his forehead.

"Melanie brought up the missing weapon in a bar? She needs to be fired," Jim says.

"No, she's the best assistant I have ever had. And we don't know that's how the leak occurred," I say.

Jim turned back around and laughed. "Really? You don't think mentioning it at a bar was how it was fucking leaked? Now we need to figure out why the reporter printed that we said it was the Navy's fault."

Gunnar stands up. "Wait." He stares at Norah. "Did you say the investigator took Sarina home last night? From a bar?"

Now all eyes turn to me.

"Yes, he said he had some questions for her. And since she was drunk, he offered to drive her home."

Gunnar's eyes widened and his mouth falls open.

"Shit. Are you talking about the investigator from Morgan Thompson Security?" Jim asks.

"That's the one," Norah says, smiling as if she hadn't just stabbed me in the back.

What the fuck is she doing?

"First of all, I wasn't drunk." Well, that may not be completely true, but I need to dig out of this hole Norah just dug for me. "Second, he had some questions pertaining to the investigation."

"What questions?" Gunnar asks.

"And why the hell would you agree to answer them? Because you were drunk? Because I remember specifically telling you we were going to handle our own investigation!" Jim yells.

Dammit. He did say that. "It was related to something he believed I purchased but I hadn't. It was just a simple question."

"That you could have answered at the bar, which has its own issues, but seriously, you didn't need to have him drive you home," Gunnar says.

Jim frowns. "Something you purchased? What does that have to do with a missing weapon system?"

I lean back in my chair ignoring Gunnar and only answering Jim. "I don't know. All I know is he asked if I purchased a hoodie."

Jim rubs his eyes. "That doesn't make any sense."

"Jim, based on how the man was practically growling when he saw Sarina sitting next to another man, I suspect the question was just an excuse to get her alone," Norah says.

"Oh no, Sarina. Did you have sex with the man investigating our company?" Gunnar asks.

Three pairs of accusing eyes turn to me. What the fuck is going on?

"No!" I shout. "He drove me home since Norah was too drunk to do it herself. And on the way home, he asked me some questions pertaining to the investigation. That was it."

"He didn't stay the night with you?" Norah asks.

Why would she ask me that? Did she see his car parked outside?

"Norah, you were drunk too?" Jim asks.

Norah blinked. "No, I just had a couple of drinks."

Why is Norah putting me on the spot like this? And why the hell did Jim care if Norah drank?

"Why would you think he'd do that?" I ask Norah.

Norah begins to tap her fingers on the table. Why is she nervous now?

"It's obvious he's into you. And I know how dedicated you are to this company. I thought maybe you'd help him see that whoever was involved in this theft is likely on the Navy side. It just seems like quite a coincidence that this article came out this morning."

Norah smiles as if she'd just complimented my work ethic instead of the thinly veiled insult she just threw down.

I stand up. "I can't believe you're suggesting I would have sex with someone to sway his investigation. I thought you knew me better than that." Turning to Jim and Gunnar. "I need a break from this."

I storm out the door before anyone can stop me. I'm too livid to stay here. Instead of going to my office, I take the elevator down to the first floor and walk outside.

It's raining lightly but enough that I stand under the covering outside the front door. The air is crisp and fresh. I suck it in, hoping to expel all this anger and hatred I feel for Norah right now. What she did makes no sense. She's been my friend. Hasn't she?

I'm remembering every interaction we've had when my phone buzzes in my jacket pocket. If that's Jim asking me to come back to the meeting, I'm not sure I can control myself from telling him to go to hell. I close my eyes. That would be one fast way to get fired.

The message isn't from Jim.

Donny: *Did your company really put out that statement?*

Sarina: *No. It was a leak.*

Donny: *Any idea who?*

Sarina: *Well, my boss seems to think the leak was me to you as you drove me home last night.*

Donny: *Shit. How'd he find out?*

Sarina: *My so-called friend Norah threw me under the bus.*

Donny: *I'm so sorry. I never thought about what that might look like.*

Sarina: *Is it true?*

Donny: *Is what true?*

Sarina: *Did I say something about the Navy that you told some reporter?*

I wait and he doesn't respond. Either I pissed him off or now that he's been called out, he's done texting.

Then the phone rings. Donny.

"Hey," I answer.

"No. No you didn't say anything about the Navy and no I didn't talk to a reporter. Nor would I. This investigation is confidential to say the least. How drunk were you last night? Do you remember anything?"

My mind drifts back to us standing outside his car. I kissed him. He backed away and stopped it. Ugh.

"Not much," I lie.

He sighs into the phone.

"Well, I'd like to remind you. But I'm tied up all weekend with this investigation."

Yeah, I'd bet a man like Donny Reis would be tied up most of the weekend. By a variety of very young, very attractive women. The idea which pisses me off.

"I have to go back to my meeting. Good luck investigating."

I end the call before he can reply.

Good luck investigating? I groan.

CHAPTER 10

DONNY

I RUB my eyes as I reread Norah Jensen's background report again. And again, I still find nothing. After Sarina told me that Norah threw her under the bus yesterday, I was sure I must've missed something. I wanted to get to the bottom of what was going on before Sarina had to start a new work week tomorrow. But I found nothing. Hell, she could be trying to hurt Sarina for other reasons. For all I know maybe they dated the same guy.

"Maverick, I need you in my office," Stormy says as he walks by my door.

"Be right there."

I hear him say the same thing as he passes Rover and CT's offices.

By the time I walk into Stormy's office, Rover and CT are already there.

"What's going on?"

"PV Transport put a tracking device on the box that housed the laser weapon system," Stormy says.

"Wait. We already asked them about that, and they said it didn't have one."

"They lied."

"What else have they lied about?" CT asks.

"This is bullshit. First the dash cam and now this?" Rover grumbles.

"Look, I'm frustrated too. But all we can do is move forward with what we have. And according to my contact, Henry, the tracking device stopped working shortly after the weapon was stolen. He believed it had been discovered and destroyed. He says that's why they didn't mention it."

I make my way further into the office and sit down in one of the empty chairs. Stormy has the largest office, which often doubles as a small conference room.

"So, if it was turned off, what good is it to us?" Rover asks.

"It turned back on this morning," Stormy says.

"And we're supposed to trust it? It's probably attached to some car driving across the country." Rover says.

"Yeah, I was skeptical at first, too. But according to what Henry put together, the tracker somehow turned off but then, this morning, it turned back on. He says there are some things that can block the tracker. The main thing being thick cement walls."

"Thick cement walls?" I ask.

"Like a tunnel," Rover says.

I stare at Rover, who shrugs.

"Whoever took this knows that?" I ask.

"I doubt it," Stormy says. "Because the tracker was located at Boeing Field."

"Shit," Rover says. "Did someone already fly the weapon out?"

"We don't know. I haven't gotten an update from Henry since last night."

I grab a glass from the middle of the table and fill it with water from the pitcher next to it. My gut tells me things are only going to get uglier. "Does that concern you? That you haven't heard from him?"

Stormy shakes his head. "No. But if I don't hear from him by this afternoon, I'll be concerned." He looks from me to Rover to CT. "Look, there are more questions than answers. The Navy is sending up a SEAL team from San Diego. They will arrive later today and will be helping with the investigation."

"Yeah, Rocco, Ace, and Phantom. We know the guys," I say.

"I'm curious, why are they sending up a team from San Diego instead of using their own guys locally?" Rover asks.

Stormy leans back in his chair. "The investigation is still ongoing, and no one has been ruled out as a suspect in all of this yet. The Navy wants to play it safe and bring in an outside team. And us. We will be providing support."

"I owe Ace after that last prank he pulled on me," CT says with a shake of his head.

"Save it for after you all solve this and get the weapon back, all right?" Stormy groans.

Rover laughs. "Please save it for later. We all know it'll just backfire anyway."

CT crosses his arms. "It won't backfire."

"It will. All your pranks do," Rover says.

CT's hackles are up; I step in before he has a chance to argue. "When do they arrive?"

"You're all due to meet up on base on Whidbey Island at eleven o'clock."

I check my watch. "We better get going. Traffic is hell getting up there."

* * *

I CAN'T STOP my grin the moment I spot Rocco. The surprise in his eyes tells me he wasn't expecting me.

"Shit, Maverick! First the phone call and now this? I figured I'd see you later in the week. Are you stalking me now?"

I pull him in for a hug.

"It's been too long, man. Good to see you. It looks like we'll be working with you guys."

"We?" Ace asks.

I turn back to see Rover and CT arguing about something as they enter the makeshift conference room we've been placed in. I roll my eyes. Those two.

"Ah shit. Is that Rover and CT? And they still bicker like that? That must drive you crazy," Rocco laughs.

CT steps up with a grin. "We aren't bickering. We were discussing whether a tuna salad should have dill or sweet relish in it."

I frown. "Neither. That's disgusting."

Ace cocks his head. "If you have to use one, it has to be sweet. No dill in tuna."

Rocco rolls his eyes then holds out his hand to CT. "How the hell have you been?"

"Good. We're all working at Morgan Thompson now."

For a moment we catch up on how we got to be working together again here in Washington state.

"You really get used to the rain?" Ace asks.

"You do. And it really isn't that bad," CT says.

Phantom laughs. "Says the man born and raised here."

"Okay, let's go over what we know. We don't have time to waste." Rocco hands over a folder. "And have you been briefed on what PV Transport discovered?"

"We have," I say. "But feel free to fill us in. Something may have been left out."

Ace nods then proceeds to relay what we've already heard.

"If the guys from PV Transport got a hit last night from the tracker, the odds of it being in the same place today are low. I know those hangers and they have several tenants. They aren't going to hang around and risk someone seeing something they shouldn't," CT ventures.

"Agreed. Which is why we got a record of all the flights out of Boeing Field from the time they were seen there until about an hour ago." Ace points to the folder Rocco now holds.

"None of the planes that flew out were big enough to transport this equipment. They were all small passenger planes," Rocco says.

"And as of an hour ago, the tracker is still sitting in the hanger," Phantom adds.

"But that doesn't make any sense." Nothing makes sense about this case, as far as I'm concerned.

"Why the hell would they be hiding it in plain sight?" Rover asks.

I whip my head to him. "That's exactly what they are doing. Hiding it in plain sight." Turning back to Rocco, I ask, "Do you know whose hanger it's in? Who rented it?"

Rocco opens the folder and pulls out a few papers. "It's a corporation created last month. None of the people named as officers nor the registered agent are real."

"So, the weapon is just sitting there. Do you have a plan to get it?" CT asks.

"We do," Ace says. "It's risky."

"Isn't it always?" It's why we do what we do. We're used to the risk.

"Well, there's more than the usual risk. It's Seafair weekend," CT explains.

"Shit." Rover's curse echoes my thought exactly.

"How does that affect us?" Ace asks.

Rover's eyes widen. "Seafair is a huge celebration here. The Blue Angels do a show and take off and land from Boeing Field. A ton of people come out trying to get an up-close glimpse of them."

Ace, Rocco, and Phantom groan.

"So not only do they have the weapon hidden in plain sight, but they have it there on the air field's biggest weekend?" I think I have a plan.

"That about sums it up," Rocco says.

I grin. "Well then, they shouldn't be surprised when some tourists accidentally poke around where they shouldn't."

CHAPTER 11

Sarina

This is the first Sunday morning I haven't been at work in months. I should be relaxing but instead, I sip on my hot chocolate, jealous of the people in this coffee shop. Their lives weren't spinning out of control like mine.

Yesterday was a clusterfuck. After I returned to the meeting, Jim took me into his office to discuss my behavior. My behavior!

He acted like I got drunk and took Donny home for a one-night stand. I made it clear that was more Jim's MO and not mine. You can imagine how well that went over.

I spent the rest of the day yesterday in my office going over my calendar and making a list of anyone that had access to my office the day my credit card was used. I knew I had it that morning when I bought a coffee. And I had it that night when I purchased some take-out. I deduced someone must have taken it just long enough that day to place the order. I still had no idea why.

My purse remained in my desk on the fourth floor. Only a small number of employees had access to that floor. And based on my meeting records, only two were granted access only for the meetings. Thankfully most of my meetings are on the third floor.

That left me with a list of ten people. Jim, his assistant Tony, Melanie, Norah and her assistant Tracy, the CFO and his assistant, and the CTO and his assistant.

In order to solve this mystery, I needed to know what was significant about this hoodie. And despite texting Donny, he hadn't responded.

I can't help but smile remembering that he made me breakfast. But the smile dies on my lips as I tell myself he isn't an option. I'm clearly still a suspect. But does he stay the night and take care of all his suspects? I close my eyes. Of course, he would if they were drunk. He obviously thought I might puke since I found a trash can next to the bed.

But I swear I remember cuddling with him that night and it feeling really good. It had to have been a dream. Right?

Melanie walks into the coffee shop and smiles when she sees me. I hate being dishonest with her but until I narrow this list down, I have to remember anyone could have done this.

After ordering a coffee she sits down, setting her purse on the table.

"Okay, so tell me exactly what happened Friday night. And please, give all the details."

She's grinning at me.

"Nothing happened. He drove me home."

Her smile falls. "Really? That's it?"

I take a sip of my cocoa as she watches me. "That's it. He had some questions about the investigation."

Please don't ask anymore because I don't want to admit I tried to kiss him, and he rejected me.

"That's actually why I wanted to meet you here," I start. "There was some unusual activity on my credit card he asked me about."

Melanie frowns. "What do you mean? Someone stole it?"

"It looks that way. But the thing was, it would have had to have been taken from my office last month. Do you know if anyone that I'm not aware of went in there for any reason?"

"No, I know how particular you are about your space."

"Any chance someone went in saying they needed a pen? Or maybe someone from maintenance?"

If it was Melanie, I've just given her a chance to point the finger at someone else. Not that I can really believe she would do something like that. But at this point, I need to rule everyone out.

She shakes her head. "No, the last time I recall anyone other than you or me in your office was during the summer when Jim insisted on waiting for you in there."

I remembered that day. That was when I got my first full taste of what working for Jim Albright was going to be like. He had pissed off a major supplier. While he kept asking me to find someone new, he would never tell me why. I couldn't understand why he was asking a Vice President to handle this. I thought it was demeaning and his way of asserting power. Until I called the supplier and found out what happened. Yes, he'd slept with the CEO's wife.

I swear that man must be known in those circles for being the go-to guy for affairs.

That supplier had been kind enough to fill me in on Jim's reputation and I discovered this wasn't his first offense. And now that he'd roped me in, it wouldn't be the last offense I had to deal with.

"Are you sure it happened while it was in your office? Maybe it was during lunch or on your way to work?"

I didn't give her the details that I never actually lost my

card. That's what told me I likely knew the person who stole it.

"I'm not sure," I lie. "I'll keep thinking about it and see if I remember anything else."

Melanie pulls her phone from her purse. "What day was it? I keep a very detailed calendar."

"October seventh."

"Well, you already know your appointments. But also that day, Jim had sandwiches ordered in for lunch. The guy dropped them off at the first-floor reception desk and I went down and grabbed them."

That would rule out her suggestion that I lost it at lunch.

"That's about it. Pretty typical day. Nothing crazy going on. I hope your credit card company doesn't charge you for whatever the thief bought."

Her phone buzzes on the table, and she lights up. I'm thankful for the change of topic.

"What's his name?" I ask.

She grins. "Noel. I've been seeing him for a few weeks."

"Really? You haven't mentioned him."

Melanie shrugs. "It's been casual, although I do really like him."

"Tell me all about him. Where did you meet him?" I prompt as I lean back in my seat.

She grins. "It was actually at one of our happy hours after you and Norah left. He's older and there's just something about him. He looks like a bad boy and it's so sexy."

No surprise there. Melanie seems to gravitate toward older men. But I do worry about her choice in men.

"Bad boy? Please tell me he has a job?"

"I'm sure he does. He's paid for all our dates."

I take a breath and try my hardest not to sound judgmental. "You've known him for a few weeks but you don't know if he has a job?"

She laughs. "Of course he does. He's out of town a lot for business. But don't worry. He's been so kind to me. And his salt and pepper hair is so damn sexy."

She stares at her coffee with a dreamy look in her eyes.

"You want more than casual with him, don't you?"

Her smile widens. "I do. I'm hoping he brings it up though. We're going out tonight and I'm planning on inviting him back to my place." She waggles her brows.

I laugh. "Please don't do that in front of him."

"I won't. I want this one to stick."

Donny's face flashes in my mind. I want something with him to stick. No, stop. I can't go there.

Fortunately, Melanie is unaware of my inner turmoil.

"Well, I can't believe I'm going to tell you this but I kind of have a daddy kink. And tonight, I'll find out if he's on board."

I'm not at all surprised by her daddy kink. She's hinted at it enough during happy hour. Whatever works for her. I'm glad she has it figured out.

"On board?"

"Yep. After I invite him up, I'm going to call him daddy. That will either end in a wild night of passion or him running out of my place."

I laugh. "Sounds like an interesting night you have planned."

"I do. Now we need to get you a date too."

I lean forward and set my cup on the table. "No. I've got enough going on in my life right now. Besides, I can just live vicariously through you."

She rolls her eyes. "I'll let it slide for now. But not for long."

"Why are you so insistent on setting me up?"

She reaches over and grabs my hand. "Sarina, you're a

beautiful, smart, brilliant woman. I just hate seeing you alone. I know the right guy is out there for you."

"You know, I might be alone but I'm not lonely. I'm fine."

Her phone buzzes again. "Like I said, I'll let it slide for now. I gotta run. I've got an appointment to get the full Brazilian."

I wince. "People still do that?"

She shakes her head as she sighs. "Oh Sarina. They do. I'll text you the name of my salon. They do a great job. But for now," she stands up and grabs her coffee, "I must run. See you tomorrow in the office."

"Don't stay up too late," I say.

"Don't worry. I will." She winks and then nearly sprints out the door.

Was I ever that excited about a man? I think back over the few relationships I have had. Not one of them had me considering a Brazilian.

But for Donny, I'd consider it. I spit out my cocoa as that thought hits me.

No. I need to keep my thoughts professional with him. But then as I lean back, I wonder why. Why can't I indulge in this little fantasy in my head? He never has to know. And it isn't like men who look like him cross my path that often.

My phone buzzes and I frown, wondering why the director of Human Resources is calling me.

"Hello?"

"Sarina? I'm glad I caught you. Can you meet me today?"

That is one part of my job I do not like—you're never really off the clock. Whatever this is, I'm sure it can wait until tomorrow.

"Actually, Mary I've gone out of town for the day."

It's a lie but I really just want one day off.

"Oh, uh. I guess I'll have to tell you this news over the phone."

I take my last sip of cocoa and close my eyes. The only time I hear from HR is when there is a problem with an employee. Not something I want to deal with on top of everything else.

"What happened?" I ask.

Mary coughs. "I'm so sorry to have to tell you this but the board met last night—"

"What? Are you sure? I wasn't notified."

Mary sighs. "You weren't notified because the meeting was about you."

My heart sinks. "Me?"

"I'm afraid I don't know the details. I only know that it has been decided that you're on a suspension starting immediately. Sarina, I'm so sorry to have to tell you this over the phone."

Suspended? What the hell?

"Was a reason given?"

"Yes. I'll read you what the board wrote. 'Sarina McIntyre is a suspect in the theft of the laser weapon system and is also carrying on an intimate relationship with one of the men investigating this incident on behalf of the Navy. The board feels it is in the best interest of Asher Vaughn to suspend Ms. McIntyre's employment until this matter is resolved.'"

I can't breathe.

"Sarina, they chose this route instead of terminating your employment because everyone here really likes you and doesn't truly believe you could have done this. It just doesn't look right, and they felt they had to make this choice."

I gulp in air. "Mary, I don't have an intimate relationship with that man or anyone. The only thing I've been intimate with in the last two years is my vibrator!"

I slap my hand over my mouth as several people turn to stare at me. One mom puts her hands over her child's ears as she glares at me.

"Oh—well...you can take that up with the board. I'm just the messenger."

I close my eyes. I just told the head of HR I use a vibrator. At this point, I couldn't show my face there again anyway.

"I understand. Thank you for letting me know."

I end the call before I can embarrass myself any further.

Suspended? The board thinks I'm a suspect. That I could steal a weapon meant for the United States Navy. I think I'm going to be sick. How could anyone think this? My mind goes back to the hoodie. I don't know what it means but I have a strong feeling I'm being set up.

CHAPTER 12

Donny

The trip to the hanger at Boeing Field had been a bust. Aside from the fact it took us two hours in traffic to even get there, the space in question was empty. Well, not empty. It was filled with goodie bags that a local business was handing out to the people who'd come to see the Blue Angels land.

According to the person in charge of the goodie bags, the space had just opened up that morning. They originally were going to be outside but with the forecast of rain all day, they were thankful they could move indoors.

But that left the question: where the hell is the weapon? According to the tracking device, it was sitting in that hanger. And no, we didn't find the device. CT, Rover, and I plan to go back tonight after all the festivities have wrapped up.

Until then, I have some time to myself. I sharpen my charcoal pencil and get back to shading in her hair. When I lean back, I can't help but smile. Sarina is smiling back at me. Drawing has always relaxed me. And while I've drawn a few portraits of friends, this is the first time I can remember drawing a woman. A woman that I'm interested in. One that I need to stay away from until this investigation is over.

I usually draw landscapes to try to remember all the places I've seen. It was something I found that calmed all the anger I carried as a hormonal teenager.

My phone lights up. I grab it when I see Sarina's name.

Sarina: *I was just suspended from my job. It's your fault.*

What the hell? What did I do?

Sarina: *The board thinks we're having sex.*

I set the phone down on the table and run my hand through my hair. Now, there are a few ways I could approach this. Most of those would be the right way.

Unfortunately for me, I can't help myself.

Donny: *Do you want to?*

I stare at my text. What the fuck am I doing? After she kissed me outside the bar, I know for a fact our chemistry is mutual. Just ill timed. Very ill timed.

Sarina: *???*

I can imagine her, flustered, typing on her phone.

Donny: *Sorry. I meant, why do they think that?*

My phone rings. And as if I haven't made enough bad decisions, I continue when I answer it. I shouldn't be having personal conversations with a suspect. But this is technically about the case because I need to know why they suspended her.

"Sarina—"

"Donny? They suspended me because Norah told them yesterday that you drove me home from the bar. Despite the fact that I explained to everyone that you were only there because you had questions relating to the investigation, they only believed it was a booty call apparently. And now I'm jobless."

Well shit. Now I feel bad. Once she texted her location Friday night, I couldn't stay away. Clearly, I didn't think it through what consequences could come from barging in there. Then seeing her with that other man, I may have overreacted.

"I'm sorry. I didn't realize how it would look to everyone."

She sighs into the phone. "Neither did I. Why did you come to the bar that night instead of waiting until the next day? If you had I wouldn't be suspended!"

She's angry. Rightfully so.

"I'm sorry. It was a bad judgment call on my part. Look, I'll talk to the board and tell them nothing happened and that we don't have a personal relationship."

She sighs into the phone. "I'm sorry for snapping. Please don't talk to the board. That would only make this worse."

"You sure?"

"I'm sure." She sighs again. "Donny, am I really a suspect?"

I squirm in my seat. She is but I know deep down she didn't do this.

"Technically, all employees of Asher Vaughn are suspects." That wasn't a lie.

And as I say it, I realize it's a good thing she turned down my offer to go to the board. Going to the board on her behalf would be more than an investigator would do for a suspect. Fuck. There really is nothing I can do for her without making it worse.

She sniffles.

"Sarina, are you crying?"

"What? No." She sniffles again. "Dammit. Maybe a little."

"Your job really means that much to you?"

"It does. But it's more than that. My phone has been ringing since the suspension was announced. Reporters keep calling. I made the mistake of answering the first couple of calls. The questions they're asking… they think I'm guilty."

I close my eyes. I know this is only going to get worse for her before it gets better.

"Can you stay with a friend? You know until this blows over?"

She laughs. "Actually, I can't. That's the problem with giving my life to this job. My friends all work at Asher Vaughn. I'd only be risking their jobs."

The need to protect this woman is strong. But I can't invite her to my place, nor can I stay with her.

"Donny, thank you for talking to me. I really appreciate it. Can I ask you something?"

"Yeah."

"Do you think I did it?"

I know I'm supposed to try to remain impartial, but my gut is screaming this woman is innocent.

"No, I don't."

She sniffles again. "Thank you."

"Don't thank me until I find the person responsible for all of this. Did you go through your credit card history?"

"I did. And there were no other suspicious charges."

"Only the hoodie?"

"Yes, isn't that strange?"

"Whoever did it hoped you wouldn't notice one odd charge. It just confirms even more for me that you're being framed."

Her end is silent.

"Sarina, you still there?"

"You think I'm being framed?"

"I do."

"Thank you, Donny. I appreciate you talking to me."

"Anytime."

She ends the call and I lean back. Anytime? Damn I'm in

trouble.

* * *

"WELL, THAT WAS A FUCKING BUST," Rover says while sipping his beer.

CT, Rover, and I came back to my place after thoroughly searching the hangar at Boeing Field again. We found the tracker. It was taped behind a toolbox. Someone is fucking with us. I think we all secretly hoped whoever had the weapon would try to bring it back there tonight after the crowd dispersed.

"I don't understand. How the hell can we not locate a laser weapon system? It isn't small," CT says before finishing his beer.

"It isn't huge either," I point out. "Do you think someone on base is involved?" I ask CT.

He shakes his head. "No. And neither do Rocco, Ace, or Phantom. No one there knew anything. All the records indicate a delivery was coming that afternoon. But based on when and where the truck was stopped, the delivery would have come that morning."

"That's odd. Do you think the pickup time was changed?" I ask.

"I don't know. That's one question I didn't ask." Rover runs his hand through his hair. "It still bothers me that the driver got out of the truck."

"Yeah, me too," CT says.

"We should question him again," I say.

Rover shakes his head. "I tried yesterday and found out he went on vacation to Barcelona."

I frown. "But he was shot less than a week ago."

"Yeah, but it was basically a flesh wound," Rover reminds me. Then he closes his eyes. "Shit. He was in on it, wasn't he?"

"Did Trip check his bank records?"

Rover shook his head. "No, he was considered a victim."

"I just texted Trip asking him to see what he can find," CT says.

Rover grabs his phone. "I'm going to call Henry at PV and see what I can learn."

He leaves the room.

"If it was the driver, then that would take Asher Vaughn and the Navy off the hook," CT says.

"Yes, it would," I say, hoping we may finally have a lead.

"And that would mean you could date Sarina McIntyre," CT says.

I glance up and see his ugly mug grinning at me.

I lean back and cross my arms. "Why would you say that?"

"I think we've all seen the article. You took her home?"

Shit. That means Stormy and Cowboy might have seen it.

"No, I was just trying to ask her some questions."

CT opens his mouth but before he can respond, Rover walks back in the room.

"PV Transport says they determine the pickup schedule and routes. The driver would have all the information they need to steal the weapon," he says.

I jump up. "Let's go."

"Where?" Rover and CT ask.

"Into the office. We need to gather everything we have on this driver."

"The sooner we confirm he is our suspect, the sooner Donny can date Sarina," CT says.

"No," I say. "The sooner we find out if he's our suspect, the sooner I can question him to find out who he's working with. Someone is setting up Sarina. What other reason would there be for someone to steal her credit card to buy a hoodie worn by the gunman?"

"You're assuming she was set up," Rover says.

"I know she was."

And it's true. I have no doubts.

CHAPTER 13

SARINA

I DISCOVERED PRETTY QUICKLY Monday morning that I don't have any interests outside of my job. After trying to watch television and being bored out of my mind yesterday, I'm now at the gym. It's quite crowded. I find I keep staring at everyone wondering why they aren't at work.

I can't even relax at the gym. When did it come to this? Of course, it doesn't help that I keep thinking about Donny. He confirmed in our call yesterday that he doesn't think I did it. I don't know why but that was really important to hear.

"Hey, need a spotter?"

I turn to find an attractive guy standing behind me.

"No, I'm good. Thanks."

He shrugs. "If you change your mind, come find me." Then he winks.

Am I depressed? Is that why I have nothing in my life except work?

"What a coincidence."

Shivers run down my spine hearing the familiar deep voice. I glance up and there's Donny standing three feet away. The man is hot in a tank top and shorts. My eyes take in every muscle, every bead of sweat that I want to lick off.

"Sarina?"

I snap out of my lust-induced state. "Huh?" I manage.

"This is your gym?" His eyes are taking in my outfit, and I give myself a mental high five for wearing the cute tank and running tights.

"It is. But I normally come in after work. I'm surprised to see so many people here this morning."

He laughs. "This is normal. A lot of people want to get their workout in before they start their day."

Of course they do. But why is he here?

"You seriously go here. This isn't some kind of trick to run into me?"

"Confident woman. I like that." He licks his lips and I'm enthralled. His lips are full, and I want to feel them on mine again.

"Really, I go here. Most days I come in early to get my weightlifting sessions in. Then I go for a run."

My eyes travel down his body to his legs. They are muscular and I can imagine he has a lot of endurance.

He chuckles and my eyes snap back up.

"Trust me, this chemistry, it's mutual. And that is why I'm standing back here and not touching you right now. I wouldn't want to stop."

His honesty sends chills up my spine.

"Plus, I suspect you might have a coworker or two here and we don't want to make things worse for your job."

"Right," I say stepping back increasing the space between us. "Did you solve the case yet?"

He arches a brow. "I'm good but no one is that good."

I nod. "I'll let you get back to your workout then. It was good seeing you again."

He nods. "You, too."

I make my way to a treadmill and run a few miles. I sneak glances at Donny who looks even sexier lifting weights.

After my shower, I head out and nearly run into the guy who offered to spot me. Fortunately, I catch myself in time and utter an apology.

On the drive home, I spot a farmer's market that I always wanted to stop at but never felt I could take the time. Today, I stop.

As I purchase a jar of fresh local honey, the hairs on the back of my neck go up. I glance around but don't see anything out of the ordinary. I move to the next shop and buy several fresh tomatoes. The feeling grows stronger. Is someone watching me?

Instead of going back to my car, I walk a few blocks over to a park and sit on a bench. The feeling is still there. I get up and retrace my steps taking in every person I pass. No one looks familiar.

Would Gunnar have hired someone to watch me? I know he's very concerned with the PR for the company, as am I. Or is it someone at Donny's company? I make my way back to my car and put my bags inside, but I don't get in. I glance around one more time. Nothing out of the ordinary. But I can't shake the feeling.

I grab my phone from my purse and text Donny.

Sarina: *Are you having someone follow me?*

His response is immediate.

Donny: *Why are you asking?*

Sarina: *I can feel someone following me, but I can't see him.*

"Either you're very perceptive or I'm losing my touch."

I spin around to find Donny grinning at me from the other side of the car.

"Why the hell are you following me?"

He stares at me for a beat, and I don't think he's going to tell me.

"I think someone is trying to set you up to take the fall."

I clutch the door handle to stay upright. I feel lightheaded.

"You mentioned that before. The hoodie. That was part of it, wasn't it?"

He nods. "Can we get in your car?"

"Of course." I get in and unlock his door.

The moment he's inside, his scent climbs over me and I'm both scared at being framed and turned on by the man at the same time. The conflicting emotions are too much. This is too confusing.

He seems to sense my turmoil and places his hand on mine, calming me.

"The man on video seen carjacking the truck was wearing a hoodie from Dave's BBQ."

I close my eyes and lean my head back.

"So, whoever did this works for Asher Vaughn."

"Why do you say that?" he asks.

"Because I went over all my movements on the day the hoodie was purchased. The only time my purse was out of my sight was when I was in meetings. Only a handful of people have access to the fourth floor, and I added in others that were granted access that day. This list is ten people including myself."

He squeezes my hand. "There's a problem with your list."

"What?"

"Someone could have copied down your card information at any time and only used it that day. The order was placed online."

I frown.

"Was your purse out of your sight at any other time outside of work over the last month or two?"

"No, of course not." But then I remember something. "Oh no."

"What?"

"I went to a conference in October. left my purse at my table during one of the dinners."

When he frowns, I feel I need to further explain.

"I got up to get my dinner. It was buffet style. On the way, I got caught up in a conversation with a colleague. I was away from my table for maybe twenty minutes."

"What was the conference about? Who attended?"

"It was primarily Asher Vaughn employees, members of the military, and some vendors. Donny, there had to be nearly two thousand attendees."

The thought that someone there could have purposely been planning on framing me for something like this. I feel sick.

"That does increase our pool of potential suspects. Text me the details of that conference and I'll look into the attendees."

Then he turns in the seat to face me. "For now, I want you to lay low."

I laugh. "What do you think I'm going to do? Give a speech? Scream from the rooftops?"

"What are you doing next?" he asks.

"Going home."

"I'll follow you."

He reaches for the door handle, and I grab his arm.

"Why would you follow me?"

He turns back and the heat in his eyes matches what my body is feeling for him. This is insane. I need to fight these feelings.

"I told you. I think someone is trying to set you up. If I can figure out who that person is, I think I can solve this."

"Okay."

I'd agree to just about anything right now to get this resolved.

"Thank you for believing me."

Donny stares into my eyes. "You're welcome."

Neither of us move. The air is electric between us and it is taking everything I have not to kiss this man again. But I won't give him another reason to pull away from me.

His face inches closer to mine.

"Donny?"

"Yes?"

He's so close I can smell his minty breath.

"What are you doing?"

"Kissing you," he says just as he leans in and we connect.

His hand is in my hair pulling me closer. My whole body is lit up as our tongues tangle. I'm lost in this man until the sound of a baby crying pulls me out of my lust filled stupor. I jerk back. That's when I notice a woman pushing a stroller with a very upset baby past my car.

I miss his warmth immediately.

Donny leans his head back on the seat.

"Shit. I'm sorry. I shouldn't have done that. This pull I feel for you is strong."

My fingers go to my lips missing his touch. "I know," I say.

"I'm still following you home."

I nod.

Donny squeezes my hand then gets out of the car.

Ten minutes later, I pull up to my home. There are a lot of cars parked on my street. The neighbor must have something going on. I park in the driveway and barely make it out of my car when at least three microphones are shoved in my face. There's a bright light aimed at me too.

"Is it true you were the mastermind behind stealing the new weapon system during transport?"

"Who are you working for? Are you selling it to terrorists?"

"Is anyone else at Asher Vaughn involved?"

I push through staring at the ground to not be blinded by that bright light. I now see a van across the street that says KMTV News.

No. The press thinks I did this? But why? It doesn't make any sense.

One reporter steps in front of me stopping me from getting to my door.

"Ms. McIntyre, are you a terrorist?"

"What? No! I didn't do this." I try to push past him, but he won't let me go. He grips my arm, a little too hard.

"How can you deny this despite all the evidence?"

I jerk my head up. "What evidence."

"Take your hands off her."

Donny is suddenly by my side removing the man's hand from my arm.

The man smiles. "Donny Reis. Former Navy SEAL and a man who would know how to sell a weapon system. How long have you two been working together?"

I close my eyes. When I didn't think this could get worse. It does.

"Come on," Donny says as he leads me to the door.

He takes the keys from my hand and unlocks and opens the door.

Once inside, he closes all the curtains. I sit at the kitchen table. Stunned.

"They think I did this? But why?"

I hear Donny talking on his phone, but I don't pay attention. I grab my phone and try to figure out what is going on. That's when I see the press release from Asher Vaughn.

It's damning. No, it is more than damning. It's a lie.

"How can they print this?" I ask holding up my screen to Donny.

He quickly reads the story.

"Wow. We're in a relationship and you're the primary suspect. Unbelievable. All lies."

"Yes, they are."

I rock back and forth. How the hell did this happen? I couldn't believe Gunnar would allow this press release. I could sue. I should sue. Damn it, but I want my job back. Is that even possible now? Clearly, I've been judged by the public and found guilty.

Donny pulls up a chair next to mind and wraps his arms around my shoulders, pulling me into him. I grab on and let the tears fall. I should be embarrassed but I'm not. I'm exhausted.

I have no idea how long we stay like that before there's a knock at the door.

I pull back. "They're knocking now?"

Donny stands. "It should be Shaw."

"Who?"

He goes to my door and opens it. A tall woman with long, dark hair walks in. She's gorgeous and I immediately wonder if this is Donny's girlfriend. That only makes me feel worse.

"Sarina, this is Shaw Morgan. She's Cowboy's wife and a damn good attorney."

I glance at the woman, who holds her hand out. I shake it.

"Nice to meet you." I glance at Donny to further explain.

"I called Shaw because it looks like you need legal advice. But more importantly, she's been where you are."

I laugh. "She's been called a terrorist?"

Shaw sets her purse on the kitchen table and turns to me.

"I was accused of crimes I didn't commit. I lost my job and the media hounded me. I was made out to be a pariah. But I fought back and I'm here to help you do the same thing."

I'm overwhelmed by all of this. Why would she help me? Because Donny asked her? Why would he help me?

But those aren't the questions that come out of my mouth.

"Who's Cowboy?"

"One of my bosses. He and Stormy own Morgan Thompson Security."

"Oh." I'm still trying to process all of this when Donny's phone rings.

He answers it and takes a few steps away.

"It isn't what it looks like," he says.

His hand goes to his hip. "Yeah, I'll be right there."

He pockets his phone and turns back to us. "That was Stormy. I have to go to the office immediately."

"Go ahead. We'll be fine," Shaw says.

Donny stares at me for a moment.

"I'll be fine," I assure him.

With a final nod, he turns and leaves.

"Okay, so let's discuss this press release," Shaw says.

"First, do you want some coffee?"

She smiles. "I would love some."

After pouring us each a cup, we sit down at the kitchen table.

"Cowboy? Is he really a cowboy?"

Shaw laughs. "Well, he owns a ranch and is from Wyoming so in some ways, yes he is."

"Do you live on a ranch?" I ask then take a sip of coffee.

Shaw smiles. "I do. But let's talk about you. I like to get to know all the guys' girlfriends."

I spit out my coffee. "Oh, I think you misunderstood. We're not dating."

She arches a brow at me. "The way that man looks at you and the way you look at him, it's just a matter of time. Besides he wouldn't have asked me to come here for just anyone."

I swallow uncomfortably.

"He told me he believes I'm being framed and if he can find out who's behind it, he'll be able to solve this case. That's all this is about."

"Mm-hmm. If that's what you want to tell yourself."

The man has admitted he is attracted to me. And our chemistry is unlike anything I've ever experienced. But why would I think it is anything more than that, attraction? I want to believe it, though.

"See, that smile right there. That's how I know."

I turn my attention to my coffee and that must be a clue for her.

"Well, you need someone here you can trust and now you're stuck with me."

"Thank you. I really appreciate it. I don't understand how I could be framed for something like this."

Shaw licks her lips. "Sadly, once the press gets a hold of something, it can snowball. I'll contact Asher Vaughn and ask them for their proof that the allegations they made in the press release are true. If they can't provide them, then I'll pressure them to retract it."

CHAPTER 14

DONNY

I HIDE my smile as I leave Sarina's. I'm happy Shaw is there with her and is willing to help her out. But the last thing I need is a photo of me smiling leaving her place.

But that's not an issue because the moment I step outside, I'm blinded by the lights. Instead of only a few reporters, the crowd has grown to at least twenty people standing on her lawn. And I'm certain I'm scowling.

"Mr. Reis, are you and Sarina McIntyre in a relationship?" One reporter asks shoving a microphone in my face.

"No comment." I push past them and get to my car. Fortunately, they get the message and don't try to follow.

It takes effort to drive the speed limit to MTS. I'm pissed. Pissed that Trip didn't find anything amiss with the driver's bank records. Pissed at how Asher Vaughn has treated Sarina. Pissed at the press. Hell, why would Asher Vaughn throw her under the bus like that? And me. It didn't make much sense unless they were trying to get the focus off of them and onto me.

This on the heels of the press release pointing fingers at the Navy. Frankly, all of this makes them look more guilty. I'd like to speak to the CEO but so far, I've had no luck. Every time I try, I get shut down. Some asshole named Gunnar left me a voice mail stating they had their own internal investigation team.

Yeah, well that isn't satisfactory, Gunnar.

By the time I make it into MTS, I'm fuming. I'm angry at not only whoever set Sarina up, but the assholes camped out in her yard. What possible news story do they think they are going to get harassing her?

But my anger melts the moment I see Stormy and Cowboy waiting for me. Despite the fact both Stormy and Cowboy started this security company together, it is rare for Cowboy to come into the office. He spends his time running his ranch and with his family.

Cowboy's face is red, something I've never seen. I'm immediately uncomfortable as I walk toward their office. I pass CT, who's sipping a cup of coffee. He slaps me on the back.

"Good luck."

Jesus, is it really going to be that bad?

Then someone plays "Taps" on their phone.

"Not funny, Peaches."

Peaches laughs. "How'd you know it was me?" he asks, peeking out from behind a desk.

I roll my eyes. How would I not know? But before I can think on it too much, I'm inside Stormy's office and the door is closed.

"Maverick, you need to walk us through everything that has happened in this case," Stormy says.

Cowboy's arms are crossed. "Don't leave anything out."

I take a seat at the conference table and pour myself a glass of water. Their withering stares have me parched. Then I tell them everything I know.

Stormy is glowering by the time I've finished.

"Wait a minute. Maverick, I think you left something out. How did these rumors start that you and this woman are sleeping together?"

I take a sip of water then set the glass down. Before I speak, I make sure I look each of them in the eye.

"No, we are not sleeping together. Nothing like that is going on. I went to where Sarina was Friday to ask her some questions. She was at a bar. I didn't realize it might be misinterpreted until we were outside and she kissed me. She'd had a few drinks too many. I stopped it."

"Shit. Well, I guess that explains the photos," Cowboy says.

"Photos?" I ask.

Cowboy turns his laptop around for me to see. Up on the screen are several photographs. One shows us kissing. And it doesn't look like I'm doing anything to stop it. Another shows me helping her into her house with my arms around her. Damn someone followed us that night. Wait, why would anyone be following us? No articles had been released yet.

Then the last photo was taken this morning as I'm leaving the house.

"Damn reporters," I say remembering how I had to make my way through them.

Stormy growls. That's when I realize what this looks like.

"No, That morning photo was taken on my way here today. Look," I point at myself. "I'm wearing the same clothes."

Stormy nods.

"Someone is trying to set us up. All I did was drive her home and we talked."

"Why the hell did you go to a bar to question her? Why not wait until the next day?" Cowboy asks.

That was a good question and one I've asked myself many times. But I know the answer. Something protective took over and, well, that's not exactly the full truth. Something protective and something jealous took over.

"I should have waited. You're right. I was just eager to solve this case."

"If someone was watching Ms. McIntyre then, then they were already tipped off," Stormy says.

"Or," I counter, "the person who spread the lies to the press also tossed that in."

Cowboy paces the room. "Friday you were at a bar with Sarina, and you drove her home. Saturday there's a news article stating Asher Vaughn believes the at-fault party is in the Navy. Now today, Monday, the press believes that Sarina is the guilty party and that you are somehow connected."

I nod.

Cowboy stops pacing. "Why would the press flip flop who they believed was guilty so quickly? What information did they receive?"

"Saturday's article, did anyone else pick it up and report on it?"

We all pull out our phones and begin to search.

"Not that I can find," Stormy says.

"Me neither," Cowboy confirms.

"I found the original story. It was on Seattlenewsnow.com."

Stormy and Cowboy both groan. "And Asher Vaughn gave Sarina shit for that?"

Seattlenewsnow.com was known for making things up in an effort to get more followers to their site. Rarely did any other news source pick up something they originated.

"They did. She mentioned a PR guy."

"Did she mention his name?" Stormy asks.

"No, but I'll find out."

I send a text to Sarina asking for the guy's name.

"Gunnar Tomlinson. I just sent the spelling to you two. Damn! That's the man that stopped me from interviewing the CEO."

"I'll have Trip see what he can find," Cowboy says.

Well, if anyone can find dirt on the guy, it's Trip.

Cowboy puts his phone on speaker.

"Sugartown Tanning, how can I help you today?"

I can't help but laugh. The man answers the phone with a different fake business each time. He claims it's for security but I'm pretty sure it's just to fuck with Cowboy. The two served together and from what I've seen, they're pretty tight.

"Damn. I'd forgotten about that place," Cowboy laughs. "But I'm afraid I don't have time to go down memory lane. I need you to run a name. I'm texting it to you now."

"Got it. I'll send you what I find," Trip says. "Too bad you don't have time for memories. You might need to lighten your load. Talk soon."

Cowboy turns to me. "About Friday night, you said you asked her questions as you drove her home."

I swallow not liking that he's back on this. "I did, yes."

"When you got to her house, you helped her to her door?" he asks pointing at the photo showing that.

"Of course."

"Did you help her inside?" Cowboy asks.

"Yeah. She passed out on the drive home."

Cowboy exhales loudly.

"How long were you inside?" Stormy asks.

"She came to as I was helping her inside. She asked me to stay. Nothing happened. I'd never take advantage of someone in that condition. But I left in the morning before she woke up."

Stormy tipped his head back and was muttering something at the ceiling.

"Jesus. Well, that explains a few things." Cowboy leans on the table. "You probably should have led with that. We're trying to do a little damage control here. The Navy is concerned that you may not be objective."

"Look. I know it looks bad. But nothing happened. I swear."

"I know, but I'm afraid we have to move you off this investigation. Since you're in the spotlight now, you'll do desk duty until it clears up."

"Desk duty? But I promised Sarina I'd find out who's setting her up."

Stormy arches an eyebrow. "Did you now?"

Shit. I realize too late how that sounds.

"I'm certain someone is setting her up and if I can figure out who it is, I'll likely have our suspect."

Cowboy takes a seat at the table.

"Tell us what you know."

Stormy and I take a seat and I tell them what I know, including the one charge on her credit card, the fact the driver flew across the world shortly after being shot, and that the press releases toss blame without any facts to support them.

"It's not the driver," Stormy says.

"Trip didn't find anything on the driver?"

"No."

"What about his family?" I ask.

Stormy paces the room then pulls out his phone. He turns it on speaker phone.

"Purfect Pets. We have all the right sweaters for your pup. How can I help you?"

I have to stifle a laugh.

"Trip, did you dig into any of the driver's family's finances?"

"No. I can do that now."

"Thank you."

Then Stormy leaned against the table and faced me. "Let's hope he gets a hit."

"Hey Stormy, sorry to interrupt but there's a delivery for you," Peaches says.

Stormy frowns. "What is it?"

Peaches walks in holding a box. "A cake."

Stormy opens the box. Sure, enough there is a large sheet cake with the words "Happy Anniversary" written across it.

"Something you want to tell us?" Cowboy asks.

Stormy frowns. "I have no idea what this is." He looks at Peaches. "Who delivered it?"

"A guy in a van that said Custom Cakes on the side."

"It must be a mix up. I'll call them later."

Stormy stands. "Everyone back to work. I'll let you know if Trip finds anything."

After Stormy leaves the room, Peaches stares at me then Cowboy. "So can we eat it?"

I chuckle. "I'm not touching something of Stormy's."

"Me neither," Cowboy says.

"Ugh. You guys are no fun," Peaches says as he storms out of the room.

CHAPTER 15

SARINA

BY MONDAY EVENING, I'm mentally exhausted. So much so that when my phone rings, I answer it without looking.

"What the hell is going on? Why are so many vehicles over there and people standing on the sidewalk?" Melanie asks.

Thankfully it isn't the press.

"Haven't you heard the news?" I ask sarcastically.

"I found out about your suspension this morning and tried to come by as soon as I could leave. But that doesn't explain all those people."

I fill her in on what I've read online and the questions the reporters asked me.

"Where the hell did they get the idea that you're behind anything?"

"That's a very good question. I don't know. This whole thing sucks."

She sighs. "It sucks more than you know."

I brace myself. “What else is going on?”

“Jim promoted Norah to your position. She kept me very busy redecorating the office and telling me how things are going to change.”

“Wait. Promote? You mean she’s in the position temporarily. The board has to approve that position and damn it, I’m suspended, not fired.”

“Norah isn’t treating it as temporary. I don’t know. We went to happy hours with her, and I thought she was cool, but I think the power is going to her head. She treats me more like an assistant than a friend now.”

I had no idea they would replace me that quickly. I thought this was a short-term suspension.

“I’m still shocked Jim filled the role so quickly. But I shouldn’t be. He doesn’t like me.” Threatening to go to the board solidified that.

But Norah is stepping in. She hasn’t even called to check on me. I really thought she was a friend.

“Has Norah asked about me at all?”

Melanie sighs. “No. I’m sorry. She’s focused on the job. But tell me about the other things they are saying. You know about you and Donny. Is there any truth to that? Did you guys get together?”

I laugh. “No. And even if there had been a spark of chemistry, I'm sure this ruined it.”

“Don’t rule him out just yet.”

“Donny’s pretty sure I'm being framed, but without me having access to anything at Asher Vaughn, I don't know how I'm going to prove anything.”

Melanie sighs again. “Damn, this is really shitty. You know if you need anything, and I mean anything, let me know.”

I hear a drawer close.

“Thank you. I really appreciate that.”

"Oh, before I forget, your brother called today but didn't say why."

Wow. Is it possible Preston read what's going on and is actually checking up on me? He's always been a bit of a self obsessed asshole but maybe this thing with our dad helped him see it.

"I hate to cut this short, but Noel texted me as soon as I got home and wants to come over."

Ah yes, the older man.

"Did you call him daddy?"

Melanie squeals into the phone. "I did and he was so into it! It was the hottest thing ever. I'm hoping for a repeat performance."

"Good luck."

"Thanks. I'm going to send you a photo of me and Noel. I took it last week and love it. Give me just a second."

She's silent for a moment.

"Huh. That's weird. I can't find it."

"That's okay. You can show me next time I see you."

"I will. Hang in there. Hopefully this suspension situation will all get sorted out soon."

Melanie ends the call and I toss the phone on the table then take a seat. Norah Jensen has taken over my role.

Shaw places a cup of tea in front of me.

"What's wrong?" she asks.

Shaw has been great. First, she talked to me about my options for suing for libel. Then when I couldn't hold back the tears, she held my hand and told me she has my back. This woman doesn't even know me, and she's been kinder to me than, well, just about anyone.

I thought Norah was my friend, but I have to face the truth. Norah has not been acting like a friend. Now I'm wondering if she was always after my job. Why else would she turn so quickly on me? Unless she believes the lies and thinks I am a traitor.

But Norah never struck me as someone who wants to climb the corporate ladder. I've been to Norah's home. She's the quintessential cat lady with three cats that she knits sweaters for. She has a separate online business she's pursuing.

Yet, she is in upper management.

I place my hands around the teacup and take comfort in its warmth.

"I just found out that someone I thought was a friend has taken over my job. It's the same woman that encouraged me to go with Donny that night at the bar, and the one who threw me under the bus at the meeting with the PR representative the next day."

"That doesn't sound like a friend," Shaw says as she sits in the chair next to me.

No, it doesn't. And now I'm wondering how far would Norah go to make me look bad? I'm about to ask Shaw if a cat lady could be an arms dealer when my phone rings. Donny's name flashes. I simply stare at it.

"You should take that. He might have news," Shaw says.

I nod then answer.

"I have bad news," Donny says.

I close my eyes.

"I'm off the investigation. I've been put on desk duty until everything blows over."

"Blows over? Why do you think it will just blow over?"

Papers shuffle in the background. "I told you I'm certain you're being framed. And I won't rest until the assignment is resolved."

"Yeah, but like you said, you're off the case."

"Well, I am on desk duty which gives me a lot of time to

dig into the background of everyone on your list that could have taken your credit card."

I take a sip of tea. "Start with Norah Jensen."

"Oh yeah? Cause she told everyone about me taking you home?"

I shrug even though he can't see me.

"Yeah." I don't have the energy to tell him she's taken over my job.

"Will do. I'll let you know if I find anything. Oh, I gotta go."

I set the phone down and drink some more tea.

My phone buzzes. A text from my brother.

Preston: *Saw the news. Call me if you need anything.*

He's trying. I have to give him that.

Sarina: *Thank you. I will.*

"Traitor!" several people shout from my front lawn.

Tears well in my eyes. I love this house and always felt so comfortable here. But not anymore. All because everyone out there believes I'm guilty of this terrible crime. They have no evidence but apparently that doesn't matter.

"You know, I can get you out of here and away from the press. Come stay at the ranch with me."

"I appreciate your offer, but I don't want to impose. I'm afraid there's no running from the press," I say pointing outside.

Shaw smiles. "Josh and I live at Horse Haven Ranch. We have a guest room where you can stay. You can enjoy the peace and quiet until Donny solves this. I'll make sure no one knows you're there."

I laugh so I won't cry.

"Donny's been taken off the investigation. He's on desk duty."

"I doubt that'll stop him from working on this."

Shaw seems so sure. Donny did say he was going to keep digging.

The chants outside grow louder.

"Seriously, this isn't healthy. Let's go."

The more I think about it, the more I realize she is right. I'm going to go crazy if I stay here.

"Okay. Let me grab a few things."

"Of course."

I pack a few days' worth of clothes, toiletries, and some snack bars. I don't want to impose but I'm not sure going out for food will really be an option. I grab my laptop and I'm ready.

Shaw takes my laptop bag from me and nods. "Let's do this. Follow right behind me."

We step outside and I lock up. Immediately, several microphones are shoved in my face.

"We will not be taking questions at this time," Shaw says as she ushers them away from us.

More people with signs have shown up. Now it isn't just *"traitor"* but also *"burn her at the stake!"*

Shaw opens the passenger door of her car and I get in, placing my bag on my lap. After she closes the door, she walks around the car and slips inside. Several people are pounding on the window as she puts my laptop in the back seat.

"Sarina, why did you do it?"

"Sarina! Is Donny Reis your accomplice?"

"Assholes," she mutters under her breath as she starts the car.

She backs out slowly. You'd think people would move out of the way, but they don't. Finally, after what feels like an eternity, we make it onto the street. Five minutes into the trip, I finally say something.

"I hate to tell you this, but it looks like some of the reporters are following us."

"I'm on it." Shaw pushes a button on the dash. "I'll call Josh and he'll take care of it."

"Shaw, where are you?" a deep voice asks.

"I got Sarina out of her house. It was getting really bad. I want to take her to the ranch, but we've got some press following us. Think you can help me out?"

"Sure thing."

"I'm heading to highway 202. I'll go south. Can you have someone meet us there?"

"Yeah, I have someone I can call."

"Thank you."

"Stay safe and call me when you get home."

"I will."

Shaw pushes the button on the dash again to end the call.

We drive for another twenty minutes before turning south on the highway. We weren't on the highway long when a semi up ahead signals from the side of the road that it's merging into traffic.

"Watch out. I think that truck is going to cut you off."

Shaw grins. "No, he's going to help us."

The semi enters the two-lane highway right in front of us. Instead of slowing, Shaw guns it and pulls into the oncoming lane to pass the semi. Shaw manages to pass the semi and cut back to our lane just in time. Then she slows quickly and takes a right turn down what appears to be a forest road. Then she whips the car to the left and cuts the engine. The lights are off, and we're surrounded by trees.

I hear the semi pass on the highway just a few feet away. Then I listen as other cars pass behind it. My skin prickles as I wait for someone to turn down the road and find us. But they don't.

After several minutes, Shaw starts the car and makes her way back to the highway. She turns back the way we came.

"That was amazing," I say.

She laughs. "Yeah. Unfortunately, in the line of work that the guys do sometimes we get press. It's an issue, so we've developed a few tricks of our own to get them to leave us alone. It's not perfect, but it works."

A little while later, Shaw pulls down a long driveway. Above is a sign that reads "Horse Haven Ranch."

A beautiful home and a very large arena come into view. There are a few guys near the arena along with a couple of horses. Shaw waves and they wave back. Then she grabs a remote from her visor and the garage door to the home opens as we approach.

"I'll get your laptop. Bring your bag this way."

I get out of the car and follow her through the garage, past the laundry room and into the home.

The first thing I see is a wall of windows looking out over pastureland with mountains in the backdrop. I see a few horses in the distance grazing on the grass.

"Oh my, this is so beautiful."

"Thank you. I love it here. I worked on the ranch right out of high school. That's when I met Josh."

"Wow, you two have been together a long time."

Her smile drops. "Actually, we haven't. But that's a long story for another time. Feel free to hang out here if you'd like or you could walk around the grounds."

"Thank you. I really appreciate this."

My eye catches on a folder sitting on the kitchen table and that's when I realize I've probably kept Shaw from working.

"Oh, I'm so sorry. You probably need to work."

She waves her hand in the air. "It's fine. I have my own

practice and work from home. It allows me to be free for the boys when needed."

"Where are your boys?"

Shaw sits down at the kitchen table. "They're with my mom. And don't worry about it. She loves having them. It worked out perfectly so I could spend the day with you making sure everything is okay. Plus, I was curious."

I sit across from her. "Curious about what?"

"You. The way Maverick talks about you, well I just knew I had to meet you."

"Maverick?"

She blinks. "Sorry, Donny. I'm so used to using his call name."

"His call name?"

"Kind of like a nickname. You'll have to ask him about it."

Now I'm curious how he got the name Maverick but right now I'm stuck on something else Shaw said.

"He talks about me?"

"When he called me."

Of course. But she must see the disappointment on my face.

"Hey, Sarina, Maverick wouldn't have called me for just anyone. You understand?"

No, I really don't but I nod anyway.

I stare into the kitchen and notice a hallway next to it with several photos hanging on the wall. I spot Donny in one and walk over.

"Are those Donny's coworkers?" I ask.

"Yes," Shaw says as she walks up next to me. "This is my husband Josh. On the other end is Stormy. They own Morgan Thompson Security. And then there's Rover, CT, Peaches, Trax, and Fox."

"Those are some interesting names," I say.

She laughs. "Yes, they are. You'll have to ask them how

they got those names. There are some pretty interesting stories. You definitely need to hear CT's story."

I'm struck by how strong and handsome all of these men are. Of course, Donny is the hottest one of the bunch in my opinion.

Shaw laughs. "Yeah, I could stare at them all day too. Wait until you're surrounded by them in person."

I can feel the heat creep up my neck. "Oh no. I mean yes, they're good looking. I doubt I'll ever meet them all."

Shaw cocks her head. "Do you like Maverick?"

I turn back to his picture and smile.

"I do."

"Good. You'll meet the guys. Don't worry about that."

CHAPTER 16

DONNY

THE LAST WEEK on the ranch has been good for Sarina. We've talked every night this week, getting to know each other. Cowboy finally realized what was going on and told me he believed Sarina was innocent too. And since I'm technically off the investigation, I have the green light to date her.

And now, I'm on my way to the ranch for a date. I'm surprised by how many cars are here when I pull up. I get out of my SUV and glance to the arena. It's full. I guess that makes sense for a Saturday. It's been a long time since I've ridden a horse. I wonder if Cowboy would indulge me sometime.

I turn my attention to the front of the house. Sarina is sitting in a chair smiling at me. She's even more beautiful than I remember.

"Hey," I say as I walk up onto the porch.

"Hey you." She's grinning.

We didn't have to see each other for this chemistry to

grow. Every night on the phone, everything I've learned, just made me want her more.

"You sound chipper," I say.

She stands. "I am. The press hasn't found me, and I've also been looking forward to seeing you."

I grin. "Yeah, me too."

I want to say more but for all I know my boss might be on the other side of the front door.

"I was hoping we could check out the pond on the property. Shaw says the views are fantastic and I thought it might be nice to get away from all of this," Sarina says as she motions toward the arena.

"Sounds great. Do we need to ride to get there?"

She shakes her head. "I've never ridden a horse. Shaw said we can take the golf cart."

I snort. "Golf cart? On a ranch?"

She tilts her head. "That's funny?"

I shake my head. "Probably just to me."

I hold out my hand and she takes it. The same shivers move up my arm that did the first day I met her.

I pull her in for a quick kiss. She blushes and that makes me want to do more. But not here.

She leads me behind the barn where sure enough, a golf cart awaits.

We get in and she drives.

"I have some news and questions," I say, breaking the silence.

"Okay, go ahead."

"Do know anything about Norah's father?"

She frowns. "Not much, but Norah did mention he's a food critic who travels around the world. She said he's written some books and does well. I've never met him, but I believe his name is Frank."

"Frank Jensen. He does have a few books out about the

food of a few countries. But they aren't doing that well. And the countries he's lived in aren't the ones he wrote about in the books."

I don't mention there are large chunks of time where Frank fell off the radar and we have no idea where he was.

She turns off the main path and onto the grass. "Sounds like maybe he isn't that good at what he does then."

I laugh. "I wish it was that simple."

"What do you mean?"

"It's just a hunch, but the countries and cities he's lived in aren't exactly known for their cuisine. They're known for being terrorist hot spots."

She turns to stare at me. "Terrorists? Do you think Norah helped her father to get the weapon into the hands of terrorists?"

"Watch out!" I point to three geese now in front of us. She swerves and misses them. I glance back to make sure they aren't chasing us. One thing I learned about geese is that they're mean as hell and will chase you down to bite you. When it's clear they're going to leave us alone, I turn back.

"Do you think Norah helped her father?"

She frowns. "I can't imagine Norah being involved in anything like that. Are you sure you have the same Frank Jensen? It sounds like it might be a common name."

"I'm sure it's the same man. Do you remember Norah ever talking about traveling to other countries? Or about having financial problems?"

Sarina parks the golf cart near a bench. Straight ahead is a beautiful small pond. The water is calm and reflects the trees.

"No. Norah usually talks about her cat sweater business. She sells them online."

Sarina steps out of the cart, but I stay still. Did I just hear that right?

"Donny? You coming?"

"Yeah, I… did you say cat sweaters?"

"Yes."

"Cats don't like clothes."

Her brow furrows. "Well, some must."

"Do you know the name of her business?"

"Kitten Kapers."

I grab my phone, thankful I have coverage and search for Norah's business.

"I found it." Then the page loads. "Oh no."

"What?"

Sarina walks around to my side of the cart to stare at my phone.

I start laughing. "These really are sweaters for cats. How the hell would you even get one on a cat?"

"I don't know. I've only been to Norah's a couple of times, and I can't say I ever saw her cats. Maybe they were hiding from a potential fashion show."

I'm laughing too hard to respond. Finally, I take a deep breath. "I'm sorry. But I grew up with barn cats and if we tried to put even so much as a collar on them, they would have shredded us. The cats in these photos look pissed."

Now she's laughing. "You're right. The cat I grew up with would never have tolerated a sweater."

Catching my breath, I bookmark the page. "Okay, I'm going to look into this later. Now I want to spend time with you."

I get out of the cart and reach for her hand.

"Actually, I need those hands to carry a few things." She grins as she points to the back of the cart.

I've been so focused on her that I didn't realize she has a cooler bungee-corded to the back along with a blanket. She grabs the blanket.

"Can you get the cooler?"

"Sure thing," I say as I pick it up.

She leads me toward the pond then sets the blanket down. I survey the area looking for more geese and I'm surprised I don't find any.

She spreads the blanket out and once I set the cooler down, she opens it up.

"This isn't anything fancy, but I thought we'd have a picnic of sorts."

"Of sorts?"

Her cheeks turn red. "Well, I couldn't go to the store to get anything, so I had to make do. Shaw helped."

Then she pulls out two juice boxes and two string cheeses.

"The only portable food she had was what the kids take to school for lunch."

I grin. This woman. "Thank you. I really appreciate the thought. Plus, I really like tropical punch juice."

"That's good. I'm happy we have a warm day. It's rare to see the sun in November." She lays back staring at the sky. I set my juice box aside and lay next to her. I clasp her hand in mine, intertwining our fingers. She turns to me and smiles.

"Donny, what happens if the real traitor is never found? What if we can't clear my name?"

"We will." I know deep in my heart; I will stop at nothing to clear her name. "Trust me."

She nods then I pull her to my chest and wrap my arm around her shoulders as she curls up next to me.

"Thank you for believing in me," she says.

I squeeze her. "It's clear to me you're being framed. We just need to figure out who and why."

I can feel her nod into my shoulder. "You think it's Norah, don't you?"

I sigh. "I know she's your friend but after all you told me about how she treated you, and then took over your job, she's on my list."

A comfortable silence envelops us. But after a few minutes, she lifts her head.

"A saw the photo of you and your team that Cowboy has hanging on his wall."

I frown. "He has a photo of me on his wall?"

Her eyebrows shoot up. "Yes, you didn't know?"

I shake my head.

"It's of all your coworkers at Morgan Thompson. Shaw said they call you Maverick. Why?"

"It's my call sign. I'd come out of the barracks one day wearing sunglasses and ran my hand through my hair. That was all it took. My wise-ass friend, Rover, said I looked like Maverick from *Top Gun*. Boom. Just like that, it stuck."

"Well, I can see why it stuck."

I laugh. "You can?"

She nods. "In the photo you're wearing sunglasses and your hair is styled a lot like Tom Cruise in *Top Gun*." She reaches over and runs her hand through my hair. "I like it longer like this."

Her hand feels so good. I close my eyes and enjoy it.

"And how did Rover get his name?"

I laugh. "That's my fault. To get him back for getting me stuck with Maverick, I started calling him Rover because when the guy gets locked onto something, he won't let it go, like a dog with a bone. The other guys liked it and that was that."

She stares at me for a moment. "And what about CT?"

I shake my head. "You need to hear that one from him directly."

CT hates telling the story, so we make sure to get people to ask him about it whenever possible.

"Okay," she says still staring at me.

I reach for her cheek and pull her closer. Then I lift up and press my lips to hers.

She's tentative at first but then she presses against me and deepens the kiss. I don't know how long we stay like that but finally she pulls back smiling.

"I wish we were somewhere more private," she says.

"Me too, sweetheart. Me too."

She cuddles close to me, and I vow to myself I will catch the traitor and clear her name. I won't rest until I do because I have no doubt we belong together.

CHAPTER 17

SARINA

I TOSS and turn half the night before I finally get out of bed. I can't sleep. Seeing Donny had been wonderful. And that kiss? It was amazing. But what has me awake is what Donny said about Frank. He really thinks the man might be behind the stolen weapon.

And that Norah might be too. I know he's wrong. There's no way Norah would get caught up in that. Would she? I have to know. I get dressed and quietly creep to the door. Cowboy and Shaw keep all their keys handy on a hook in the laundry room. I feel bad sneaking out without asking but I need answers.

I quickly write a note letting Shaw and Cowboy know where I'm going in case they wake up and wonder.

I'm on the road minutes later. I drive past Norah's house, surprised her car isn't in the driveway. I then drive to her rental. She stopped here once when I was in the car, so I recognize it as soon as I pull up. It also helps that Norah's car is in the driveway. Why is she here? It's odd. Norah always brags about waking up every morning at five. She usually leaves our happy hours early so she can get to bed.

The lights in the house are off. I shake my head. She's probably staying here tonight. This is none of my business.

I pull forward and that's when I notice light and movement coming from the back yard.

I drive past the house and park two blocks up. Then I slowly make my way to the back yard, being careful not to step on anything. Fortunately, it's a clear night, and the moon is nearly full so I can at least see a step or two in front of me.

The light is coming from a detached garage in the back yard. I creep to the side of the building next to the fence where I spot a window. There are voices coming from inside, but I can't make out what they're saying. I crouch down under the window, then slowly stand up and realize I'm too short to see inside.

"Shit," I mutter under my breath.

I take a few steps toward the back of the building and spot a crate. Fortunately, it's empty and I'm able to carry it back to the window. I flip it over and that's when I notice the writing on it.

"Property of Asher Vaughn."

What the hell? I've seen these crates in the factory. I snap a photo with my phone, cursing when the flash goes off. I'm squatted low to the ground so I doubt anyone would see it.

Then I step up on the crate and peer through the window. The moment I see it I clasp my hand to my mouth to keep from screaming. The laser weapon system is sitting on a large table in the middle of the garage. Two men stand at the end of the table talking. Their voices are muffled, and I can't make out what they are saying.

I turn off the flash on my phone and snap a photo. Then I slowly step off the crate and send both photos to Donny. I type out a message with the address just as someone covers my mouth and nose behind me. It smells funny. I try not to breathe and fight off whoever it is. But he's too strong.

* * *

DONNY

I PACE IMPATIENTLY in the conference room at Morgan Thompson Security. The moment I saw those photos from Sarina when I woke up, I knew she could be in trouble. But when she didn't answer her phone and Cowboy confirmed that Sarina had left the ranch, I knew something bad had happened. She'd left a note for Shaw but why hadn't she texted me where she was going? I have to figure out where the photos were taken.

"I know you're frustrated but if you keep pulling at your hair like that, it's going to fall out."

I turn to see Peaches arch a brow at me.

"You must really like her. You're never this wound up for a mission," he says.

Peaches is a good guy but he's a talker. I'm not. The only thing I want now is the location of Sarina's cell phone.

"Got it," Trip's voice booms through the phone on the conference table.

He relays the address and I'm almost out the door when Rocco walks in followed by Ace and Phantom.

"We got here as soon as we heard. You found the weapon?" Rocco asks.

CT steps in front of me. "We have an address thanks to Sarina but she's missing. We think whoever did this took her or is holding her. We can't go in all guns blazing," CT says.

"Got it," Ace says. "We'll follow you."

CT nods then turns to me. "Let me drive. I know you're in a hurry, but it won't do you any good to get pulled over and be delayed."

I nod and hand him my keys. As we hop into my Yukon, I glance around and notice Rover's motorcycle isn't in the lot.

"Where's Rover?"

CT pulls out onto the road. Ace, Rocco, and Phantom are close behind.

"He's taking a couple of days of personal time. All he said is family issues."

I nod. It must be his sister. Rover is fiercely protective of her. It's been just the two of them for years. I'll have to call him. Later. Once I have Sarina back.

Twenty minutes later, we drive by a house.

"This is it," CT says.

There are no cars in the driveway nor on the road in front. CT parks a couple of houses down. Ace pulls up behind us.

We walk back to the house. Ace and I walk down the driveway to the back yard while CT goes to the front door with the other two guys.

In the back, there's a detached garage. The main door is open and inside is an old car. The engine has been removed and is in the corner on the floor.

CT steps into the garage. "It doesn't look like anyone is in the house, but the guys are being thorough."

CT stares at the car and the engine. "What the fuck?"

"Exactly. It looks staged."

"Yeah, that's a Ford, and that engine is for a Toyota."

I stare at the ground and notice the tire marks on the cement floor appear to be still wet.

"Well, maybe they left something behind," Ace says as he begins to go through the boxes on the work bench.

I step outside. The photos Sarina took were from outside

of the garage. I walk around the side and find the crate she snapped a photo of.

I grab a stick and use it to push around the overgrown grass. That's when I spot her phone. My stomach sinks. This confirms someone took her.

I try to see if she took any more photos, but its password protected. Of course. Next to her phone, I find a blue shop towel folded a couple of times. Using the stick, I pick it up and catch a whiff of something.

Fuck. They had chloroform? Why were you here, Sarina? And who the fuck has you?

At least there's no sign of a struggle, no blood.

I walk to the back of the house as Rocco exits through the door.

"No one is here but there's something you're going to want to see."

I follow him to a back bedroom. On the bed are several passports and identification cards. Without touching anything, I scan it all. The photos are all of the same man although sometimes his hair is blond and other times brown. Then I read some of the names. Frank Jensen stands out.

"He has this many aliases?" I ask.

"Yeah, recognize that one?" Phantom says pointing to an ID card.

"Holy shit." Francis Bernhardt.

Francis Bernhardt had been one step ahead of them for the entirety of a mission several years ago. Francis worked with a local terrorist group in Somalia, a group that Rocco and his team along with me, Rover, CT, and the rest of our team were trying to take out. While they rounded up most of the guys, they never could find Francis. They believed he was American but based on what their interviews of other suspects, some thought the man was from Algeria. Others thought he was from Germany. A master of accents, one suspect had nicknamed him. And he had been in our town, under our noses.

“Why the hell would he leave all this behind?” Ace asks.

“He wasn’t expecting Sarina last night. Whatever they had going on, they felt they had to get out of here in a hurry,” Phantom says.

“Looks like he was already planning on getting out of here. His suitcase is packed.” Rocco nods to the door where a suitcase stands next to it.

“We better call this in,” I say.

We walk back outside, and I call Stormy and explain what’s going on. He says he’ll reach out to his contact at the CIA.

I walk over to the other guys.

“We need to find Norah and make her tell us where Sarina might be,” I say.

“Her address is in her background report,” CT says pulling it up on his phone.

“If she’s not there, we can then go to Asher Vaughn,” I say.

CT crosses his arms. “So, the five of us are just going to barge into her house and then maybe Asher Vaughn and demand answers?”

“That’s exactly what we’re going to do,” I say as I march toward the street.

“Hey, isn’t that Cowboy’s?” I point to a car parked a couple of houses up from mine.

We all turn to look and sure enough it’s Cowboy’s car. CT gets to it first.

“Locked. I’ll text Cowboy and let him know where it’s at.”

Thirty minutes later, we reach the gate at Asher Vaughn. There had been no answer at the door.

“How can I help you?” the guard asks.

“We’re here to see Norah Jensen,” CT says.

"Just a minute." The guard closes the window and picks up a phone. A minute later he reopens the window.

"Ms. Jensen is not on the property today. I can't let you in."

Not on the property?

"I bet she called in sick," I say.

"You can do a U-turn here," the guard says pointing to a spot just in front of the locked gate.

"Thank you."

CT took the U-turn as I pull up the background report on Norah on my phone.

"Where the hell is she?" I ask.

CT's phone rings from the console. When I see it's Trip, I answer it. "Hey let me put you on speaker phone."

"You guys are keeping me busy today," Trip says. "So, there isn't too much I can find on Frank Jensen other than he had a child with Marilyn Jensen. There were court documents filed trying to get child support from Frank. It appears he never made any attempt to be in Norah's life or support her."

I snort. "Well obviously something changed there."

"It did. I'd bet it happened after Norah got the job at Asher Vaughn about ten years ago. Around that time, Norah started taking trips overseas. Prior to that, she'd never traveled outside the United States."

"Any chance they were work-related trips?"

"It's possible. But it seems doubtful Asher Vaughn would have reason to send an employee to Egypt and Afghanistan," Trip says.

"Shit!" I slam my hand against the steering wheel.

"You think Norah is with Sarina?"

"I do now. And we need to find her."

CHAPTER 18

Sarina

I open my eyes but it's still black. The air is moist and smells musty with a hint of farm animals. All I can hear is the distant sound of dripping water. Where the hell am I?

The last thing I remember is peering in that garage window and seeing the weapon stolen from the Navy.

No. I remember someone coming up behind me. I was caught.

I move my hands to my face. No blindfold and my hands aren't bound. A shiver runs through my body. It's cold.

A small bit of light comes through what appears to be a vent several feet above me. The light grows just a bit brighter, and I realize there are several vents along the walls.

Wait. I scan the space, what I can see of it. It looks like it might be the inside of a trailer. I stand up and make my way to one end. It must be a door that opens. Feeling around the edges and the middle for a handle, I find none. Then I walk to the other end and find a handle. I'm just about to try to turn it when I hear voices approaching.

Quickly, I return to where I was and lie back down. The door opens and I close my eyes pretending to still be unconscious.

"What the fuck are we going to do with her?" a male voice asks.

"I don't know. But she's seen too much," a deeper male voice says. "You know this is your fault. As far as I'm concerned this is your problem."

"My fault?! I'm not the one that knocked her out and put her in this trailer!" the first man shouts.

"Oh, what the hell was I supposed to do? She took a picture of the damn thing in my garage. She knew where the house was. We both know she was going to call the cops."

"And where is that phone?"

I hear shuffling of clothing. "Shit. I think I dropped it."

"Fuck! You're so fucking incompetent. Maybe if you'd covered the damn windows in the first place this never would have happened!" the deeper voice shouts. "None of that shit matters. What matters is what are we going to do now?"

"Lee, I didn't sign up for murder, so you better come up with something else," the first guy says.

I'm relieved. At least I might survive this.

The other guys laugh. "Didn't sign up for murder? Well, it's a little too late now, Frank, or did you forget about the guys in the trucks? Or Wally and Pete? That's on you just as much as me."

"Oh fuck no it isn't! I didn't ask you to kill them!"

"And exactly how did you think I was going to get a multi-million-dollar weapon away from trained and armed guards?"

When the first guy doesn't respond, the deeper voice says, "That's what I thought. And you should be fucking appreciative. Wally talks too much. And at least with him and Pete gone, now we only have to split the money two ways."

"What the fuck, Lee? This is more than I bargained for," the first guy muttered. "How long do you think she'll be out for?"

There is silence for a moment.

"Maybe another thirty minutes. Maybe less. We need to get ready to move."

The door slams shut, and I open my eyes. It's lighter in the trailer now and I'm relieved I can at least see my surroundings. As their footsteps shuffle away, I quietly get up and peer out one of the vents.

The two men appear older, both with graying hair. One is taller and broader. The other is thinner and balding.

They enter a barn. I walk to the other side of the trailer and stare out. I'm on someone's private property. To my right stands a dilapidated house. To my left is the barn. It's a newer barn. The sun is rising in the sky which means I'd likely only been out for a couple of hours.

My hands go to my pockets. Of course, I didn't have my phone. The guy said he dropped it. I hope Donny sees the photos I sent him. Damn. I never did send him the address.

Okay, I need to get myself out of this mess. I try to open the door, but it won't budge. It was locked.

Glancing up, I study the vent. What are the odds I can push that vent out and climb out? I push as hard as I can, but the vent won't budge. I try to open the main door again, but it won't budge either. Then I hear voices. The men are talking and based on the footsteps in gravel, walking this way. If they don't know I'm up, I can jump out and just start running. Hopefully, I can outrun them. I have to.

I wait for my moment. The latch in the door moves. As soon as the door swings open, I jump. Then I run.

"Hey! Get back here!"

I look back to make sure they aren't too close, but I only see the balding man. When I return my gaze to what's in front of me, I see the taller guy run at me. Then I see his fist right before it connects. I go down hard and as everything starts to go black, I realize this is the end.

* * *

Lee

THANK fuck Frank finally listened to me. Not that he hadn't already fucked up our entire plan. I told Frank to bring the damn weapon to this property to start with. But no, he just had to store it ten minutes from Asher Vaughn. It was like he just wanted to fuck with that security team. This thing should have been on that plane at Boeing Field and already out of the country.

But no. Fucking Frank. He's taken too many chances. It's like this is a game to him.

I should not have worked with him but my contact vouched for Frank. Now I get to drive hours into the middle of nowhere in eastern Washington. It doesn't help that it's fucking snowing and I don't have chains for the tires. At least the damn mountain pass was open. I can't get out of here soon enough.

I smile picturing Frank getting off the plane in Mexico and wondering where I am. By the time he realizes I'm not showing up, I'll be collecting my millions.

A light on the dash catches my eye. Fuck. I need to find a

gas station now. Easier said than done out here. Fortunately, I spot one off the next exit.

The pump says pay inside. Of course, it does. I glance in the cab of the truck. She's still out cold. And even if she does come to, she's not going to be able to get the ropes off her wrists.

After paying and pumping, we're back on the road. What the hell am I going to do with this woman beside me?

She stirs.

"Where am I?" she asks.

I don't respond as she shifts around becoming more alert.

Then she realizes she's bound at the wrists and ankles. Her eyes widen.

"Where are you taking me?"

I still don't respond.

"You don't want to kill me," she says.

I turn on the radio hoping it will shut her up.

"My dad, he has money. He would pay you to get me back. A lot."

Well, this is interesting. Too bad I didn't have more time. I glance over at her. Maybe I can take her with me.

I chew on that idea for the rest of the drive. She keeps rattling on, but I don't pay any attention.

"Hey!" she yells.

That got my attention.

"What?"

"I have to pee."

Great. I can't very well walk her into some bathroom all tied up, so I pull off at the next exit and drive until I find a long driveway. Fortunately, with all the farms out here, that doesn't take long. I park the truck and get out.

I open her door and lift her out and onto the ground.

"Go," I say.

She looks around. "Here?"

"Yeah."

She stares at her hands. "Can you untie me?"

I don't move.

"If you don't, I'll probably pee all over myself and you will have to smell it."

Shit. She has a point. I untie only her hands.

She rubs her wrists then goes to pull her pants down but stops.

"Can you turn around please?"

I turn and walk to the back of the truck, grabbing my phone out of my pocket. We have less than thirty minutes to go. I text my contact to make sure the plane is ready to go and to let him know there will be one more passenger.

I turn back and the woman is gone.

"Shit."

I see her hopping up the driveway. I chase after her and knock her to the ground. Her head hits the ground hard and begins bleeding profusely.

"Fuck." She better not die. Not after she told me about her dad's money. I had already decided to take her with me, for insurance.

I scoop her up and put her back in the truck, tying her hands again in case she is alive.

By the time we make it to the airport, she's still out. I can see her breathing so that's good.

My contact is waiting for me, and we load the weapon onto his private plane. Then I grab the woman and toss her over my shoulder.

"Whoa. Wait a minute," he says. "I'm not into human trafficking."

"That's not what this is. Let's go."

He stares at me for a minute but then motions for me to get on the plane. I put the woman in a chair and seat belt her in. As I sit back down, I hope like hell she wasn't lying. But if she is, I'll just leave her in Canada. I smile as the plane takes off. Despite Frank fucking everything up, I'm still going to get this sale done. After this, I'll be so rich I won't have to take any more jobs.

CHAPTER 19

DONNY

WHERE THE FUCK IS SHE? My team at MTS has been trying to find her since she disappeared yesterday. We went back to Norah's and searched inside, finding nothing. A noisy neighbor popped over to chat as we were leaving. At least we found out Norah had left town. A vacation she had told the older woman. Trip was working on tracking her down.

Today, Rocco, Ace, and Phantom are joining us.

"What do you know?" Rocco asks as he steps into the room.

"Jack shit," I say.

Rover is back, thankfully. As much as Rover and CT bicker, I know they have my back on this. CT fills the other guys in on where we have searched and how our tech guy Trip is working on locating Sarina, Frank, or Norah.

"Let me call in Tex," Rocco says.

"That would be great. I know Trip is great, but no one has the contacts Tex has," I say.

Rocco nods. "I'll give him the names of all three. If anyone can find them, he can."

Rocco steps out to make the call and Ace comes up and clasps my shoulder.

"I'm sorry man. I know this sucks. When my daughter was kidnapped, I couldn't see straight. But I promise you, we'll get her back."

I'd heard about Ace's impromptu marriage and family long after the fact, including what happened to his daughter. Thankfully, she was returned, safe. I'm hoping like hell that's the case for Sarina.

"Thank you." It's all I can manage to say.

Peaches walks in and shakes his head.

"Damn it." I pound my fist on the table.

Peaches and Rover were following a lead that I had hoped would turn up something.

"Norah's car was located abandoned in a temporary lot at the airport," CT says.

It made no sense why she wouldn't simply park in long term parking. Unless she had no plans to return.

Rocco stormed into the room.

"We found Frank. He bought a ticket for a flight to Mexico City. He landed this morning."

My stomach sank. "Just one ticket?"

Not that Sarina would willingly go to Mexico with them but if Frank was in Mexico, where the hell was she?

"Yes, just one. We'll find her. You have my word," Rocco says.

All I could do was nod. I knew his word was gold. But the more time that passed, the more likely she might not be alive. Then I remembered the other woman.

"Melanie! We need to find her."

"Who?" Rover asks.

"Sarina's assistant but also her best friend. Sarina might have sent her a text too," I say.

"I'll drive," Peaches says.

Stormy walks into the room. "CT, I need you to stay behind."

CT glances around.

"It's okay. I think we have enough manpower to question Melanie," I say.

He gives me a nod then follows Stormy out of the room.

"I'm going to stay behind too," Phantom says. "I'll check in with Cramer and see if he's learned anything new."

Rocco nods. "Sounds good. I'll call if we learn anything."

We make our way out to Peaches' minivan and get in.

"Peaches, you have kids now?" Ace asks.

"No," he responds.

I see the confusion on Ace's face and despite my shitty mood I can't help but laugh.

"He got a minivan to haul his band's equipment in," I fill in.

Realization dawns on Ace. "You're in a band? I mean, I remember you said you played guitar, but I guess I figured you meant by yourself."

Peaches shakes his head as he pulls out onto the road. I've punched in Melanie's address from the background report I have on her.

"I enjoy playing so I play with some guys at a bar here and there."

"He's actually pretty good," Rover says from the back seat.

I turn around and realize we have five guys in the van.

"You know we probably didn't all need to go see Melanie," I say.

Rocco shrugs. "Maybe we just like hanging out with you."

Ace reaches his hand to my shoulder. "We're here for you until we find her. Got it?"

I nod. "Thank you."

Ace nods and leans back in his seat. "Or until we have to go back to California."

"Well, we better find her fast then," Rocco says.

I stare out the window as we drive, thankful to have these guys with me. I knew they had my back on this.

We pull up to a condo building and get out. I walk straight to the entrance and buzz Melanie's unit number.

"Hello?" she answers.

"Melanie, it's Donny. I'd like to talk to you."

"Of course. I'll buzz you up."

Once inside I take the stairs two at a time with the guys right behind me. I find unit two eighteen right away.

When she opens the doors, her eyes are wide.

"Oh, I thought it was just you."

"Sorry, I should have mentioned it. This is my team. This is Peaches, Rover, Rocco, and Ace."

She smiles. "It's very nice to meet all of you."

The woman is drinking in my friends, clearly happy to have the chance to stare at them. Where is her concern for her friend?

"Have you heard from Sarina?" I ask.

Her gaze moves to mine. "No, I haven't. But that's not unusual. Sarina likes to take a day or two now and again to recharge. Her family has a cabin near the mountains." She motions to her living room. "Please everyone have a seat."

The space is small but between the couch and two chairs, we all fit.

"Would you like something to drink?" she asks.

Before I can say no, Rocco speaks up. "Yes, some coffee would be great, thank you."

"Okay, anyone else?"

"Yeah, that would be great," Peaches says. "Oh, do you happen to have any pumpkin spice creamer?"

Rocco raises a brow.

"As a matter of fact, I do," Melanie says. Then she turns to Ace.

"None for me," Ace replies.

"No thank you," I say. The last thing I need is to be hyped up on caffeine. I've got enough adrenaline running through my veins to keep me going.

"And you?" Melanie practically purrs at Rover.

"No, thank you."

"I'll be right back."

Melanie goes to the kitchen and Rocco leans over to Peaches.

"Pumpkin spice?" Rocco asks.

Peaches smiles. "Yes, it's delightful. You should try it sometime."

Rocco shakes his head. "No thank you."

"She doesn't seem too concerned, does she?" I ask.

"That's exactly what I was thinking," Ace says.

Peaches leans in. "Maybe she's just one of those women who put men before friends."

Melanie returns with a tray and three coffees, pumpkin spice creamer and sugar. Then she sits on the arm of the chair Rover occupies.

"Here is the address for the cabin. I've been out there a few times with her. She says it's the one place she can relax," Melanie says.

I take the address. It's in Fisher Springs. Now I'm itching to drive out there and check it out.

"Thanks," I say.

"Does she go to the cabin often?" Peaches asks.

Melanie shrugs. "A few times a year."

I lean forward. "Wouldn't she tell you if she was leaving town? You are her best friend, right?"

She shifts uncomfortably. "Usually, she'd mention it at work. But since her suspension, I haven't talked to her daily."

"You think Sarina went to the cabin and didn't tell anyone?" Rocco asks.

Melanie shrugs a shoulder. "Well, I'm sure she told her dad or maybe her brother."

I glance at Rover, and he shakes his head. That was the lead he and Peaches looked into this morning.

"Have you guys found the weapon yet?" Melanie asks with a smile.

"Not yet," Rocco says.

She reaches for one of the coffees and takes a sip.

"Have you heard anything more about Norah and where she might have gone?" Ace asks.

She puts the cup back on the tray. "No. I've gone over everything in my mind. Her up and leaving is so out of character, even if she is kind of odd, you know?"

"What do you mean?" Rocco asks.

Peaches chuckles. "I'm guessing you haven't heard. She is a cat lady times ten."

Rocco frowned. "How does that make her odd?"

I am frustrated to be discussing Norah's life habits when I needed information to find Sarina.

"Norah makes clothes for cats and sells them online," I say to Rocco. "Now Melanie, when was the last time you talked to Norah."

"Three days ago. She was in the office and asked me to reschedule some meetings she had the next day. She never said she was taking any time off."

"Cats wear clothes?" Ace asks frowning.

"She knits sweaters and little mittens for their feet. It's all really cute actually," Melanie says.

Ace's brows shoot up.

"We can discuss the cat clothes later," I say to Ace. "Did

she pack up her office or take anything home with her that would indicate she didn't intend to come back?"

Melanie stares straight ahead for a moment.

"No, she didn't that I know of. But she keeps her top desk drawer locked. Anything she values would probably be in there and I don't know if she took it home or not."

I meet Rover's gaze. I know he's thinking what I am. We didn't find anything incriminating at Norah's place. But if she were going to keep it somewhere, then where better than inside the walls of Asher Vaughn. That place has better security than the white house.

"Do you find it odd that both Norah and Sarina seem to be missing?" I ask.

Melanie frowns. "Missing? You think they're both missing?"

I watch as her concern grows. Could she really never have entertained that possibility?

"Did you ever meet Norah's father?" Ace asks.

"Frank? I did. He showed up at a company picnic a couple of years ago. Very nice man."

She wouldn't think he was so nice if we told her what was really going on.

"Asher Vaughn has company picnics?" Peaches asks.

"We did that year. Our old CEO decided to try one to see if it helped employee morale. He thought it would be good for the coworkers to bond at a picnic. But since he didn't allow children to attend, there weren't too many there. The board of directors came, though."

"He wouldn't allow kids at a picnic?" Ace asks.

Melanie shakes her head. "No. And since hardly anyone showed up, the company figured it was a waste of time."

A couple of years ago Sarina wasn't working there yet.

"Who did you work for before Sarina came on board?" I ask.

"I was the assistant to Sarina's predecessor, Matt Burns."

I make a mental note to look into Matt Burns.

"Why did he leave the company?" Rover asks.

Melanie's eyes well with tears. "He had a heart attack at his desk and died. I found him but it was too late."

"Oh, I'm sorry," Rover says reaching out to touch her hand.

Her frown changes to a smile as she stares at their connection.

I stand up. "Thank you, Melanie, but I think we should all be going."

Peaches and Rocco put their coffee cups back on the tray and everyone stands.

"Oh, okay. Well do you want my number in case you have any more questions?" She directs her question to Rover.

Look, I get it. The guy is good looking. But her friend, no her best friend, is missing and all she can do is flirt?

A familiar tune plays from Peaches' pocket.

"Damn it, guys!"

"Is that Justin Bieber?" Ace asks.

"I love that song!" Melanie says. "It always makes me crave peaches."

CT laughs.

"You did this, didn't you?" Peaches says to CT.

CT holds up his hands. "I swear I didn't."

Rover shakes his head then turns to Melanie. "We know where to find you. Thank you for your time."

None of us speak until we are back in the car.

"Can she really be that clueless?" I ask.

"If Sarina took off for a day or two at a time, then why would she think this is any different?" Peaches asks.

He might have a point. It's not like she had to cancel work meetings since she was suspended.

“We need to get into that drawer in Norah’s office,” Rocco says.

“Yes, we do. That’s why we’re going inside Asher Vaughn tonight,” Ace says.

"We’re in,” Rover says.

“Good. After the PV Transport driver came back from Spain and neither Tex nor Trip found that any of his family had any sort of windfall, we’ve hit a dead end in our investigation. We know Asher Vaughn has more information than they’re telling us. But their attorneys got involved and said they have nothing more to say,” Rocco explains.

I glance from Rocco to Ace.

“But you think they do?”

“We know Norah is involved. And Frank. But Frank didn’t work at PV Transport so how did they know which route those trucks would be on? According to the PV rep, they don’t share that information with anyone, especially not Asher Vaughn or the Navy. They said the fewer that know what they’re transporting and where, the better,” Rocco says.

“Maybe we’ll get lucky with that locked drawer in Norah’s office. Maybe she keeps a journal,” Ace says.

I laugh. “Yeah, cause all the bad guys do that.”

“She’s not your typical bad guy,” Peaches says as he turns into the parking lot at MTS.

That is very true.

“I’m going to the McIntyre cabin in Fisher Springs to check for Sarina. But I’ll be back by tonight. I want to go with you,” I say.

Ace grins. “Figured you would want to.”

CHAPTER 20

Sarina

Why is my body shaking? I force myself to open my eyes and find I'm buckled into the seat on an airplane that feels like it is going through rough turbulence.

"Ma'am, it's just turbulence. It will be fine."

My eyes meet a man sitting across from me. He's wearing a suit. An expensive suit. And he's smiling at me.

I glance down at my situation again and realize my wrists are bound and my ankles are bound. My head hurts and I wonder if I was struck in the head.

Turbulence. Shit. I'm on an airplane. I've been kidnapped. Everything with the man from earlier comes to the forefront of my mind. I told him my dad would pay him. So why am I on a plane? Did he sell me to a higher bidder? This man?

The man must sense my fear.

"Relax. Lee is just taking you to Canada," the man says.

"Canada? I don't want to go to Canada!"

I pull against the restraints but it's no use. How the hell is he getting me out of the country? Isn't there security at airports? That's when I take in the plane. It's small. A private jet.

"Well, you'll have to take that up with him."

I turn my gaze back to the man. I'd bet it's his plane.

I lean my head back and close my eyes as the turbulence finally subsides. I hear a door latch behind me.

"Shit. Why the hell didn't someone warn me! I was in the fucking bathroom!"

I recognize that voice as my kidnapper.

I keep my eyes closed trying to assess my situation. I was tied up on a plane to Canada with two men who wanted god knows what.

"She still out?" my kidnapper asks.

"No. The turbulence woke her up."

Someone nudges my foot and I open my eyes. I glare at the man.

"Haha! Lee, I think you've made a friend."

The man takes a seat across the aisle from me.

Lee. I remember the other gray-haired man called him that too. I get the chance to really study him now. In the truck, sitting next to him, I didn't want to stare. I suspect I'm only still alive because of what I said about my dad having money. Time to find out.

"What do you want?" I ask him.

"Right now, a little peace and quiet."

I glance out the window but all I see are clouds.

"Where are we going?" I ask.

Neither man answers so I turn my gaze to the man across from me.

"You said Canada. Where in Canada?"

"Fucking hell. Really, Jared? You can't keep your trap shut?" Lee asks.

The other man's eyes narrow. "Watch yourself. Or you might not make it to the destination."

Interesting. Lee isn't the one in charge. Time to negotiate.

"I told Lee that my dad would pay a nice ransom for me. But he didn't even call him. Why do you think that is?"

Jared stares at me. "How much?"

I shrug. "We didn't get to discussing that."

"Lee. A word in the back."

Jared is up and out of his seat before the other man can answer.

As soon as their eyes are off of me, I get to work at loosening my restraints. Fortunately, Lee is no expert knot-tyer and I get them loose quickly. But I don't take them off. No, they need to be convinced I'm subdued until we land.

When I hear them return, I begin to moan.

"What the hell you bitching about?" Lee asks.

"My head hurts."

"Try to sleep," Jared says.

Well, that's bullshit advice but I'll do whatever it takes to make them think I'm too weak to even try to overtake them.

I keep my eyes closed until I feel the plane touch down. I glance out the window and all I see is farmland.

"Are we at an airport?" I ask.

Jared laughs. "A rural one, yes. Now about this ransom. I think your friend was too quick to pass that up. How about we find a phone and give your dad a call. Yeah?"

"That man is not my friend."

"I didn't pass up shit. I just hadn't gotten around to it yet. And I don't appreciate you stepping on my game."

Jared rolls his eyes as he unbuckles his seat belt. Then he unbuckles mine.

"Do you think you can walk?" he asks.

Lee bends down and scoops me up. "In case you failed to

notice, her legs are bound so no, she can't walk. Now let's get the hell out of here."

Lee carries me to a trailer truck like the one we were in earlier. He tosses me in behind the front seats and closes the door. The truck shakes and I can only assume they are loading the weapon into the trailer in the back. I get the ropes off my wrists as they get into the truck. Lee gets into the driver's seat as Jared gets into the passenger seat.

"How far is this place?" Lee asks.

Jared punches something into the GPS and a voice announces, "You will reach your destination in one hour and one minute."

"Nice!" Lee says. He leans forward and stares at the GPS. "It looks like another airport."

"It is. We will trade them the truck and trailer upon payment and fly their plane home. They'll drive here and fly my plane back to the US."

"Sounds like you have it all worked out," Lee says as he drives out of the airport.

As I sit and wait for the right time to try to escape, I think over what Jared said. And it doesn't make sense to me. Why would we take a risk of driving a weapon around on the road and why take it to a place of higher security? Why wouldn't the buyer just drive to us?

Is Jared trying to screw Lee over? Maybe I can use this to my benefit.

I push up to look out the window. All I can see is farmland. We truly are in the middle of nowhere.

"Jared, why are we driving a stolen weapon to a different airport? Does it have higher security?" I ask. "Why aren't the buyers driving to us?"

I see Lee's brow furrow. Jared shifts uncomfortably.

"It's a matter of trust," Jared explains.

"How so?" I ask.

"Yeah, how so?" Lee asks. His grasp on the steering wheel tightens.

"Well, uh," Jared starts.

Neither one notices as I slowly pull the restraints off my ankles. Dad would be so proud that all the classes he insisted I take on self-defense are paying off.

With no warning, I wrap the rope around Jared's neck and pull tight. It takes him by shock.

"Pull the car over now," I order Lee.

Lee glances at Jared as he struggles to grab the rope but fails.

"Or what? You'll kill that asshole? Go ahead. Sounds like he's trying to screw me over anyway."

Shit. That wasn't the plan. I keep my grip until the man passes out. I let the rope go loose. I don't want to actually kill him but hopefully Lee can't tell the difference.

Lee turns on the radio and sings along like he doesn't have a care in the world. Why is he not worried I'm going to do the same to him?

"Don't even think about trying that shit on me," Lee says.

"Why not?" I ask.

The man slams on the brakes sending me forward between the two front seats. He has my arms back in the restraints so fast I don't know how he did it. Then he gets out of the truck and yanks me out, too.

"I'd love whatever money your dear old dad has but honestly, you aren't worth it."

He tosses me to the side of the road, and I roll down into a ditch. I hear the passenger door open and another thud. Then the truck tires squeal as he tears out of there.

Okay, so that wasn't what I was expecting. And now I need to free myself before Jared wakes up and realizes I tried to kill him. I didn't. I could have. But I didn't. But something tells me he's not the kind of man that distinguishes those types of differences.

Fortunately, Lee still sucks at tying knots and I'm able to break free of the rope. I put it in my pocket in case I have a need for rope, laughing because even in this precarious situation my dad's words of 'waste nothing' are sticking with me. I crawl up out of the ditch thankful that nothing is broken. I'm sore, no doubt, and my head really hurts. Reaching up, I try to massage the pain in my head but only make it worse when I press on a knot that has formed.

I glance across the street. Jared is still lying on the ground. Turning, I take in my surroundings. Farmland as far as the eye can see. Where is a barn or a house? There is a grouping of trees in the distance. It could be providing protection for a house. At the very least, it isn't farmland. I begin the long walk down the road.

After walking about a quarter mile, I realize those trees are further away than I originally estimated. I shiver. The sun is going down and my light sweater isn't thick enough to fight off the chill. I have no idea how far north I am but mid-November at night in Canada I'm betting gets pretty damn cold.

"Hey!"

No. I turn to see Jared about three hundred feet behind me. There is no way I can let him catch me. I turn back and begin to run but I don't see the pothole. I go down hard on the asphalt. Forcing myself back up, I know something's wrong. I put weight on my left foot, and I go down again.

Shit. I either twisted or sprained my ankle.

Turning to face Jared, I clutch the rope in my hand behind my back.

He's moving at a good pace, but he's limping. When he's about twenty feet away, he drops to the ground.

"What the fuck happened? Where's Lee?"

Does he not remember or is he testing me?

"He tossed us out of the truck and left."

"Fuck!"

He rubs his head. "That explains my headache and my twisted knee."

He pulls up his pants to examine his knee and I take the moment to examine my ankle.

"Why are you walking this way?" he asks.

"Had to pick a direction. Why not?"

He stares at me and must sense my fear.

"I could care less about getting a ransom from your dad so stop staring at me like I'm going to pounce. What I need is to find Lee before he gets that weapon to my client. Fuck I can't believe I gave him the address."

Jared pulls his phone out of his pocket and holds it up.

"Damn it. No reception here either."

My ankle hasn't swelled so that's a good sign.

"Who is your client?" I ask.

"Doesn't matter. What matters is Lee has something worth a hell of a lot of money in that truck."

A hell of a lot is an understatement.

"He's driving. We're walking. You can't beat him there."

Jared nods. "True. But if I can get my phone to work, I can stop him." He holds up his phone again then stares at me. "Any chance you have your phone on you?"

I laugh. "I've been held captive for the last forty-eight hours. No, I don't have a phone."

Jared winces. "Oh right. Sorry. But remember, that wasn't me."

No, it was Lee and it's pretty clear he screwed both of us over.

"Well, we might as well try to keep going. The sooner I

can get reception, or we find someone with a phone, the sooner we can get back home," Jared says.

Home. Visions of Donny float through my mind. I wonder if he's looking for me. There's no way he would know I'm in Canada. It looks like I'm going to have to save myself.

CHAPTER 21

SARINA

MY TEETH ARE CHATTERING as we walk along the roadway. The sun has gone down and it's almost dark. We find a driveway but after we walk down, we discover a house that had been nearly burned to the ground. Now, back on the main road, I'm losing hope.

"Do you see any lights?" I ask.

Jared has his hands in the pockets of his blazer, but I can tell he's shivering too.

"No."

"You know, I refuse to believe I got away from Lee just to freeze to death out here."

"I hear you. I need to find that bastard."

A twinkle in the distance caught my eye.

"Hey, is that a car?" I say pointing.

Jared stares. "I think it is. Oh, thank god."

As the car creeps closer, my hope returns. We won't freeze out here after all. Fortunately, the road is fairly straight, and the driver is able to see Jared jumping in the middle of the road.

The car slows and the passenger window rolls down. An older woman with her dark hair pulled up in a bun frowns at us.

"What the heck are you two doing out here? Your car break down?"

"Something like that," Jared says through chattering teeth.

"Well, get in. You'll freeze to death out there."

I grab the back door and pull it open. Right now, I just want to get my ankle elevated in the back seat. Jared must be thinking the same thing about his knee because he glares at me as he opens the passenger door. I dive in and am met with a warm, wet tongue.

"Don't mind Jasper. He's friendly."

I turn and stare into the eyes of a very large Doberman Pinscher.

"I hope so," I say under my breath.

Once we're in the car, the woman drives down the road.

"I'm Patty. What are your names?"

Before I can speak, Jared answers for us. "I'm Jackson and this is my girlfriend, Kaley."

What the hell? Jared turns back and arches a brow. I guess that's his way of saying go with it.

"Nice to meet you. Where are you two headed?"

"The United States," I say.

Patty whistles. "Well, you aren't going to make it tonight. Mighty nasty storm coming in. And there aren't any motels around here. Fortunately for you two, I have a guest room."

Room? As in one? Hope Jared likes the floor.

"You can stay the night and then we'll see if the roads are drivable in the morning."

"If?" Jared asks.

"You really didn't hear about the storm? Yeah, really

unusual to get that kind of snow this early in the season. They say it will be big. But they could always be wrong. Anyway, I'll have you to my house and warmed up in no time."

Patty turns on the radio and country music blares from the speakers in the back. Jasper decides I'm okay and lays his big head on my lap. I struggle to keep my eyes open as Patty turns down one road then another.

"How much further is it?" Jared asks.

"Oh, another twenty minutes."

I just hope we are going closer to the border and not further. I close my eyes and miss the rest of the journey.

"We're here!" Patty chirps.

I open my eyes to find a lovely log cabin. Well, this might be better than I thought. I step out of the car and look around. It's dark and I see nothing, no city lights, no lights from other homes.

"Don't you have neighbors?" I ask.

Patty laughs. "Not close. I have one hundred acres here and I love it. Although I recommend you don't go walking around at night."

I glance at Jared who shrugs.

"Why not?" I ask.

"Cougars. Well, one that I know of. He's been coming down the hill and eating my chickens. I had to bring them all inside. Damn cat. Now let's get inside."

We follow Patty up the stairs to her front porch and into her home. Jasper follows closely behind and once inside, retreats to a dog bed.

"Are you hungry?" she asks.

"Yes," Jared says. "I hate to trouble you."

Patty waves her hand. "No trouble at all. I made a big batch of chili earlier today. I'll just heat some up."

I watch as she goes to the kitchen and then I turn my

attention to the rest of the house. It's one grand room with the kitchen, a dining room table and living room. There's a fireplace near a recliner chair and a floral couch that screams to be taken back to the nineteen eighties.

"Have a seat," Patty says pointing to the dining room table.

Jared leads the way and sits down. I sit down across from him. We might be in this together but I still don't trust him.

Patty brings over two bowls of chili and spoons.

"I hope that warms you up. Now tell me, where were you coming from?"

Jared shoves a spoonful of food in his mouth, so I answer.

"The airport."

"Timmins?"

I have no idea what airport it was, but I can't tell her why.

"Yes," I say before scooping a heap of chili into my mouth.

Now it could be because I'm starving but this is the best chili I've ever had.

"This is really good."

Patty beams. "Thank you."

"It is," Jared agrees. "Is this ground turkey?"

Patty shook her head. "Nope. Squirrel."

I spit my mouthful back out into my bowl and began to cough.

Jared swallows his down but looks like he is going to be ill.

"What?" he asks.

"Squirrel."

Patty frowns. "Oh, don't look disgusted. There is nothing wrong with eating a little squirrel now and again. We have too many out here and they do add a little something extra to the chili."

Jared scoots his seat back. "I'm actually quite tired. Do you mind if I go to bed?"

"Me too," I say as I stand up.

"Of course. You two must be exhausted after all that walking."

Patty takes our bowls to the kitchen then turns back to us. "Follow me."

We follow her down a hallway.

"On the right is the bathroom."

I glance in. Nothing out of the ordinary. No stuffed squirrels hanging on the wall.

"And in here is the guest bedroom."

She opens the door to reveal one double bed and not much else.

"I'll be down the hall if you need anything."

"Thank you," I say.

Once Patty retreats to her room, I close our door and turn to Jared.

"I think I'm going to be sick," I say.

He's still looking a bit green. "No shit. I mean, I've tried exotic foods but squirrel? Can we get rabies from eating that?"

"How the hell should I know?" I yell.

"Shh!" he says. "The last thing we need is for her to come running in here."

"You're right. Does your cell have service here?"

He shakes his head. "No. I checked as soon as we pulled up. Nothing."

I take in the room. "You're sleeping on the floor."

He's about to open his mouth to protest but I stop him.

"You allowed a man to kidnap me from the United States. If you don't want me sharing that with Patty, shut up, and go to sleep."

Jared nods. "Okay. Okay. No need for threats. I'm so tired I could sleep anywhere."

Jared takes the comforter folded at the end of the bed and

one of the pillows and makes a makeshift bed on the floor. I lay in the bed and stare up at the ceiling.

All I can think about is Donny. Is he looking for me? Does he have any idea where I am? How could he?

"Tomorrow we'll ask Patty if she can drive us to the airport. My plane should still be there," Jared says from the floor.

"And can I trust you to actually fly me home?"

"Yes."

Like I have any other choice. It isn't like I have any money on me to buy a ride from anyone else. I shiver and think about Patty's storm prediction.

"What are we going to do if it really does snow too much to drive?"

I hear him sigh. "I don't know."

CHAPTER 22

SARINA

THE MOMENT MY EYES OPEN, I jump out of bed. But Jared is already at the window shaking his head.

"What's wrong?"

"It snowed last night."

"Yeah? So?"

"Come look."

I get up and go to the window. It's half covered in snow.

"There is no way it snowed that much. I'm sure the wind just pushed it against the house. I'm going to check."

I shiver. Damn. Is the power out? I pop out of the room and walk down the hall. The aroma of coffee wafts in the air. Wait. Maybe the power is on.

"Good morning. Did you two sleep well?" Patty asks.

"I did. I was coming out to check on the snow." I stutter to a stop when I see the snow at the back sliding door.

"Yeah, it looks like we got three feet last night and it's still coming down."

"Is the power on? It's so cold in here." Jared asks rubbing his arms.

"No, unfortunately not. I often lose power when it snows a lot. I heated up water using my propane camping stove." Patty points to it sitting on the counter.

Jared's eyes widen. "You used that inside?"

"I did. Works great. Want some coffee?"

Jared stands rooted to his spot with his mouth partially hanging open as if he is just now realizing Patty is a bit quirky. Well, quirky might be understating it.

"Yes, I would love some coffee. Thank you, Patty," I say thankful to hold anything hot.

She beams and grabs a mug from the cabinet and sets it on the counter. Then she grabs a plastic thing that looks like a coffee filter and scoops some ground coffee in. I watch as she then takes the kettle of hot water from her propane stove and slowly pours it over the coffee. When she's finished, she returns the kettle and hands me the mug.

"Cream or sugar?"

"No thank you."

I take a sip and quickly turn away so she can't see my face. But Jared does. It's the worst coffee I've ever had.

"Jared, would you like coffee?"

"No thank you. Can you take us to the airport? I figure we can catch a flight out today."

Patty laughs. "Oh, that's funny."

"I'm afraid I don't see the humor in it," Jared says.

Patty cocks her head. "We can't get off my property much less make it to the airport. And I guarantee you even if we did, it's closed."

Jared's hands went to his hips. "You don't know that!"

"I do. They won't plow this much snow. And even if they did, I doubt the airport has power."

"Shit." Jared turns away and walks to the fireplace.

Patty's large dog is sprawled out in front of it soaking up as much heat as it can. The dog glances up at Jared then lays its head back down to sleep.

"At least here we have a warm fire, plenty of firewood, and enough bread and peanut butter to last for the week."

Jared spins around and meets my eyes.

"Week?" I ask.

Patty sighs. "Yeah, that's how long they think this snow will stick around."

"A week?" Jared asks. "I can't miss a week. I have a company to run."

Patty shrugs. "Maybe the forecast will change. Until we have power, we won't know for sure. Anyway, I've got to go check on my chickens. There's bread and peanut butter on the table there. Help yourself."

She walks to the door, puts on a parka, and then turns back to us.

"You know I'm really glad you two are here. I really miss having company."

Then she walks out the door.

"Tell me this isn't happening," Jared says. "Pinch me. Wake me up from this hell."

I pinch him. Hard.

He jerks his arm back. "Ouch! What the fuck?"

"You asked me to."

Jared walks to the table. "Do you think this is really peanut butter? Or do you think she put some squirrel essence in here to make it better?" He takes the lid off the jar and smells it.

"I don't know but it doesn't look like we have much choice but to eat it."

Jared falls back into one of the chairs. "Hopefully not for a whole week. Want to join me?"

No, but if I want to eat, I have to.

I walk to the table and grab a piece of bread. "Someone is looking for me. He'll find me."

Jared laughs.

"What? He will."

"I'm sorry. I don't mean to laugh but I'm afraid he won't. If he somehow manages to figure out you were on that plane, he'll be at the wrong airport."

"What do you mean?"

He sighs. "My pilot filed a flight plan, but he listed the wrong airport for landing."

I sit up. "He can do that?"

"I don't know how it works but he said he did."

"So, no one will be looking for us here."

"I'm afraid not."

I stare at my bread, suddenly not hungry anymore.

"Hey," Jared says.

I glance up.

"You should eat what you know now and skip what you don't know later."

He has a point. I spread a thick layer of peanut butter on the bread and take a bite.

Jared leans forward. "I'm going to find a way out of this place even if I have to steal a tractor. You in?"

I swallow. "Yes. I think I'd rather stay at the airport than here. Something about this place gives me the creeps."

Jared grins. "Could it be that?" He points over my shoulder.

I turn and find a stuffed raccoon staring back at me. I jump.

Jared laughs.

Then I take in the rest of Patty's cabin in the light of the day.

"How did I not see this last night?" I ask noticing the row of what appear to be stuffed, once live, rodents.

"No idea. I didn't see them either."

I turn back to my bread. "Let's get out of here today."

* * *

THREE DAYS later and we are still trapped at Patty's house of horrors. Sadly, another few feet of snow fell making the use of the car impossible. Jared found a tractor in a shed, but it wouldn't start.

There could be something in the barn, but it's been locked every time we check. Jared's been going through drawers every chance he can, looking for a key, but he's had no luck.

Patty walks into the house interrupting my thoughts. "I've been saving this for a special occasion, but I'd rather share this with friends." She's holding a frozen, foil wrapped item.

"What is it?" Jared asks while glancing at me.

After three days and nights of peanut butter on bread, I'm craving anything else.

"Now don't freak out. I guarantee you this will be the best thing you've ever tasted. Just have an open mind."

I close my eyes. This can't be good.

"Opossum. Now don't worry. I didn't kill it. I know those critters do a lot of good around here. I found him on the side of the road. He'd been struck by a car, but it had been below freezing and he was frozen solid."

I had to take deep breaths to not get sick. We were going to be stuck here all winter. I can't live on peanut butter alone. Why the hell does she not have any jelly!

Jared grabs my arm.

"Kaley, you all right?"

I almost didn't respond then I remember that is the fake name he gave me.

"Kaley, I think you're having a panic attack. Look at me," Jared says.

"Now why would she have a panic attack over this?" Patty holds up the offending package.

"She's vegetarian. Still a bit traumatized from the chili."

I take several deep breaths and stare at Jared. This man may be my foe but now, we have to rely on each other to get the hell out of here. He squeezes my arm as I calm my breathing.

"Oh well, why didn't you say so? I'll save this bad boy for another time."

Patty walks back out the door to put the carcass back from wherever she found it.

"We have to get out of here," I say.

"Agreed. Grab a coat."

I snag a coat off a hook near the door, and we step outside.

"If we can make it to the main road, I'm guessing it has to be plowed by now. This is Canada. They're used to snow."

I nod. What he says makes sense.

We walk past the barn when I hear voices. I stop and turn to Jared.

"Do you think someone else is here?" I whisper.

Jared shrugs and then walks to the barn door. I follow. For the first time since we got here, not only is it unlocked but it's open a crack. He peeks in, then waves for me to join him and do the same.

I can't believe what I see. Patty is sitting on a chair facing a television that is on. And next to her is a portable heater; that is also on.

Jared turns to me and puts his finger to his lips to make sure I remain quiet. Then we walk back toward the house.

"What the hell?" I ask.

"She has power."

"Why would she lie to us?"

"That is a very good question and one I really don't want to find out. You know what this means?'

He's smiling.

"The airport is likely to be open and running."

He's right. We can get the hell out of here.

"Come on. We need to get to the main road before she figures out we're gone," Jared says.

While we thought Patty was tending to her animals and farm, we now know she was staying warm in the barn. Based on the last few days, we have a few hours.

CHAPTER 23

DONNY

IT'S BEEN four days since Sarina sent those photos and disappeared. Four agonizing days of dead ends. The locked desk drawer of Norah's turned out to be a bust. It was empty. And I haven't heard anything about Frank. I don't know if he's still in Mexico or if he was extradited to the US. I've asked Stormy nearly daily if he's heard from his CIA contact, Agent Harding. Each day he says he hasn't had any updates. I'm about to go out of my mind, I feel so helpless.

"Hey, you're here early."

I look up to find Rover, standing in the doorway to my office, looking like shit.

"You all right?"

"Couldn't sleep," he says.

"Neither could I."

I've barely slept since Sarina went missing.

He steps in and takes a seat in the chair across from me.

"You took some time off?"

Rover nods.

"Want to talk about it?"

When he doesn't respond I figure that means no but then he leans forward.

"It's my sister."

"I figured it must be when you said it was a family issue."

Rover runs his hand through his hair, pushing it off his face. "She may or may not be dating a guy that's really bad news. And despite my warnings, she's not listening to me."

"Well, in her defense, you've had something against every guy she's dated."

Rover jumps up. "No. This guy really is bad. I just don't know how to get her to see it before it's too late." Then he sighs. "Sorry, you have enough of your own shit going on. I don't need to pile mine on, too."

"Hey," I say. He meets my gaze. "I'm always here for you, got it?"

He nods. "Got it. Same for you. Now tell me, do you have any leads?" he asks, nodding at the papers in front of me.

"Trip sent me a list of every property Frank Jensen owns. There are actually quite a few."

Rover frowns. "Anything local?"

"Yeah, one I'm planning on checking out."

"I'm going with you."

"Thanks. I appreciate that. And seriously, I'm here if you ever want to talk."

Rover nods. "Well, if I can't figure something out, I'll let you know."

I stand and Rover follows me out.

"If Frank owns something local, why was he staying in Norah's rental?"

That's a good question. "Maybe we can figure that out when we see this place. It's out on Paradise road."

The property is thirty minutes from Norah's rental house and when we get there the hairs on the back of my neck stand on end.

"Before we go digging around, we should probably introduce ourselves in case the property is rented out." Rover nods to the house at the end of the driveway.

The sun is beginning to rise, and I realize how creepy we would look rolling up at this hour if there's some innocent person renting the place.

"Sounds good."

I park the car and Rover makes his way to the front door. I step out of the car and notice from this angle the house is in terrible condition. I doubt anyone lives there. Then I turn and spot a barn to the right. By contrast, it's new and looks to be in great condition. It's also padlocked. The driveway turns and continues back further into the property.

Then I notice the deep tire tracks in the dirt.

"No one answered the door," Rover says as he comes up beside me.

He notices the tracks, too.

"Those are deep."

I nod. "Like something heavy drove through here."

"You think the weapon was here?"

"Gut feeling says yes, and Sarina was here."

Rover claps my shoulder. "Well, let's start looking around. I'll take the barn."

"I'll take the driveway."

After what feels like forever, I rub my eyes. Nothing. Rover walks out from behind the barn shaking his head.

"I found a way in but there's nothing in there," he says.

I walk back toward the house and the sun glints on something, catching my eye. As I step closer, I see it's a gold chain.

But when I bend down and pick it up, I'm nauseated.

"Rover."

He sprints over. "What'd you find?"

I hold up a gold chain with a gold four-leaf clover attached.

"This is Sarina's."

"Are you sure?"

I nod. "She played with it when I first interviewed her." I place the necklace in my pocket. "She was here."

We both stand there taking everything in.

"After she sent me those photos, someone brought her and possibly the weapon here. We don't know how long they waited before leaving or when they left," I say, thinking it through.

I spin around and stare at the house. "We need to go inside."

Rover's hands go to his hips. "Yeah, we do. From this angle though, there's no way someone could be living in there."

"No, but they might have taken her in there. She might…"

"Hey, don't even go there. We will find her. Got it?" Rover says.

I give a curt nod. I'm trying really fucking hard not to let my mind go to a lot of places. Sarina has been missing for four days. And the guys that stole a multi-million-dollar weapon during transport aren't going to want to babysit someone who knows too much.

"Seriously, stop. Let's go." Rover leads the way to the house.

Fortunately, the property is heavily treed, and the house is set back from the road. No one can see us. While that's good for what we need to do, it's bad for whatever happened with Sarina.

He makes quick work of the lock; we step inside and find nothing. Seriously nothing. The house is empty. It doesn't even have a refrigerator. Clearly no one is living here.

"Damn it!" I would throw something but fuck, there's nothing to throw.

His phone rings and he pulls it from his pocket. "It's Rocco."

"Hey Rocco. Are you still in town?"

Rover frowns then pulls the phone from his ear.

"Hang on. Maverick's here. He needs to hear this too."

He turns his phone to speaker phone.

"Maverick, any word on Sarina?" Rocco asks.

"No. What news do you have?"

"We got the weapon back."

"That's great, where was it?" Rover asks.

"Wait, you didn't find Sarina?" I ask.

There's a pause. "No Maverick. I'm afraid not."

Rover pats me on the arm, but I step back. If she's not with the weapon, then where the hell is she?

"We retrieved the weapon at a small airport in Canada," Rocco starts.

"Canada? They got it out of the United States?" Rover runs his hands through his hair. We both know how bad that is.

Rocco continues. "The buyer rented a private plane from upstate New York and set a flight plan for Canada. It turns out the CIA has been after this guy for alleged terrorist acts. He was also on a watch list in Canada. Once his plane landed, he was detained by Canadian authorities until the CIA arrived."

"The CIA?" Rover asks.

"Yeah, and guess what they found at the small rural airport this guy landed at? Our missing weapon. It was in the trailer of a truck. That's when we got called in."

Rover glanced up at me, keeping his gaze on me, and asks, "Was anyone in the truck?"

"No," Ace says. "But the truck is registered to a Fred

Johnson with an address out on Paradise road. I'll text it to you so you can check it out."

I close my eyes. "Another one of Frank's aliases." The name matches one of the identification cards Frank had left at Nora's rental.

"No need. We're here now," Rover says.

Ace laughs. "What—did you learn to teleport since you got out?"

Rover explains the property is owned by Frank so we came here to check it out and that I found Sarina's charm but not her.

"Frank's house on this property is empty. No one lives here. There's a barn that could hide a truck and trailer, so we think the weapon and Sarina were brought here."

"Were," I say. "Where the fuck is she now?"

"Maverick, we'll find her," Ace says. "But you should know Tex did a check on Lee Danvers. It's an alias and he has quite a record. He's even made the FBI's most wanted list."

"Shit. Can you send me the address for this airport? I think I need to go check it out," I say.

Rover arches a brow. "You think Frank flew her to Canada with the weapon?"

"It's possible. Since she wasn't in Mexico with Frank, this is the only other lead I have," I say.

"We'll check it out since we're here," Ace says.

My phone rings in my pocket and my heart leaps in my throat when I don't recognize the number.

"Is it her?" Rover asks.

"I'm not sure," I say then answer the call. "Hello?"

"Donny!"

"Sarina?"

"Oh, I'm so glad I reached you."

"Where are you?"

"Canada. But I'm flying home."

What the hell? I look at Rover who is frowning.

"I thought you were kidnapped."

"I was. It's a long story but the guy who did it, Lee, got away. He tossed me and Jared out into ditches in the middle of nowhere."

"Jared?" The last thing I should be is jealous after the ordeal she just went through but the idea that some other guy has been comforting her doesn't sit right with me.

"He owned the plane we took to Canada. He feels bad for what happened and is flying me back. I'll be at Boeing Field by nine tonight. Can you come get me?"

"Of course," I say. I'll be there by eight so I can make sure to meet this guy. "Do you know where Lee is?"

"No, he was driving to some other airport but that was days ago."

At least he isn't a threat at the moment.

"What's Jared's last name?" Maybe I can learn something about him first.

"I don't know but it's his phone I'm calling from. Oh, I have to go. They're ready for us to board."

And the phone cuts off before I can ask anything more.

"That's good news. At least you know she's safe," Rover says. "You guys catch that? Sarina's been found."

"That's good news. Hey, I have to go. We need to wrap up here," Rocco says.

"Thanks for calling," Rover says then ends the call.

"You want any company tonight when you pick her up?" he asks.

I shake my head. No, I need to find out what the hell happened.

"Wait. Actually, I do. We don't know enough about this Jared guy. We need to know if he was involved in trying to sell the weapon."

"I'll call CT and we'll have your back."

I need to trace this phone number and figure out who the hell this Jared guy is.

CHAPTER 24

DONNY

JARED COOPER. That's the owner of the phone and apparently the plane Sarina is now on. I looked him up. A billionaire entrepreneur who's often photographed in exotic places surrounded by half naked women. Yeah, I know his type. He thinks he can get whatever he wants. But he isn't getting Sarina.

But what if he is what she wants? She's career driven and maybe she likes guys like him.

Maybe I should back off and let her decide. I lean my head against my seat. This is why I avoid relationships. I sit back upright. Are Sarina and I in a relationship? Neither one of us said so much but it certainly felt like it.

I guess tonight will be a moment of truth.

Speaking of truth, I need to know how she was kidnapped by one man and ended up being rescued by another.

I wasn't sure where to wait so I'm parked outside the

arrivals door of the main building at Boeing Field. Just after twenty-one hundred, Sarina walks out the doors of the building with a tall man next to her. I exit my car and walk to them.

"Donny!" She runs to me and jumps into my arms. "I'm so happy to see you. Did you get the photos I sent?"

She pulls back and I lower her. "I did. The weapon has been recovered."

She sighs into me. "Oh, thank god. Where did they find it? Lee drove off with it after tossing us out."

"A rural airport. What happened to you?"

The tall man coughs.

"Sarina, I'm glad you made it back. I need to get going to the office."

"Wait," I say. "I'm Donny."

Jared sticks out his hand. "I'm Jared."

I shake his hand. It's sweaty.

"So are you two friends?" I ask.

"Sorry, I need to go," Jared says.

I stare at the man and his forehead beads with sweat. He's nervous.

"We're not friends," Sarina says. "He watched Lee carry me onto his plane. I was tied up."

"You helped Lee kidnap her and fly her to Canada?"

I take a step forward, balling my fists.

His hand goes up as he moves back. "Look, I made a mistake. I've tried to apologize. Now that we are all back, maybe we can just forget about it." He smiles and I suspect he's used to getting his way.

I don't smile back.

He winces. "Look, I got to go. I've been missing for nearly a week. We can chat later."

Jared steps away. I don't go after him because I spot Agent Harding and a few other agents walking toward Jared.

"What are they doing?" Sarina asks.

"Likely asking questions. We need to know if he was involved with trying to sell the weapon."

"He was. I appreciate his help in helping me escape Patty, but he was the one who knew who the customer was. He never said their name."

"Wait, Patty? I thought your kidnapper was named Lee."

She shakes her head. "It's a long story."

"Come on, let's go back to my place and talk."

"Sounds good."

Once we're on the road, I'm wondering if she fell asleep but then she turns to me.

"I thought Lee was going to kill me."

I squeeze her hand. "I'm sorry."

"I had just sent you those photos when someone came up behind me and next thing I knew, I woke up in the back of a trailer. There was no way out. Then I heard Lee. Well, I didn't know his name then. He was talking to another man."

"Did you see him?"

"Through one of the vents. They both were older. He called the other man Frank."

"Any chance it was Frank, Norah's dad?"

She sighed. "I wouldn't know. I've never met the man."

I was about to ask her about the company picnic but then I remembered, she was new to Asher Vaughn and didn't work there then.

"I overheard the other man tell Lee he didn't agree to murder. Then Lee..." she shakes her head. "He's killed people."

My jaw clenches as I realize how dangerous this man likely is.

"I have some photos to show you when we get to my place," I say. I need to know for sure it was Frank.

"Okay. I tried to escape but Lee hit me and then I tried to

escape again, and he knocked me down. I woke up on the plane. Then he shoved me in a truck but changed his mind because he threw us out of the truck and Jared and I were walking so long in the cold, I really thought I was going to die."

I grip the wheel, angry that I couldn't have done more. Angry that she had to rely on a kidnapper to get her home.

* * *

AFTER I GET her to my place, she showers then walks into the living room wearing the T-shirt and shorts I set out for her.

"I really like you in my clothes," I say without thought.

She blushes.

"I thought you might be hungry, so I ordered a pizza. I hope you like it."

"As long as it doesn't have squirrel, I'll love it."

I raise a brow.

"If it weren't for Patty, we would have frozen to death. But then things got really strange."

We eat pizza while she tells me all about Patty and how they were trapped there for days.

"I can't tell you how happy I was when we made it to the road near Patty's and it had been plowed. And the first car we waved at, stopped for us. I knew then I would make it home."

I take her plate from her and put it on the coffee table next to mine. Then I scoot closer to her on the couch and take her hands in mine.

"Sarina, when I couldn't find you, I've never felt so helpless. I've been on missions, and I've rescued many people. But the thought of losing you was more than I could bear."

She squeezes my hands. "Donny, I really missed you too."

I squeeze her hand. "I need to have control over situations

but when you were gone, I had no control over what was going on with you. I've never felt such a strong need to keep someone safe as I do with you. I've felt this connection from the moment I met you. And I'm sorry if I'm coming on too much, too strong, too soon. But I had to let you know."

I stare at our hands, feeling raw, having laid myself bare for this woman.

"When I was walking along the road thinking I might freeze to death, you were all I thought about."

I lean forward and press a kiss to her lips.

"I found something of yours."

I walk over to my bookshelf and grab the necklace. When I return, I hold it up. Tears well in her eyes.

"I thought I lost it forever." She fingers the charm. "Thank you."

"Do you want me to put it on you?"

She nods then turns her back to me and holds up her hair. I place it around her neck and make sure the clasp in back is secure.

"This was my aunt's necklace. She gave it to me when I was young and said it would bring me good fortune. I had it on when I got the job at Asher Vaughn. And when I met you."

"I remember."

"My aunt was like a second mother, and this is one of the few things I have from her. It means a lot. Thank you for finding it."

She turns back and launches into my lap to hug me.

Before I'm ready to let go, my phone rings. I pull it out of my pocket and check who's calling from over her shoulder.

"It's Stormy."

I answer. "Hey, what's going on?"

"Sarina should hear this, too."

I pull the phone from my ear and put it on speaker phone.

"Okay," I say.

"Hi, Stormy."

"Glad you're back. You gave our guy quite a scare."

"Thank you. I'm very happy to be back."

"What's going on?" I ask.

"Frank was detained in Mexico City several days ago. He has since been turned over to the CIA and questioned. He immediately turned on Lee. He said Lee was behind everything. When asked about Sarina, he said she had nothing to do with any of it. That information has been shared with Asher Vaughn."

She closes her eyes and breathes a sigh of relief. "Have you talked to Asher Vaughn?"

"Yeah, I spoke to some guy named Gunnar."

She rolls her eyes. "I can imagine how well that went."

"He wasn't very cooperative, so I asked Shaw to call him up. I don't know what she said but he promised a press release later today stating Sarina is no longer a suspect. He couldn't promise that her suspension will end soon but I'm sure it's being discussed. You don't mess with Shaw."

Her eyes well with tears.

"What's wrong?" I ask.

She shakes her head. "Thank you. Thank you all so much. I value your support more than you can ever know."

"You're welcome. I'll let you go so you can celebrate the news," Stormy says.

"Wait," she says. "What did Frank say about Norah?"

"He said she knew nothing about what was going on. Trip did a full check and there hasn't been any money transferred to her. It really looks like she wasn't in on it."

"Then where the hell is she?" I ask.

"You mean Norah?" Sarina asks.

"Yeah, she's been missing for a week."

She furrows her brow. "Missing? She's not at the cat expo?"

I run a hand down my face. "The what?"

"The cat expo. It's this week. Norah's been planning to go for some time. She wants to find a pet store that'll sell her cat apparel."

"And where is this expo?"

"Los Angeles."

"I'll have Trip check," Stormy says.

"Thank you and thanks for letting us know about Frank," I say.

"Enjoy your weekend."

I set my phone on the coffee table and turn my attention to Sarina.

"Do you believe Frank that Norah isn't involved?"

She stares at me for a moment. "I do. She has her flaws, but she's devoted to Asher Vaughn. I really don't think she would be okay with all this."

I nod. My gut tells me Norah is innocent too.

She smiles. "It means the world to me to have you and your friends on my side. Through all of this, my dad hasn't even called to check on me."

I frown. "What? Doesn't he read the news?"

"I'm sure he saw. He follows the news and this industry. And I'm sure my brother told him." She shrugs. "We've never been much of a touchy-feely family since my mom left. Then when I quit his company, I don't know. I think he took it personally. He hasn't spoken to me since then."

I pull her until she's cuddled up next to me.

"I'm sorry."

She yawns.

"We should get some sleep," I say.

She nods. "Can I stay here with you?"

I stand and hold out my hand. "I planned on it."

She takes my hand and I pull her into my arms and kiss her.

"I could really get used to having you here."

"I could get used to being here."

My heart cracks open just a little more at her words. Staring into her eyes, I realize I'm falling for this woman.

"Thank you for standing by me through all of this."

"I knew you were innocent."

She frowns.

"What's wrong?"

She shakes her head. "I don't understand Norah. We were friends and then she threw me under the bus and according to Melanie, redecorated my office. It was like she was just waiting for me to leave."

"I'm sorry. Sometimes people aren't what we think they are."

She nods.

"Does this mean you've talked to Melanie today?"

She shakes her head. "No, she told me this before. I sent her a text letting her know I'm safe and that I plan to call her tomorrow."

CHAPTER 25

Sarina

My phone buzzes, waking me from a very pleasant dream. I sit up and remember I'm in Donny's bed. I smile remembering how he held me last night. But he's gone and his side of the bed is cold.

I sit up and stretch my arms up over my head. My phone buzzes again. I've missed messages from Donny and Melanie.

Donny: *I didn't want to wake you, but I had to go into the office this morning. I'll be back around lunch.*

I check the time.

"Almost noon?" My eyes widen. "How the hell did I sleep that long?"

Of course, I wasn't sleeping well at Patty's so I shouldn't be surprised.

I click through Melanie's messages. She's sorry for not realizing something had happened to me at first and hopes I can forgive her. But my eyes catch on her last text.

Melanie: *Check out the news. AV put out the press release. It looks like I'll see you Monday!*

I type my name in the search box and sure enough, there is Asher Vaughn's press release.

"They did it!" I shout to no one.

Asher Vaughn put out the press release clearing my name.

As if on cue, my phone rings again. It's Mary from human resources and I answer.

"Mary?"

"Sarina, I'm glad I caught you. Look, I'm sorry about all that's happened but after the news about that man came out, the board met and agreed to reverse your suspension. We're all hoping you can return to work Monday."

I can't help but grin. While I'm pissed at the board for what they did, I understand and likely would have done the same thing. The reputation of the company is important in this industry. I'm just happy this has been cleared up and I can return to work.

"Yes, I can do that."

"Great!" Mary says. "I'll see you Monday morning."

I set my phone down. I can't wait to tell Donny. He'll be back soon, so I shower and get ready for the day.

By the time he opens the front door, I run for him.

"Great news!" I say jumping into his arms. He closes the door then spins me around and presses me against it, kissing me hard.

After a few minutes of the most delicious kiss, he leans back grinning.

"It's good to see you, too."

"My suspension has been lifted. I go back to work Monday."

His eyebrows shoot up. "Already? That's great. Although I'll miss you."

"Yeah? What, do you think I'm going to work twelve-hour days?"

He shrugs. "Maybe. But now that things are resolved, I'll probably get a new assignment soon."

"Tell me about your job. Are all your assignments like this one was?"

He releases me and steps back. "No. Sometimes I have to go places that I won't be able to tell you about."

He pushes a strand of hair behind my ear.

"Why can't you tell me?"

"Morgan Thompson sometimes works with the military and goes in and does things they can't."

"Can't? What do you mean?"

He frowns. "I'm sorry but you don't have the proper clearance for those details."

I grin remembering our first conversation.

"Yes, but I have a pretty high security clearance."

He leans forward and kisses me gently. Then he leans back and says, "You have Asher Vaughn clearance, not military clearance."

"You'll be in danger." I know enough about what the special forces do to know he'll be in very dangerous places.

I can't help the tears from welling in my eyes. The idea of losing Donny after I just found him is overwhelming.

He lifts my chin. "Hey, listen. I'm trained for all of this, all right?"

I nod, then sniffle.

"I'll always come back to you, Sarina. I know we haven't been together long and that might be too much to say right now. But I've never felt this way for anyone. You're it for me."

The intensity of the emotion in his eyes has my stomach fluttering.

"I feel the same way, Donny. And I'll be honest, it scares me. You're right, this is fast. But it feels right."

I lean towards him and kiss him lightly. Then pull back. But then I see the heat in his eyes, and I kiss him again. Harder this time. His arms go to either side of my head, pinning me to the door as he deepens the kiss.

My hands find their way under his T-shirt and my fingers work over the ridges of his abs and up his chest. He steps back and removes the shirt and my eyes feast on him.

This man is the sexiest man I've ever known, and his body is amazing.

"If you're having second thoughts, we can stop at any time," he says.

"No second thoughts," I say as I lead him to his couch and push him down before crawling over him, straddling him.

I kiss him and let the kiss build as I grind into him. He grips my hips tightly and moans as I press down.

I need more so I pull my shirt off and his hands immediately go to my cotton bra. For a second, I wonder why the hell I wore a cotton bra but then his mouth is on my nipple, and I forget everything except how good this man feels under me.

He unhooks my bra and tosses it aside. Then his mouth goes back to my nipple. I grind harder wanting more of him.

Next thing I know, he's flipped us around and I'm lying on the couch with him above me. He kisses my neck and works his way down. When he reaches my stomach, he undoes my jeans. His eyes are on mine the entire time.

I help him shuck off my jeans then reach for his belt.

He stops me.

"Not yet. I need to taste you first."

He pulls my panties off and before I can respond, he dives in. His tongue licks over my clit and I buck my hips.

"Mmm. So good." He continues to lick and suck as I reach for his hair. I pull and he groans; the vibrations of it feel really good. Then he inserts a finger inside me, and I feel my orgasm building.

"That's it. Come for me, Sarina."

His words are my undoing as I go over the edge. He doesn't let up and it's the most intense orgasm I've ever had.

I catch my breath as I come down. He leans up and kisses me; my scent over his scruff and I love it.

"Let me return the favor," I say.

He shakes his head. "Not this time. I really need to be inside you. Is that okay?"

"Yes, please. Now!"

CHAPTER 26

DONNY

I CHUCKLE AT HER EAGERNESS. I love it. Sarina is so responsive, and she felt so tight when I had my fingers inside her.

I stand up and pull a condom out of my pocket. Then I remove my pants and underwear. I roll the condom on.

She reaches for me, and I can see her smile fall. Her eyes meet mine.

"Go slow, okay?"

I nod. I know I'm a bigger guy and the last thing I want to do is hurt her.

I lower myself back above her and then enter an inch at a time. It takes all my control to not thrust all the way in. But by the way she's breathing, I know she needs me to go very slow.

"If it's too much, just tell me and I'll stop."

She shakes her head and then her hands move down to my ass, pushing me further in until I'm deeply seated. We both moan.

"You feel so good."

"You do, too. Please move now."

I pull back and thrust in again. I'm not sure how long I'm going to last, this feels so good. She reaches down and strokes her clit, which almost does me in.

"Faster," she says.

I oblige. Then I feel her spasming around me and she cries out my name. I'm a goner. I thrust in and chase my own release.

We remain like that for several minutes. I stare into her eyes and there is no doubt I'm falling in love with this woman. I want to tell her but the last thing I want to do is scare her off. Instead, I get up and take care of the condom.

I return to the couch and pull her into my arms.

"Now that is a great way to start the day," she says.

I laugh. "Start? It's lunch time."

And as if on cue, my stomach growls.

"We should eat. I also wanted to ask you something," I say as I caress her back with my hand.

"What?"

"CT is having a bunch of the guys over this afternoon for a Friendsgiving sort of thing. Want to go?"

She sits up. "But Thanksgiving isn't till the end of the week."

"True. But Rocco and the guys fly out tonight so he put this together really quickly so we can say goodbye."

She rubs her eyes. "Sounds like a guys' thing then."

"No, Shaw will be there."

"She will?"

I grin happily that those two hit it off so well.

"Yes, she will."

"Okay. But we need to bring something. Ask CT what he needs."

I lean forward and kiss her. "Will do. I'm going to hop in the shower first."

She leans back. "Okay."

A few hours later we show up at CT's house. I'm holding a huge watermelon and Sarina is playing with the charm on her necklace.

"You're nervous?" I ask.

She blinks at me. "Of course I am. You've told me these guys are like your brothers and I'm meeting them all at once."

"Yeah, but you've met a few of them already."

"True but that was not as your..."

She trails off and her cheeks turn pink. It's so cute. I lean over and kiss her lips gently.

"My what?" I tease.

She shakes her head. "I don't know." She looks down causing her hair to fall over her face.

"Well, I'd like to introduce you as my girlfriend."

She peeks out from her hair but she's smiling.

"Good. Because I'd like that, too."

"What's this? CT not answering his door?" Phantom asks as he walks up behind us.

"No, we haven't knocked yet," I explain.

He nods. "I get it." He turns to Sarina. "Donny doesn't like to introduce us in case you like one of us better."

"Hey, not funny," I say but with a grin, so he knows I'm kidding.

"It's true. You'd be better off with Rover or even CT."

"Fuck off," I'm growing more serious.

Rover has always been a magnet for women once they discover he rides a Harley. I never understood the appeal. My SUV is much more practical.

"This is Phantom," I say.

Sarina cocks her head. "Phantom? What an interesting name. It's nice to meet you."

"Likewise." Phantom winks at her.

"That's enough," I say.

Before Phantom can reply, the door flies open. "Are you all going to just stand here or are you going to knock?" CT asks.

"Phantom's too busy trying to sell my girl on you and Rover to knock."

CT's eyes widen. "You looking for someone new? Well, I can be your man." He winks at Sarina.

"Come on," I say to Sarina as I push past CT. "You need to meet the ones that aren't assholes."

Phantom and CT laugh behind us.

"Wow, you actually found a watermelon this time of year?" CT says.

"Yeah, we went to three stores, but we found one," I say.

CT grins. I knew the moment I asked him what we could bring he'd mess with me. But when he said a watermelon, I didn't even think how hard it would be to find one in November.

"Everyone's out back," CT calls.

Outside? It's cold out. I set the watermelon on the table, and we make our way out the sliding door to the back yard.

Instead of walking into his back yard, we walk into a covered tent that has several long buffet tables set up with chairs and another buffet table where caterers are currently arranging hot containers of all the food. There are several heat lamps keeping the space warm as well.

"Wow, I thought this was casual," Sarina says to me.

"Yeah, he really went all out."

I shouldn't be surprised. CT never does a party half-assed even if it's one he threw together at a moment's notice.

"Should we offer to contribute? This must have cost him a lot," she says taking it all in.

"No, he's good." Most outside of us guys don't know but CT is loaded.

He's not normally one to flash his money around but when it can be used for something good like this, he always steps up.

"Donny, good to see you. And this must be Sarina?" Rocco asks.

"It is. Sarina this is Rocco and Ace. They're heading back to California with Phantom tonight."

Rocco shakes her hand.

"It's good to meet you. Thank you for everything you've done on this case. I'm so happy you were able to retrieve... the item."

Rocco smiles. We all know what Sarina is talking about and I love how she's trying to be careful with her words. Not that anyone here is a security risk.

"I'm happy we got to come up here and see these guys again," Ace says. "It's been too long."

"Yes, it has," CT says. "If you guys need any help in the future, ask your commander to think of us."

Phantom stepped up to the group.

"Hey Phantom, is it true you've softened up?" CT asks.

Phantom glares at him. "No."

Rocco chuckles. "Don't let him fool you. He's a softie when he's with Kalee.

Phantom grunted.

CT shook his head. "All of you and your women. You all turn to mush when you talk about them. And that's why I won't be settling down."

I know CT has issues when it comes to intimacy. His parents didn't do him any favors in that department practically leaving him alone to raise himself.

"You might not get a choice," Ace says. "When you meet

the right person, you just know. And you'll do whatever you can to be with her."

CT smiles. "Not gonna happen."

Phantom shakes his head. "Go ahead and live in denial." Then he turns to me. "Do you still draw?"

Sarina cocks her head. "Draw?"

"Yeah, he used to sketch landscapes and he did a drawing of me one time. He's really good," Phantom says.

"Really?" Sarina asks.

I shrug. "It relaxes me."

"Have you drawn me?"

I grin. "Maybe."

"Oh! Did you hear that?" Rover says as he steps up. "Maverick drew a woman!"

The rest of the guys all say "ooohhh!"

"Is that a big deal?" Sarina asks.

"Yes, it is," CT says. "Tell her Maverick, how many women have you drawn?"

I don't know why but my face feels like it's on fire. There's nothing to be embarrassed about.

I turn to Sarina. "You're the only one."

Her eyes well with tears. "Can I see it?"

I nod. "Now let's get off the topic of me. I'm sure Rocco has some stories he'd like to share."

"Actually there is one story I'd love to hear," Sarina says.

All eyes turn to her. She turns to CT. "CT how did you get your call sign?"

Rover chokes on his beer and I try but fail to bite back my laugh.

"Yeah, CT, tell her the story about your call sign," Ace says grinning.

CT rolls his eyes. "It's a stupid name. I keep trying to change it but these assholes won't let it go."

Rocco throws a balled up napkin at CT. "Stop complaining and just tell her."

The guys are all grinning, except CT.

CT throws his hands in the air. "Fine. I'll tell the story." He takes a deep breath before he begins.

"I was out with the guys drinking one night and someone spiked my drink."

"Lies!" Rover yells.

CT arches a brow at him. "Anyway, I was a bit tipsy."

"The man was drunk!" I say.

"We were walking back and I decided to take a shortcut and climb a fence."

Rover sets his beer down. "It wasn't a shortcut. CT just wanted to show off. I will say he climbed that chain link fence really fast."

"It was really fast," CT grins. "But something went wrong when I went over the top." His smile falls.

"When he tried to get over, he got stuck!" Rover wipes his eyes as he laughs. "I can still see you hanging there."

CT wipes his hand over his face. "My underwear got stuck on the top of the fence."

"Then he began to flop around trying to get loose," Rover says.

"I felt bad for the guy being stuck up there so I said *'Hey, let's help Camel Toe down,'* and it stuck," I say as I try but fail to hold back my laughter.

Rover wipes his eyes again. "I love that call sign. But since calling him Camel Toe in public isn't the best idea, we call him CT."

"Assholes," CT says.

Rover looks over at me and we both erupt into another fit of laughter.

"What is your real name?" Sarina asks.

"Ford."

"I like that," Sarina says.

"Yeah, but you can't call him that," Rover says.

"Why not?" CT asks.

Rover grins. "Only your woman can call you that."

CT rolls his eyes. "Well then I guess no one will ever call you Dax again."

"Ohhh!" Rocco says.

Rover points his beer at CT. "Fine with me. Better to be called Rover than Camel Toe."

"Oh yeah?" CT says.

"Enough!" I say. "Let's let the other guys get a word or two in before they have to go."

If I didn't cut these two off, they could go all night. Fortunately, that ends their bickering and we spend the next couple of hours sharing stories until the guys have to leave.

I take that as my cue to take Sarina home. While I should stay and let Sarina bond more with Shaw, all I want is to get her home and have her to myself. I don't think I've ever felt so content.

CHAPTER 27

Donny

I walk into Morgan Thompson with a huge smile on my face. Sarina and I are official, and she got along with all the guys. She's everything I could want in a woman. And I had a great time hanging with Rocco, Ace, and Phantom the other day before they left.

But the moment I see Stormy, I know something's wrong. I step into his office.

"What's wrong?"

"Frank's been released."

I stare at Stormy not believing what he said.

"Released?"

"Yes."

I begin to pace in front of the man. "No. No. That's not possible. Frank was detained by the CIA for potential terrorist activities. There is no way they would let him go."

Stormy tosses his pen on his desk as he leans back.

"I don't have all the details, but I'm told he hired a damn

good attorney who filed motions stating his civil rights were being violated."

"Civil rights? That's bullshit."

Stormy nods. "It is. But it was enough to get him released last night."

"What if he comes after Sarina? She's a witness."

"You can ask one of the guys to watch her when you're not available if you're worried."

I sit back down. "Thanks."

"There's more."

Of course, there is.

"According to Trip, the CIA froze all of Frank's accounts once they detained him. We have no idea how he got the money to pay for that attorney. And before you ask, no, it isn't pro bono."

"Someone's paying that bill."

Stormy stares out his window. "That's what concerns me. Who would do that?"

"Maybe his daughter, Norah."

He shakes his head. "No, she's been quite vocal about how much she disapproves of what her father did. I think she's trying to prevent losing her job."

"Well, if it wasn't Norah, who the hell was it?"

Stormy leans forward. "That's a good question and as soon as Trip has an answer for us, I'll let you know."

"It could be a number of people he's done business with. And if it is, I doubt even Trip will be able to trace that trail," I say.

"True. In the meantime, you're off desk duty. I don't have a new assignment for you yet, but I will soon."

There's a knock at the door. "Sorry to interrupt. You wanted to see me?"

I turn to see Rover standing at the door.

"Yes. Maverick, did you have any further questions?"

I stand up. "No, thank you for telling me."

Stormy nods and I fist bump Rover on my way out of the door.

Rover closes the door once I'm in the hallway and I can't help worrying about what they're talking about. Rover has been dealing with a lot lately. I feel like a shitty friend for not being there for him. My mind has been on Sarina and keeping her safe.

I head to my office to wrap up some paperwork.

"Maverick, glad you're off desk duty."

I glance up and find Peaches grinning at me.

"Yeah, how'd you hear that? I was just told."

"Stormy's door was open. I overheard."

"So, you heard Frank was released then?"

Peaches nods. "It isn't right. I wonder if Agent Harding knows about it." He shakes his head. "You know I should call her just to be safe."

I laugh.

"What?"

"You don't need an excuse to call her. Just ask her out already."

Peaches frowns. "It's not like that."

I lean back and stare at him. He squirms in his seat.

"Okay, so it is like that. I don't think she even knows my name. I never get the opportunity to talk to her."

"Then make an opportunity."

He nods. "I'll figure something out. But back to this case. I'm happy the weapon has been retrieved. But this case still feels unsettled to me."

I know exactly what he means.

"Hell, maybe it's because of Frank's release. I don't know."

"Do you think he'll run?"

Peaches snorts. "Of course, he'll run. With all those contacts around the world? He could go anywhere."

"Do you think Frank and Lee planned this alone?" I ask.

He leans back in his chair and stares at me. "What happened to the other two guys? The transport driver said they had four guys."

"I haven't heard. There's your excuse to call Agent Harding," I grin.

"Or we can just wait until Rover comes out of Stormy's office and ask him. If anyone is asking too many questions about this investigation, it's him." Peaches' smile drops and he grows serious. "How's Sarina doing?"

"Good. All things considered. She's been staying at my place the last couple of days."

He whistles. "Does this mean you two are official then? I mean I figured you probably are since you brought her to CT's Saturday."

"Yeah, we're official."

"Good for you. I'm happy for you man."

"Thanks."

Rover walks past my door, his head down, and he doesn't even look up or say anything. I jump up to catch him but he's out the door before I can ask him how his meeting with Stormy went.

"What's going on with him?" Peaches asks. "He's been acting strange lately."

"I think he's worried about his sister." I don't want to share his private business, but I know Peaches; if I don't tell him something, he'll dig.

But now I'm worried about Rover. Maybe things have taken a turn with the guy his sister was seeing. I should have followed up and asked him about that.

"Hey, have you seen the news?" CT asks bursting into the room.

"Stormy told me that Frank was released last night."

"And now he's dead," CT says.

I turn to CT. "Dead? Are you sure?"

"Positive. He was declared dead at the scene. Apparently, Norah found him. She went to visit him this morning and he was hunched over his kitchen table. It looks like a heart attack."

"Damn it!" I shout. "He was our lead to tracking down Lee."

"Norah is stating publicly she doesn't believe he had a heart attack and that he was murdered," CT says.

I glance at Peaches who looks just as stunned as me.

"Does she have any evidence?" I ask.

CT shrugs. "Not yet but she demanded an autopsy be performed. Her story was picked up and it's going viral."

"Viral?" Peaches asks.

CT leans into the doorway. "It isn't every day the guy accused of trying to sell US weapons to terrorists on home soil conveniently dies before he's about to be arraigned."

"Yeah, but the man was older, and he was probably stressed that whoever he promised the weapon to might come back and take care of him," Peaches says.

"Well, according to Norah, that's what they did," CT says.

"I'll call Rocco and find out more about the guys they caught trying to buy the weapon. But if it isn't them, who else would it be?" I ask more to myself than anyone else.

"Let's see what Rocco and those guys have to say first before jumping to any conclusions," CT says.

CHAPTER 28

Sarina

I walk into my office to find a large bouquet of flowers waiting for me. My first thought is to wonder did Donny do this? But then Melanie steps into my office.

"Surprise! A bunch of us chipped in to make sure you know we're very happy to have you back."

She's beaming at me. And I have to be honest. I really appreciate the welcome. I wasn't sure how everyone would react to my return. Yes, I'd been cleared, but that's not always enough for some.

"Thank you. I really appreciate it."

My eyes move back to the flowers then to the rest of the office. What the hell was Norah thinking? I was merely suspended, and she had the office repainted? And where are my things?

"I've got all your stuff in a box under my desk," Melanie says. "I packed up Norah's items before you got in."

"She didn't waste any time, did she?"

"No, she didn't. Now, I'm sure you have a lot of emails to catch up on. IT assured me that you have access to your email and Norah's so you can get caught up."

"Norah's? Won't she need that for work today?"

Melanie's smile fell. "She's not coming in. You didn't hear?"

I shake my head. I have been so focused on Donny and getting back in here this morning, I haven't paid attention to much else.

"Her father died."

I lean against my desk. "Frank died?"

"They think it was a heart attack. Norah called me this morning crying. She was the one that found him."

As angry as I am with Norah, I can't imagine finding your dad, dead.

"She says her father was murdered and demanded an autopsy."

Wow. This is a lot to take in for a Monday morning.

"Thanks for telling me."

At least I won't have to face Norah. After everything she did to get my job, I'd rather put off that confrontation as long as I can.

"Okay, well, I'm so happy you're back," Melanie says then steps out of my office.

"Melanie!" a familiar voice shouts. "Why didn't you email me my calendar this morning?"

Well, I guess that confrontation gets to happen now, ready, or not.

"Norah? What are you doing here?" Melanie asks.

"What kind of question is that?"

"I mean, you called earlier and were so upset. I thought you were taking a day."

"There's nothing I can do until after the autopsy results come in. I figured I'd throw myself into work until then."

That's when I step into the hall.

"Sarina? What are you doing here?"

Melanie glances from Norah to me.

"Norah, didn't Jim call you?" Melanie asks.

Norah arches a brow. "No. I actually tried to reach him about a matter, and he made it clear he wasn't available this weekend. What's going on. Why is she here?"

She speaks as if I can't talk for myself.

"Her suspension has been lifted. She's back," Melanie says, her eyes moving between the two of us as if she anticipates a fight.

I reach for my four-leaf clover charm, wishing for good luck right now. I still don't know what the hell is going on with Norah, but I do know her acting like my friend all those months was a lie.

Norah doesn't hide her shocked expression, but it quickly turns to a smile.

"Oh Sarina, welcome back. I hadn't heard. We should probably meet to discuss what I was in the middle of," Norah says as if we're friends again.

"That won't be necessary," Jim says as he walks down the hallway toward us. "Norah, a word please?"

Jim looks pissed. I don't know what Norah did to him but I'm just happy it isn't directed my way.

"Sure," Norah says as she sidesteps past me.

"Welcome back, Sarina," Jim says and flashes me a fake smile.

They walk down the hall into Jim's office where he closes the door.

Melanie turns to me. "That was tense."

"Yeah. Any idea why Norah pretended to be my friend all those months?"

She sighs. "I think she wanted your job the entire time. I mean, before you got here, we thought she was a shoo-in for it. But once you were hired, I thought she was fine with it. And then she came to the happy hours; I really thought we could all be friends."

"I thought we were," I say staring down the hall. "Well, I better get to work and see what I've missed."

"Good luck." Melanie spins around and heads toward her desk. I stare into my office from the hallway and shake my head. I'd deal with the decor later.

Jim's door swings open, catching my attention.

"Screw you!" Norah yells.

I glance down the hall to catch her exiting Jim's office.

"Norah!" Jim yells.

Norah spins around to face him. "I should have known. We all know your reputation. But you made me feel special. Why would you do that? I really thought what we had was special."

Norah turns back around, and her eyes are red, and tears are falling down her cheeks.

"I'm sorry you misunderstood, Norah."

She flips him off as she runs down the hallway.

I turn my attention to Jim. He's shaking his head and he goes back into his office and closes the door.

"Holy shit!" Melanie screeches. "They were doing it?"

I can't help but laugh. Melanie's word choices are funny.

"Did you have any idea?" she asks me.

"No, I thought he only slept with married women."

Melanie laughs. "I'm sorry. I shouldn't laugh but that's so true!"

I walk over to Melanie's desk.

"Do you think she convinced Jim to persuade the board to send out the press release about me and hire her into my position?"

Melanie's eyes widen. "You think she slept with Jim to move up at the company?" She bites her lip as she stares down the hall. "No, I mean the board is the one that decided to suspend you. And Gunnar was the final approval on all press releases."

This is one thing I really like about Melanie. She always sees good in people which means she isn't likely to see the bad. I'm not as certain about Norah's motives in sleeping with Jim as she is. But then I work closer with Jim, and I don't know why any woman would want him. He's kind of an asshole.

"Oh, I have news!" Melanie says. "I haven't had a chance to tell you yet."

"I hope it's good."

She's smiling. "It is. Noel and I have been dating for a couple of months now and last night, he told me he loved me!" She jumps up and down. "I really think this is it!"

"Wow, I'm so happy for you. I'd love to meet him. Maybe me and Donny can go out to dinner with you two?"

She claps her hands together. "Does this mean you two are official?"

I grin. "It does."

She jumps up and down. "Yay! We can double date now. I'll ask Noel about his schedule when I see him tonight."

"Sounds great."

I spend the rest of the day playing catch up and trying to undo what Norah had done. For some reason, she found a new supplier for the Allen project but unfortunately, they were a supplier off of our do not use list. Their quality is subpar. Thankfully, no contracts had been signed yet. I am able to end that relationship with minimal yelling on their part and find a more suitable supplier. Yes, it'll cost more, but it's necessary.

But I can't help my mind from returning to Norah yelling at Jim. Why the hell would she try to date the man? She's heard my many complaints about his affairs. And the fact she never mentioned it at our happy hours…how long was it going on? Did she want to keep it a secret? I know it's none of my business, but I can't help myself.

Next thing I know, I'm face to face with Jim's assistant.

"Is he free at the moment?"

Tony smiles. "Well, no one is in there if that's what you mean. I can call and check."

He picks up the phone and lets Jim know I'm there to see him.

"Send her in," he says loud enough I can hear.

"Thank you." I walk into his office making sure to close the door behind me.

"Sarina, is everything all right?"

I nod. "Yes, I think I found a solution to the Allen project, and it looks like I've worked through most of Norah's changes."

I don't miss the scowl on his face at the mention of her name.

"That's actually what I'm here to talk to you about."

He frowns. "Her changes? I'm afraid she didn't discuss those with me."

I sit down in the chair across from him. "How long were you and Norah dating?"

His brows shoot up. "Oh well, you're digging right in then." He coughs then takes a drink of water. "I'm not sure it's really any of your business."

I don't say another word but continue to stare at him. It's one tactic I found works with Jim. He hates awkward silences.

"I wouldn't call what we were doing dating," he finally says.

Okay, now I'm sorry I asked.

"I thought she understood. I mean it's no secret I'm not a relationship type of guy. But somewhere along the line, she developed feelings. And as you saw earlier this morning, it didn't end well."

I lean back. "So, it was just a fling then?"

"Yes."

I don't miss that he didn't answer my original question. "How long did the fling last?'

He stares down at a paper on his desk then waves his hand. "A few weeks maybe."

"Why Norah?"

He glances up. "Excuse me?"

"Why Norah? You had to have known she was a bit different than most women. She really doesn't strike me as fling material."

Jim leans back and crossed his arms. "Well, that wasn't the impression she gave me. She came on to me. I went with it. I am a man after all." He smiles.

I can't help rolling my eyes. What the hell did Norah see in this guy?

"Now if you'll excuse me, I have a meeting to attend." He stands up and walks past me but before he reaches the door, he turns around. "And I hope you still aren't thinking about going to the board with your concerns about me."

I stand and turn to face him but don't respond. I hadn't thought about it because I've been too focused on playing catch up.

"Because I'm afraid you've lost all your credibility with them. Do you really think they would listen to you after you had your own affair with the main investigator in this case?"

He smiles then opens the door and walks out leaving me wanting to punch him. But damn it, he's right.

CHAPTER 29

DONNY

"ANY SIGN OF LEE?" I ask Trip over the speaker phone.

"No. He hasn't shown up anywhere I've looked," Trip says.

"Agent Harding hasn't found anything either," Stormy says. "But it's possible that he never made it out of Canada. He wasn't with the truck and as Sarina told us, it gets very cold up there at night. Too cold for most to survive."

That was a good point. And if Lee died, we might never know. Or he might have had help.

"What about Jared? Could he have flown Lee out?" I ask.

"No," Stormy says. "Jared has been in custody."

I smile. "He has?"

Stormy nods. "According to Harding, once they had the buyer detained, he sold out Jared hoping to get some kind of deal."

I rub my temples. "I saw Harding at Boeing Field when I picked up Sarina."

Stormy nods. "My understanding is Jared has been in custody all this time. He's considered a flight risk."

"Did he mention Frank or anyone else?"

Stormy shakes his head. "Harding said Jared swore he only dealt with Lee. And for what it's worth, he claims he had no idea about Sarina until she was already on the plane."

As much as I don't like the guy, he did help Sarina get back to the states.

"And since we won't have the final autopsy results back for Frank for a while, we need to move on. Most of this one is wrapped up," Stormy says as he paces by the end of the table in his office.

"Yeah, but what if Frank was murdered? We need to be ready to investigate if he was," Rover says.

Stormy stops. "Actually, no we don't. We were hired to locate the missing weapon. Rocco and his team did that. We searched and found Sarina because she's Donny's woman and we would do that for any of you."

"And searching for Lee wasn't going beyond that?" Rover asks.

Stormy leaned forward on the table. "No. The man kidnapped Sarina. We had to make sure he was no longer a threat."

A song plays from Peaches' phone about peaches in a can. "Dammit guys!"

He silences his phone.

Stormy arches a brow, but no one says anything else. I'd love to know who is messing with his phone and how they're doing it. The guy has the thing glued to him twenty-four seven ever since the first time someone changed his ring tone. I have to say, I'm surprised how many songs there are about peaches.

"Moving on then," Stormy says.

For the next hour we discuss a new assignment in

Mexico. Peaches, Trax, and Fox are assigned to go Friday. Stormy made sure they would at least get to have Thanksgiving with their families first. Rover, CT, and I are tasked with catching up on paperwork from this last assignment.

"Rover, did you ever find that college administrator that went missing?" Stormy asks.

"Joseph Taylor? No. Trip says he'll let me know if he turns up at any airports or anywhere else."

"Hmm. Okay, I'll keep that file closed for now. That's it."

"Wait. Stormy, did you ever figure out who sent you that cake?" Peaches asks.

Stormy shakes his head. "No, it was misdelivered. I just feel bad for whoever didn't get their cake that day. Now, everyone enjoy your holiday."

Rover rubs his hands together as we walk out of Stormy's office. "Okay guys, one last game before we take a break?"

"Break? We aren't getting a break," Peaches says glancing at Trax and Fox.

"No but Maverick is, and I can't go a week without knowing I crushed him at paintball," Trax says.

Peaches breaks out into a big grin. "Yeah. Let's play."

Thirty minutes later we're set up, divided into our usual teams.

"Maverick, I'm coming for you!" Trax shouts.

"Why does he have it so bad for you?" Rover asks as he peeks through the trees.

"Because I always get him first. Drives him nuts."

I turn and move further back into the woods. I know every inch of this place and I use that to my advantage. What Trax doesn't know is that I've sketched these woods many times and know every nook and cranny.

I make my way to a big maple tree that's in the middle of a clearing of sorts. I climb up about six feet and wait. I know Trax will come through here. I feel it in my bones.

I hear CT cursing in the distance. One man down. Then I hear a twig snap and turn too late. Fox spotted me and has taken aim, hitting me.

"Dammit!" I shout as I climb out of the tree.

"Too predictable, Maverick."

"I'm losing my touch," I tell him.

I make my way back toward the building when I hear Rover shout. I guess we're out.

By the time I get to the back patio, Trax is standing there grinning, CT wears a scowl, Rover walks in with a limp, and Fox and Peaches are joking about something.

"What happened to you?" I ask Rover.

He shakes his head. "Peaches hit me in the calf and gave me a fucking Charlie horse. Hurts like hell."

Peaches laughs. "You're getting weak old man!"

I laugh. Peaches is three years younger than us but the way he talks you would think it was at least ten.

"Old man? I'm not the one with gray hair," Rover says.

Peaches' hand goes straight to his hair. "There's no gray, asshole."

"Hey, there's nothing wrong with gray hair," Stormy says as he steps out onto the patio. Then he runs his hands through his own salt and pepper hair.

"Not when you're fifty, no. But in your late twenties, yes," Peaches says.

Stormy moves so fast; Peaches doesn't see it coming. He grabs Rover's paint gun and hits Peaches right in the chest catching him off guard.

"What the hell?" Peaches asks. He was still wearing his protective coveralls, so I know it didn't really hurt him. Too bad, anyway.

"I'm not fucking fifty," Stormy says with a grin.

Sometimes Peaches talks without thinking but fortunately he only does that around us. Around strangers, the man is silent.

"Hey," Trax says as he sits on the bench next to me. "Are you going to be okay with us leaving tomorrow?"

"I'll be just fine but it sounds like you're going to miss me," I say grinning.

Trax chuckles. "I meant with Sarina. I know everything seems to be wrapped up but what if Frank's daughter is right and he was murdered?"

I shrug. "A lot of people could've gone after Frank that aren't related to the weapon investigation. You saw all his passports."

Trax nodded. "You're right."

"Speaking of Sarina, are you two spending Thanksgiving together?" CT asks.

"We are. My parents are on a cruise and my brother didn't get leave so it'll just be the two of us."

"What about her family?" CT asks.

I shake my head. "She said her brother will be with his girlfriend and her father hasn't even called to check in on her."

"You mean since she was kidnapped, flown to another country, and feared for her life?"

I nod, holding back the anger I feel toward both her brother and her father. At least her brother checked in but instead of being here for her, he's leaving town. And don't even get me started on her dad.

"Nope."

CT crosses his arms. "That's cold."

"She says they never spend Thanksgiving together so it's no big deal."

But even as she said it, I could tell it bothered her.

"What about Christmas? Does she see them then?" Rover asks.

I shrug. "We haven't discussed that yet."

"Well, you know she's always welcome at our Christmas party," Rover says.

I laugh. Our Christmas party is all of us getting together sometime around Christmas for a white elephant gift exchange. Not all of the guys have family they can get to and we all enjoy it.

"Thanks. I'll let her know."

* * *

Sarina

ASIDE FROM THE confrontation on Monday, I'd so far been able to avoid Norah this short week. Just a few more hours and I would have the holiday weekend to avoid her. But I knew my luck would run out sooner or later. And it did the moment she knocked on my door.

"Do you have a moment?" she asks.

I want to say no. The sight of her makes me angry. But I'm trying to be a forgive and forget kind of person but it's hard. I take a deep breath to steady myself.

"Sure. Come in."

She steps in, closing the door behind her. Instead of sitting in the chair, she stands there rubbing her hands together.

"Look, I'm sorry. I was an asshole. It's just that I really wanted your job. I thought you knew but Melanie filled me in that you didn't. Before you got here, I was told I was being promoted to the VP position. I went home on a Friday, called my mom, told her the great news and was happy. But then Monday, I came in and you were here. I didn't understand. Jim was kind and explained the board made the decision and it was out of his hands. That was when things slowly began to change with Jim. I cried and he held me. We began to have morning coffee together. Two months later, we were dating."

She shakes her head. "But that doesn't excuse my behavior. But I can assure you after a couple of weeks in your job, I know now I don't want it. And as for Jim, well, I guess that was the universe giving me the karma I deserve."

She finally looks up and meets my gaze. I'm stunned. This is not like the Norah I know. I'm not sure what to say.

After a moment of silence, she takes a breath. "Okay, well I just wanted to tell you that. If you'd rather not speak to me, I understand."

She reaches for the doorknob.

"Wait."

I stand and walk around my desk.

"Everything you did was because you wanted this job?"

She turns back to face me. "Yes. I'm sorry, but I had it in my head you didn't deserve the job and only got it because you're... you know."

"Because of my military experience?"

She shakes her head. "No, because of your dad. I thought maybe he paid someone off."

My dad is well known for his wealth, but I've never known him to pay anyone off for anything. He especially wouldn't for his kids. Just thinking of him pisses me off so I take a deep breath to remain calm.

"But the board made the hiring decision."

She laughs. "It was ridiculous, yes. But I convinced myself."

I cross my arms. "And now why the sudden turn around?"

She leans against the wall. "Well, Melanie handed me my ass last night but even before that, after doing your job while you were suspended, I realized I don't want to run interference like you have to do. It doesn't interest me. I was more interested in the title and prestige than the actual work itself."

She wipes her palms on her pants. "And I want us to be friends again."

My mouth falls open. Friends? Is she kidding?

She holds up a hand. "Look, I know that won't happen overnight and you have no reason to trust me. But hopefully, down the road, we can go to a happy hour again."

The idea of confiding in her holds no appeal. I'm certain now that Melanie is behind this. Melanie hates conflict. And there shouldn't be conflict. I've learned holding onto anger doesn't help.

"And you think we were friends before?"

She nods as her eyes become glassy. "I think so. Just think about it okay?"

"I'll think about it."

Being friends with Norah again? Not going to happen.

She nods then leaves my office. The door barely closes and then reopens, and Melanie runs in all smiles.

"So, are you two friends again?"

I walk back to my chair and flop into it. "No. And don't push this."

Her smile falls. "Oh. Okay. I'm sorry."

"Look, I know you hate conflict but I'm not going to be friends with that woman again."

Melanie nods. "I guess that means you won't be joining us for happy hour today?"

I rub my temples. Why the hell is Melanie so quick to forgive Norah? "No. I won't. Besides I already have plans."

Melanie sits in the chair across from me. "Is it with that hottie of yours?" She leans forward. "Well, that smiles says it is."

I can't help but smile when I think of Donny.

"It is. I'm meeting him for dinner." Then because I can't help myself, I ask, "You and Norah are going to happy hour?"

Melanie sighs. "Yeah, is that okay with you? I mean yes, what she did really sucks but I'm hoping we can get past it since we all have to work together."

"It's fine but no guarantees that I will ever want to have happy hour with her again. Are you heading home for Thanksgiving?"

Melanie's family is from Oregon, and she drives down there occasionally to see them.

She shakes her head. "No, I'm spending it with Noel. We agreed to order pizza and keep it simple."

"Things are getting serious between you two, aren't they?"

She's beaming. "They are. And I hope you can meet him soon."

"I'd like that. Maybe after the holiday weekend."

Melanie claps. "Yes! You and Donny can come over for dinner. Noel will be out of town next week so maybe the week after. I'll figure something out and text you."

"Sounds good."

"And are you spending the big day with Donny?"

I smile. "I am. Just the two of us. And I can't wait."

CHAPTER 30

SARINA

I CURL up next to Donny, reluctant to get out of bed. The last two weeks have been bliss. Since Thanksgiving, we've taken turns staying at each other's houses. The more time I spend here at Donny's the more I have to admit it's beginning to feel more like home than my house. I think that has a lot to do with the fact that since I was trapped at home with the press outside, it has sort of tainted the place for me.

Then there is the fact I feel closer to Donny than I have ever felt to anyone, including my dad and brother. And even Melanie. But then I realize why. I've kept my guard up, even if just a little with everyone. Somehow Donny breaks through it all. Or maybe I let him.

"We better get going," he says, pulling me closer. "It's getting late."

I glance at the clock and it's almost noon. "I wouldn't be in bed so late if you didn't keep tempting me to come back."

He chuckles.

Today is the big day we get to meet Melanie's man, Noel. I've never seen Melanie so nervous as I did yesterday at work. She asked me three times if crab cakes would be okay for lunch. I finally told her to just breathe.

After a quick shower, I walk into the kitchen to find Donny eating pizza.

"Pizza? You better be hungry for Melanie's crab cakes," I say.

He shrugs. "No problem."

"Huh."

I don't understand how he can eat so much food and still have all those abs.

"Here, try a bite," he offers holding up a slice.

I lean in and take a bite. I force myself to chew and swallow.

"It's cold!"

He glances at the pizza then back at me. "Yeah, of course it is."

I shake my head. "Not for me, thank you."

He leans forward and gives me a quick kiss. "I made coffee, too."

"Thank you."

Less than an hour later, we're ready to go. I grab the chocolate cake from the counter. I'm no baker but I can follow a box mix and I know chocolate is Melanie's favorite.

Donny's phone rings before I make it to the front door.

"It's Rover, I have to take this."

He steps into the kitchen as he takes the call. I send Melanie a text letting her know we're on our way.

A moment later Donny walks back into the room, and I can tell by the look on his face I'm not going to like what's going on.

"Sarina, I'm so sorry but something has come up and I have to help Rover."

"Oh. Okay."

He cups my cheek. "As soon as I'm done, I'll meet you over there. This'll probably take an hour or so."

I nod. While I'm disappointed he won't be going with me, I can't help but love this man. He would do anything for his friends. I set the cake down on the table and turn to him.

"It's okay. I know your friends are important to you."

"They are. Thank you for understanding."

I nod as I wrap my arms around his neck. "Is Rover in trouble?"

He shakes his head then kisses my forehead. "No, but he's having some family trouble and he's always been there for me."

"You don't need to explain. I get it. I'll let Melanie and Noel know you're running late."

"You sure?"

I nod. "Just text me if you aren't going to make it."

He smiles. "Okay." Then he leans down and gives me a tender kiss. When he pulls back, he has a serious expression.

"I love you," he says.

The very words have my heart fluttering.

"I know this is fast and I don't want you to feel any pressure to say it back."

"I love you, too."

He smiles. "Yeah?"

"Yes."

Then kisses me again.

"Damn. Now I just want to take you back to bed." He sighs. "Tell Melanie I'm sorry to be late."

"I will."

I give him one more peck then turn and head to the door, grabbing the cake on the way out.

I shoot Melanie a quick text explaining Donny won't be with me then I blast my music on the drive to her apartment. By the time I arrive, I'm singing at the top of my lungs.

A woman a few parking spots over stares at me. Oops. The volume must be louder than I thought.

I'm practically walking on air to Melanie's door. I can't help it. Being with Donny is the best feeling. And I decided I'm not going to hold back with my friends anymore. I'm going to let Melanie know what she means to me.

I knock and the door opens. But Melanie isn't there. That's odd. She isn't one to leave her door open. But she is expecting me.

"Melanie?" I call out as I walk into her apartment.

I go to the kitchen and set the cake on the counter.

"In here," she calls from her bedroom.

I walk down the hall and push open the door. I jump back when I see Melanie tied to a chair in the middle of the room.

"Melanie! What's going on!"

But it's too late.

"Hello Sarina."

I turn and come face to face with Lee.

"What are you doing here? I thought you'd be long gone in Canada."

I step back but hit the wall of the hallway. I'm shaking. How the hell do I get out of here?

"Well, I should be in Bali, but my plans didn't work out. Then I remembered you mentioned your dad had money and I decided to go with plan b. Oh and be thankful your boyfriend couldn't make it. I was going to kill him."

I close my eyes. This man knows Donny isn't coming to rescue me.

Lee is standing next to Melanie. I could run for the front door. I might make it. The weight of my purse on my shoulder reminds me I have my phone.

"I can see you thinking through your options. Let me sum

it up for you," Lee says as he pulled a gun out of his waistband. "Run and I'll shoot your friend."

My eyes meet Melanie's. Tears are streaming down her face.

"I'm so sorry, Sarina. I had no idea who he really was."

Lee laughs. "No, she had no idea."

I turn to Lee. "You didn't force your way in here?"

Lee laughs harder as Melanie's tears well more.

"You want to tell her, or shall I?" Lee says as he leans over and kisses Melanie on the cheek. She flinches away from his touch.

"I thought his name was Noel."

The reality of the situation hits me.

"Noel? The man you were dating?"

"Yeah, I've been watching you for a while, Sarina. Frank thought you were the one who knew the contact at PV Transport and likely knew the route the transit team would take."

I take a small step back, hoping he doesn't notice. "I didn't know. PV Transport doesn't share their routes with us. It's part of their protocol."

Lee leans against the chair Melanie is tied to.

"Yes, I learned that. But at the time, I thought you might be useful. I was planning on how to talk to you at the bar one night when this woman sidles up next to me giving me those big doe eyes. That's when everything clicked into place."

I feel sick for Melanie. She really thought she'd found her one. And he was using her all along.

"You really should train your employees to be more discreet. She left her laptop open all the time. It was so easy to go in and read your schedule. And the best part? This little tiger," he nudged Melanie, "is probably the best lay I've ever had. Thank you for that sweetheart."

Melanie leans over and heaves, sending vomit onto Lee's shoes.

"Shit. Fuck! That's disgusting." He jumps back and I take the moment of distraction to turn and run for the door. I'm almost there when a sudden pain emerges from the back of my head. Then everything goes black.

I wake up staring at the ceiling. My head hurts like hell and I try to rub my temple, but my hand won't move. I turn to see I'm tied to the headboard of Melanie's bed. I move my right leg, but it doesn't budge. He managed to knock me out again. I fight the tears that want to fall. I won't let him win.

"I'm so sorry," Melanie says from somewhere in the room. "I had no idea. Until this morning. He tied me up. Stupid me, I thought it was a sexual thing. Then he told me his name wasn't Noel. It's Leon."

"Don't blame yourself. He tricked us both."

I try to turn my head to take in the room.

"Where is he?" I ask.

"His phone rang, and he left to answer it."

I pull on the wrist restraints, but it only seems to tighten them. Damn, he might have gotten better at knot tying.

"How late do you think Donny will be?" she asks hopefully.

"I don't know. He might not come at all."

"Shh!" Melanie says. "Noel...I mean Lee doesn't need to know that."

"Have you seen my purse?"

"You had it when you ran but when he carried you back in here, it was gone."

Shit. I remembered how I ran to the front door. It was probably there, dropped when he hit me.

"Do you have a phone in here?" I ask.

"No. And I can't break loose. I've been working on it all

morning but whatever knots he tied, they tighten as I try to wiggle out of them."

I turn my head to get a better look. Lee used Melanie's scarves to tie me up and sure enough, it's exactly what I expected.

"Stop pulling. He used an arbor knot which means the more you pull, the tighter it will get."

Melanie groans. "Well, it can't get much tighter. And how the hell do you know that?"

"It's a fishing knot. I learned it from my uncle. He used to take me and my brother fishing when we were younger."

My uncle was the only person who made my dad seem human. Whenever my uncle was around, my dad would actually smile and laugh. But I shake that thought out of my head. I need to focus on the knots.

"How do you undo the knots then?" she asks.

"Well, I've never untied one with one hand. I'm not sure it's possible."

Before I can work too hard at it, the bedroom door opens, and Lee stands there with a phone in his hand.

"Time to call daddy!" he says as if he is Jack Nicholson in the *Shining* trying to creep us out. News flash, I'm already creeped out.

"What is your father's phone number?" Lee asks holding his fingers over his phone ready to dial.

The odds my dad would take my call are slim. His assistant would likely just take a message no matter what I said.

Instead, I give him Donny's number. Before he hits the call button, Lee turns to me.

"Tell him you've been kidnapped, and he must listen to my instructions. Nothing else. If you deviate, I will kill your friend, which I should have already done after your little escapade."

I nod and get ready to talk fast before Donny says something that would give him away.

The phone rings. "Sarina?" Donny answers.

"Dad! I'm so happy you answered. I know you're so busy with work and all."

Lee growls then nudges his chin to the phone in a hint to get to it.

"Sarina, are you all right?" Donny asks.

"I'm calling because I've been kidnapped by Lee, and you're supposed to listen to his instructions."

Before I can say more, Lee pulls the phone away. "My name isn't necessary."

Then he puts it to his ear. "Is this Sarina's father?"

There is a pause. "Good. If you want to see your daughter alive again, you will bring two million dollars cash. We will meet at ninety-four ninety-four Paradise road. In one hour. The girls will be in the barn. You drop off the money in front of the house, take the girls, and we all go our happy ways."

She could hear Donny talking.

"You have an hour," Lee says.

I hear Donny arguing on the other end.

"Well, that isn't my problem. Figure it out. And if I see so much as one policeman, I'll shoot her."

Lee ends the call.

"A man as rich as your dad and he was trying to say he can't get cash that quickly. Bullshit."

I know better than to argue but I also know it's true. You can't just walk into a bank and ask for two million without raising some eyebrows. Besides the fact my dad didn't keep the bulk of his money in a bank. But I wasn't going to educate Lee on the finer points of investing.

"Okay, we need to get there before they do so let's head out."

Lee unties Melanie.

"If either of you tries to run, I'll shoot the other." He holds up his gun to emphasize his point.

I know he won't shoot me. Not until he gets his money. But I'm not willing to risk Melanie's life. I can't imagine what's going through her mind right now.

Once Melanie is free from the chair, he takes a knife and cuts my restraints free.

"Go to the parking lot." He uses the gun to point the way.

I follow Melanie outside and to the parking lot.

"Melanie, go to my car."

She goes to a large, older car. He pops the trunk and then says, "get in."

I look at Melanie and her eyes widen in fear.

"Get in," Lee repeats. "I'm not going to say it again."

I glance around and the way Lee has parked, no one will see us get into the trunk. He had this planned. Now I believe him, he really was going to kill Donny.

I take the lead and step into the trunk. It's quite large and both Melanie and I fit.

Lee closes the trunk and whistles as he walks to the driver's seat.

"I've always hated this car," Melanie says. "He says it's a classic."

While Melanie is going on about the car, I'm searching for a way out. I push and pull hoping something will cause the trunk to pop open.

Lee starts the car and it's loud. Then he begins to drive, and I realize we're going to need to hold on to keep from bumping our heads.

"I'm so sorry," Melanie says to me. "I had no idea."

"Don't be sorry. He was using you. How could you have known?"

Melanie sniffles. "He asked about you a lot. I thought he

was just showing interest in my job. Now I realize I was wrong."

"Melanie," I keep my voice low. "I called Donny, not my dad. Just hang on, okay?"

"Really?" her voice brightens.

"Really."

We hold on for what feels like an hour but was probably twenty minutes. Then he parks the car. The moment the trunk pops open, I shut my eyes. The light is blinding after being in the dark.

"Get out," he orders.

Melanie crawls out and I follow.

"Go to the barn," he juts his chin in the direction behind us. We turn to see a barn.

Oh no. Not this place again. I grip the car to hold myself up.

Lee laughs. "I see you recognize this place."

"You've been here?" Melanie asks.

"I was locked in a trailer."

"Shut up and get in the damn barn."

We follow his instructions and once he undoes the padlock on the door, we go inside and sit down against a post. He ties us to it.

"Now wait here. Once I get my payment, I'll leave, and your daddy can save the day."

Lee grins at me then turns his attention to Melanie.

"You know, it wasn't all fake. I really did like you. In a different world, I think we'd be great together." He leans forward and kisses her on the lips. She turns her head away.

Lee jumps up. "Well, good luck ladies. Hopefully I'll never see you two again."

I squeeze my eyes shut. Tears fall down my cheeks. Please Donny get us out of here.

CHAPTER 31

DONNY

"Son of a bitch!" I shout as I pocket my phone.

"What's wrong?" Rover asks after he takes a sip of his coffee.

Rover had needed to talk to someone about what was going on with his sister. After talking it through, he realized there isn't much he can do right now. I was just about to head over to Melanie's to surprise Sarina when she called me.

"Sarina's in trouble. Fucking Lee has her and is demanding two million dollars for her release."

Rover jumps up. "Why the hell does he think you have that kind of money?"

"He thought she was calling her dad. But she called me instead."

"Smart move."

"He wants her dad to bring the money to the property out on Paradise road."

"No shit? Let's go."

This is why I love these guys. They think just the way I do.

"We should call CT," I say.

Rover shakes his head. "We can't. He's still on desk duty for shooting that guy Ted at the Gardiner house fiasco. We can't risk getting him involved in anything else."

CT and Rover helped out another security company on a case they were working in our area that was essentially babysitting a college administrator, but it turned deadly when Rover and CT were in the middle of it. This Ted guy shot someone and almost shot another man, but CT was able to stop him. Until that case is closed, CT can't help us out.

"That's bullshit."

Rover nods. "Yeah, but Stormy is just being cautious until the investigation is over."

I shoot a text off to Stormy letting them know what's going on.

We're in the car and halfway there as I think through if we will beat Lee to the property.

"Melanie's apartment is about twenty-five minutes from the property."

"And we're about twenty minutes out."

We both know that's cutting it close.

"Did he say any more?"

"Yeah, he said to put the money in front of the house, the girls will be in the barn, and to do it all in one hour from the call."

"Hold it. Girls?"

"I'm pretty sure he has Melanie too."

"Shit."

We continue to drive as I map out a plan.

"You go into the barn and stay out of sight. I'll find a place near the house and take out Lee the first chance I get."

Rover is about to object; I can tell from his expression but my phone rings. I answer in case it's Sarina again.

"Hello?"

"Maverick." It's Stormy. "Agent Harding and her partner are on their way. They want Lee alive."

"How far out are they? The guy will be there in less than fifteen."

"They won't get there in time, but they'll be careful going in."

I close my eyes.

"I'll do my best but if he goes after Sarina—"

"I get it," Stormy says.

I end the call.

"I heard. CIA is coming too, huh?"

"Yep, Harding."

Rover shakes his head. "Good thing Peaches isn't here. I'm pretty sure he has a thing for her."

I turn to see Rover grinning. "She seems too badass for him."

Rover laughs. "Don't let him hear you saying that."

When we get to the property, no one else is there. Rover drives up the road to the next house and parks in front of it. Then we both quickly make our way back. I'm relieved to see no cars are here yet. Rover goes into the barn, and I take the wooded area beside the house where I can see the entrance.

And just like clockwork, an old Chevy Nova pulls in five minutes later. Lee gets out of the driver's side, but I don't see anyone else in the car. I pull out my phone to text Rover what I see but then Lee pops the trunk.

"Get out," he says.

A leg falls over the edge and I spot Melanie climbing out, her hands tied. Then Sarina climbs out after her. Her hands are also bound.

Sarina's eyes widen and I can see her fear at being back here.

That's when I notice the gun he's holding.

I text Rover that Lee has a gun and is headed his way with the women.

After they disappear inside the barn, I listen but hear nothing. I hate not going in but if he leaves them in the barn with Rover, they're safer there than if I rush in.

Five minutes later, Lee comes out of the barn alone.

Rover: *They're tied to a post. I have eyes on them.*

Lee walks across the driveway to the house. He pulls a set of keys from his pocket and unlocks the door and goes in. I check the time. Thirty minutes before he expects Sarina's dad with the money.

My phone buzzes again.

Stormy: *Harding is five minutes out.*

Maverick: *Sarina and Melanie are tied up in the barn. Rover is hiding in there too. Lee just went into his house.*

I hear a car drive up the roadway and I'm certain it's Agent Harding.

But after a few minutes, I don't hear anything.

"Maverick," Harding whispers.

I turn to find her right behind me. How the hell did she sneak up on me? No one can do that.

"We need to stay here until it's time," she says.

I frown. "Time for what?" I ask.

"You'll know." She grins at me then takes off further into the woods.

I turn my attention back to the barn. There's no sound coming from there. I can only hope that Rover is freeing them as we speak.

After standing there for what feels like forever with nothing happening, I glance at the time. Five minutes until the drop. What the hell is Rover doing? Has he snuck them out the side of the property?

A car pulls in the driveway. Shit. Who would be visiting now of all times? Did Lee call in reinforcements?

But then I recognize the car and the man who steps out of it. Stormy. What the hell? He's carrying a duffel bag.

Lee steps out of the house.

"Are you the man I'm supposed to see?" Stormy asks.

Lee crosses his arms. "Depends. Are you Mr. McIntyre?"

"I am. I have what you requested. Now let me see my daughter."

Lee walks up to Stormy staring at him.

"You look a little rougher than your photo online."

Shit. Of course, Sarina's dad's photo would be online. He owns a damn company.

"That was photoshopped. My publicist insisted."

Damn, that sounded convincing.

Lee nods.

"Do you want to discuss other photos of mine or can we get this over with?" Stormy demands.

"You're right. Put the duffel on the porch. Your daughter is in the barn."

Stormy walks hesitantly toward the porch. This man should win an Oscar. He actually looks nervous and scared.

"How do I know they are really in there?" Stormy asks.

Lee laughs. "You're gonna have to trust me."

"I don't," Stormy says. "I need to see her first."

Lee frowns. Then he pulls a gun out of his waistband and points it at Stormy.

"All right but don't try anything."

"I won't."

Lee walks down the stairs and then nods to the barn.

"Go."

Stormy walks to the barn, still clutching the bag. Lee follows.

"Open the door," Lee instructs.

As Stormy reaches for the door, he swings around with the duffle bag and knocks the gun out of Lee's hand.

"What the hell?" Harding yells as she runs to Lee. "That was an unnecessary risk."

Harding has Lee on the ground and handcuffed before I get over to them.

Stormy drops the bag and crosses his arms. "It was necessary. He had a gun."

She hauls Lee upright.

"And what if you missed?" she asks.

"I never miss."

A new car pulls up and a man in a black jacket gets out. I don't need to see the back of it to know it likely says CIA.

"Agent Winston," Harding calls as she hauls Lee toward his car.

I turn my attention back to the barn as Rover walks out of the barn with Sarina and Melanie.

Sarina sees me and runs towards me. When she reaches me, she jumps into my arms. I hold her tight.

"I'm so sorry I didn't go with you to Melanie's," I say.

She pulls back to look at me. "No, don't be sorry. There was no way to know. It turns out Lee was Noel, Melanie's boyfriend."

I'm stunned. I glance at Melanie whose eyes are red and puffy.

"She had no idea. He used her. She thought he was her one."

I hear a scuffle behind me and turn to see Lee running down the driveway toward the street, still handcuffed.

Agent Harding and Agent Winston chase him. Winston takes him down hard.

I can't help but wince at the loud thud when he hits the ground.

Both agents drag Lee back to the car. And I mean literally drag. The man is not making it easy. Once they've thrown him in the back seat of Winston's car, Harding walks over to us.

"Thank you. I don't know how you pulled this off so quickly. But thank you," I say to Harding.

"No, I need to thank you guys. Both my agency and the FBI have been looking for this man for years. In addition to a host of other crimes, he's been trading our military weapons for the better part of a decade. This was the first time he tried it on US soil. I'm happy he'll finally get what's coming to him."

"Fucking Frank!" Lee shouted from the back of that car.

"Shut up," Winston says.

"Frank's daughter, Norah, has been saying she doesn't believe her dad really died of a heart attack. Any chance Lee could be behind it?" I ask.

Harding stares out over the property as she mulls that over. "You think Lee killed Frank?"

"It's possible."

"I'll look into it," she says.

"Harding, there's something back behind the barn you need to see," Rover says. "I saw it when I was trying to bust into the barn."

"Mind waiting here for a moment?" she asks.

I nod.

Sarina pulls away from my arms and turns to Stormy. "Thank you. You don't look like my dad but thank you for doing this."

Stormy grins. "I'm just glad this worked out"

"Yes, thank you," Melanie says.

"I don't know, Sarina. I think Stormy here resembles your dad quite a bit," I say while biting back my laugh.

Stormy shakes his head. "No, I don't, I would have to be fifty. I'm not fucking fifty."

I grin. "Well, you certainly passed for fifty for Lee."

Stormy mutters under his breath. "I just happen to have a little gray hair."

Melanie sniffles, wipes her eyes, and smiles at Stormy. "You know salt and pepper hair is sexy."

I cough to stifle my laugh.

Stormy arches a brow. "Uh. Thank you."

"Melanie, baby! Can you help me out?" Lee shouts from the car.

"I said shut the fuck up," Winston says.

Melanie turns her back to the car. "I think we should go," she says.

Harding walks back with Rover.

"Have any of you been in the woods behind the barn?"

We all shake our heads.

"Good. It looks like there might be two bodies buried back there. I'm going to call it in."

"The PV Transport driver said there were four men who ambushed them, and we haven't been able to find the other two," Rover says.

Harding nods. "I'll keep Stormy posted if it's related."

"Is there any chance we can take Sarina and Melanie home? They've been through a lot," I ask.

Harding nods. "Sure, but I'll want to question each of you later."

"Thank you," I say.

"I'll ride with you," Melanie says to Stormy.

Stormy glances uncomfortably to Rover. "Rover, I'll drive you, too."

Rover grins. "You sure? I could ride with Maverick."

"Get in the damn car," Stormy says.

I turn back to Sarina. "Are you hurt?"

She shakes her head. "Just shaken up. Let's go to your place."

I pull her close and walk her to the car.

"It's all over now, right? Now that Lee has been caught?"

"They can't hold me. I'll get a lawyer and sue their asses!" Lee shouts.

I walk Sarina away from the area and toward the road.

"They have enough to put Lee away for a long time," I say.

Hopefully Harding will find out from Lee who his contact at PV Transport is. Then it will all be over.

CHAPTER 32

Sarina

From the moment Donny spotted me at the property, he hasn't taken his hands off me. It's as if he has to hold on. If he lets go, I'll fly away. I'm appreciative of it all. He's my lifeline. When Lee led me and Melanie into the barn, my eyes went straight to the tools he had in there. A hatchet, an ax, some other sharp tools that I have no idea what they are for, but it looked like a torture chamber. My initial thought was that Melanie and I weren't making it out alive. We could identify Lee. Or Noel. All of the stories Melanie told me flashed in my head while I was tied up. She really thought he was the one. I can't imagine the agony she's going through.

I glance over at her. She's smiling at Stormy as they walk to his car, but it's fake. I know her well enough to know that. And her flirting with the man, I'd bet my paycheck she only did it to convince us that she's fine.

"Melanie," I call to her.

She turns to me, smiling.

"Are you all right?"

She walks over to me and puts her hand on my arm. "Not really but I will be. I know this might sound weird but if there was anyone in the world I could be kidnapped with, I'm glad it was you. I think I would have passed out from panic with anyone else."

I reach over and give her a hug.

"Me, too. You're my best friend and I'm so sorry you got stuck in the tension between me and Norah."

"Oh honey, I know." She smiles. "I know you keep your walls up and I shouldn't have pushed you into anything involving Norah. I'm sorry."

"Well, my walls are coming down when it comes to you. We could have died today."

"And it would have been my fault. I'm so sorry!"

Tears well in her eyes.

"No, it wasn't your fault. Lee lied to you."

She nods.

"Do you want to come with us?" I motion toward Donny.

"No. You two go. I'll be fine."

I nod, unsure if she is telling the truth. But I'm so raw right now. She's probably better off with Stormy and Rover.

On the drive to his place, Donny is silent, but he keeps a firm grip on my hand. I appreciate it. The last thing I want is to be grilled on what happened as I'm still processing it all.

He parks in his driveway then leads me inside.

"Let's go bandage up your cut," he says.

Cut? I frown.

"On your forehead."

I reach for it, and he stops me.

"You can see in the mirror. I want to clean it up first."

He leads me to the bathroom, and I'm surprised by the image staring back at me in the mirror. I had been tossed in the trunk so that explains the black streaks of dirt across my face. On my forehead is a cut. Not deep enough to need stitches but enough that I should have been aware of it.

He pulls out some cotton pads and rubbing alcohol.

"This will sting a bit," he says, then dabs at the cut. I wince.

"Sorry. I'll be quick."

I hold my breath as he finishes cleaning it up.

"They say if you take long slow breaths it helps reduce the pain."

I laugh. "That sounds like bullshit."

He shrugs. "Works for me."

I stare at this man. I don't know much about his time in the service, but I suspect he's had his fair share of injuries. The telltale scars scattered on his body indicate that.

He unwraps a bandage and adheres it to my forehead. Then he leans forward and kisses my temple.

"Good as new."

"Thank you. Any chance I could get a glass of wine?"

Donny frowns. "That's not a good idea. You might have a concussion."

"I don't have one, I promise. Just a cut."

He stares at me for a beat.

"Really. I'm fine."

"Sarina, when you called me and then Lee got on the phone..."

He closes his eyes and when he opens them again, I'm surprised to see wetness.

"I let you down and I'm so sorry."

I reach out and run my hand along his cheek. "Donny, no. You didn't let me down. You saved me."

He shakes his head. "I shouldn't have had to save you. I should have been with you then this never would have happened."

I place my other hand on his other cheek and force him to look at me.

"If you had gone with me, Lee would have shot you. He told me that as he showed me his gun. Then I'd be worse off."

"He wouldn't have."

"And before you say you would have gotten him first, remember this was supposed to be a nice day at Melanie's. Neither one of us had any reason to be on guard."

He places his hands over mine. "All I know is I almost lost you. Again."

The determined look in his eyes has me nervous. "Well, I don't plan on getting kidnapped a third time. I mean if I was, I think I would qualify for the *Guinness World Records*."

I smile, hoping to make light of the moment.

"Sarina, I know this is fast, but I want you to move in with me."

Move in?

"Donny, I appreciate that you want to protect me, but you can't keep an eye on me all the time."

He brushes a lock of hair behind my ear as he smiles. "Sarina, I'm not asking you to move in so I can keep tabs on you. I'm asking because what I feel for you is strong. I know you're it for me."

I'm not sure what to say. He's it for me too. I know this is going fast but it feels right.

His smile falls. "I don't mean to pressure you. You can think about it if you need to."

"No."

His brows pull together.

"I don't need to think about it. I'd love to move in with you. If you're sure about it."

His smile is huge, and he picks me up at the waist and spins me around. Then his lips meet mine.

When he pulls back, he's still smiling.

"Oh, I'm sure."

"I agree it's fast, but it feels right," I say.

"It feels very right."

He leans in and kisses me again but this time he doesn't pull away. I deepen the kiss. I love this man and I want to show him in every way.

I reach for the hem of his T-shirt and pull it up. He takes the hint and pulls it off over his head with one arm. Then I reach for his belt.

He grins and picks me up and tosses me over his shoulder.

I laugh then smack his ass.

"Where are you taking me?"

I feel the deep rumble of his laughter. Instead of answering, he takes me to his bedroom and lays me on his bed. Then he climbs over me and kisses my neck in a way that sends goosebumps all over my body.

I wrap my arms around his neck and inhale his scent. I want to remember everything about this moment. He lifts his head and stares into my eyes.

"I love you," he says.

"I love you, too. But I'd love you more if you were naked." I wink for effect.

He laughs as he sits up. "All right but this needs to come off first." He gently pulls at my sweater. I nod.

He stands up and undoes his belt and for a moment I don't move. This man is the sexiest man, and his intense gaze has me frozen with desire as he takes off his pants and boxer briefs.

Then he quirks a brow. I quickly strip down to my panties and bra and stand next to him.

"Fuck, you're so beautiful."

Then he leans down and pushes my bra down exposing a nipple that he then takes into his mouth. He looks up at me mischievously as he sucks on it, and I feel the wetness pooling between my legs. One look from this man can turn me into a pile of mush.

He pops his mouth off and lowers me to the bed.

"There is so much I want to do to you right now, but I really need to be inside you," he says as he leans over me.

"Yes, please." I run my nails gently down his back.

He closes his eyes and takes a breath. Then he opens them. He pulls my panties off and then his fingers are on my clit moving back and forth. It doesn't take much and I'm right there. But then he stops.

I frown. "Don't stop."

He leans over to this nightstand and grabs a condom. He puts it on quickly then is back over me.

"I want to feel you come on my cock."

He lines up at my entrance. "Are you ready?"

I wrap my legs around his waist and nod.

He thrusts in all at once. I groan, loving the feeling of this man inside me. But after a moment, I need him to move. I buck up to give him the hint.

He smiles and begins to move in and out slowly. He doesn't take his eyes off of me. The love emanating from his eyes is intense. Almost too intense. I can feel tears welling. The emotions I feel for him are stronger than anything I've ever felt.

He stills. "What's wrong?"

I shake my head. "Nothing. I just love you so much."

He takes my lips in a scorching kiss and his fingers find my clit. He rocks me over the edge, and I can't help moaning into our kiss. A few strokes later he pushes in and breaks our kiss as he groans, finding his release.

He then presses his forehead to mine.

"I love you so much too, Sarina. And I can't wait until you are moved in, and we can do this every night."

He gets up and takes care of the condom.

"Every night?" I shout to him in the bathroom.

He walks back into the bedroom and shrugs. "It's good to have goals to aim for."

He crawls back into bed but his smile falls. "Maybe not every night. I'll have to leave for assignments sometimes. Stormy said we have one coming up in a few days."

I trace his ab muscles. The man's body is so damn sexy.

"How long will you be gone?"

"We think a week."

I move my gaze to his eyes.

"I'll be fine, you know."

He nods and pulls me into his arms.

"I know. It's just after everything that's happened, I'm a little overprotective."

I snuggle in. "I get it. But I'll be fine."

"I'm going to leave you with all the numbers of some of the guys and Shaw just in case you need to call anyone."

"Thank you. And I have Shaw's number. I owe her a lunch really soon. I can't believe I took her car."

He squeezes me. "She's not upset about that. We're all just happy you're okay."

"I'm just happy to be here with you."

"Me too."

That's when sleep finds me. When I'm wrapped up secure in Donny's arms.

CHAPTER 33

DONNY

AS TRAX DRIVES, my mind wanders to Sarina. This was my first assignment away from her and I'm nervous about how she'll react when I get home. It was only a week so if that was too long for her, we will have a problem.

"I got a text from Peaches that a new guy started at the office while we were gone."

"Cody?"

Rover told me the guy he'd been working on a case with was hoping to transfer to our team.

"I heard his name is Pig Pen."

I laugh. "Yeah. That's the same guy. Rover knows him. Says he's from California and we'll like him."

Trax nods. "As long as Rover vouches for him, I'm good."

We pull up in front of my house and I stare at it for a moment.

"This is your first time away since you two have been together, isn't it?" Trax asks.

I take a deep breath. "It is."

"You worried she's going to tell you she doesn't like it?"

I nod. "A little bit."

"Well, I don't think she's going to complain about you being gone so I wouldn't worry. If I were her, I'd complain about you coming home."

I turn to see him wearing a shit-eating grin. "Thanks a lot."

"Anytime."

I open the door and step out.

"Hey," Trax calls. "Almost forgot to mention, CT is having a party tonight to welcome the new guy. Will I see you two there?"

While all I want to do is stay home with Sarina, I know it's a good idea to go and give her a chance to get to know the guys better.

"Sure. I'll see you there."

As I walk to the front door, the smell of pine is strong. That's when I spot a bucket of pinecones. I bend down and sure enough, they're the source.

I open the door and almost don't recognize the place. Christmas music is playing and the smell of something fresh baked is in the air. But what really catches my attention is the large six-foot tree in the middle of my living room that is fully decorated.

"Donny! You're home!" Sarina says as she runs to me.

The moment she reaches me, I lift her up and spin her around kissing her. On the entire flight back, she was all I could think of. Everything we'd been through, and I am so thankful to have her in my arms now. And if she'll have me, I'll hold her always.

She pulls back with a smile. "I hope you don't mind but I got in the Christmas spirit."

I chuckle. "I don't mind. But how did you get this tree in here?"

"My brother actually. He's still feeling guilty about leaving for the Thanksgiving holiday. Especially after he heard that Lee kidnapped me again. So, he called and said he had some time off if I needed anything."

I watch her. She's smiling.

"And I'm happy he did. We were able to really talk. It's good."

I'm still not certain about her relationship with her brother. But as long as she's happy and they're getting along, that's all I can ask for.

"What's baking? It smells great."

"Chocolate chip cookies. Later we can make sugar cookies and decorate them."

She spins around and walks toward the kitchen. I follow her. Up on the counter, she has an assortment of snow globes and hanging off the oven handle is a red towel with a candy cane pattern.

"You're really into Christmas, aren't you?"

She smiles. "I am."

"And you really think we can eat all these cookies?"

"Of course not. I figured we could share with your team. Plus, Shaw called to tell me a new guy started last week and he's bringing his girlfriend to CT's party tonight."

"Wait, you know about CT's party?"

"Yes, Shaw wanted to make sure I'd be there to welcome Lucy."

"Lucy?"

"Cody's girlfriend. Shaw said he's the guy Rover was working with recently."

"Yes, Rover called it the babysitting job."

"Babysitting?" she asks.

"Yeah, Rover was asked to help another guy basically

babysit an administrator from Havenwood University. But then they lost him."

She pulls a cookie sheet out of the oven and my mouth is watering over the sweet smell.

"They lost him?" she asks.

"Apparently he escaped while at the hospital and last I knew no one had heard from him since."

She removes the oven mitt then turns off the oven before spinning back to face me.

"Well, you can ask Cody all about it later today."

Then she stalks toward me. "But that's later. Right now, I need to welcome you home."

She snakes her arms around my neck.

"Is that so?" I love the smirk on her face.

"It is. But first, tell me, do you like the decorations? Or is it too much?"

While holding her in my arms, I spin us around to take it all in.

"I love it. This is the first time my house has really felt like a home. Thank you."

I lean down and kiss her.

Pulling back, I add, "and thank you for moving in. I don't want to spend any more time away from you than I have to."

"Good. Because I feel the same way."

Sarina

I SPOT Shaw right away as we walk into CT's. The first thing I notice is the men are missing.

Shaw must see me looking around because she laughs.

"One thing you'll learn right away: the men all gather at

the grill. Apparently, they're all grill experts and any time someone uses the grill, they must all be out there to give their full opinions on what the hell the others are doing wrong."

Donny laughs then leans in and kisses my cheek. "It's true. I better get out there before CT ruins the burgers."

I shake my head as I stare out the window at the covered porch that eight men are crowded onto. My gaze then moves to the kitchen I'm standing in. The last time I was here, I was so focused on the outdoor tent that I didn't take it all in. It's large and gorgeous. There's a six-burner stove and double ovens. If I had to guess, I'd say CT loves to cook.

"Sarina, I'd like you to meet Lucy. Lucy is here with Cody. He's the new guy on the team. Lucy, this is Sarina. She's with Maverick."

"Nice to meet you," I say, holding out my hand.

She shakes it. "Nice to meet you, too."

"Cody? Is that his call name?" I ask, suspecting it isn't.

Lucy laughs. "No. It's Pig Pen."

I glance at Shaw who shrugs. "Pig Pen like the one in the *Peanuts* cartoon?"

"That's the one."

A beautiful blond woman pops out from the hallway. "I heard the door. Is he here?" she asks then her eyes land on me.

"Connie is Lucy's friend. Connie, this is Sarina."

Connie smiles. "Hi, nice to meet you."

"She's hoping to see Dax."

"No, I'm not," Connie says.

I frown. "Dax?"

Shaw leans toward me. "Rover."

"Oh. Sorry, I guess I don't know all their real names."

"That's fine. I'm sure they'll answer to both," Shaw says.

Then I remember what Donny mentioned on the way over.

"Oh, I'm afraid Rover won't make it. He had something come up with his family."

Connie smiles. "Good, now I can relax. I'm going to get a drink. Do you guys want anything?" She steps to the kitchen counter and pours herself a glass of wine.

"No, I'm fine," I say. While the wine does sound good, I know if I have one in the middle of the day, I'll be asleep before dinner.

Lucy watches her friend but doesn't say anything. I don't know Rover that well, but the man is a good-looking guy and I'm sure many women would love his attention. But it looks like he pissed off Connie somehow.

"Lucy, have you and Cody been together long?"

She laughs. "Well about a week this time."

"This time?"

"We were high school sweethearts. It's a long story but Cody lost his chance to go to college and enlisted. Without telling me. He broke it off and I didn't see him again until this year."

"Wow. And you just reconnected?"

"No, it wasn't that easy. But we're together now."

Shaw pours herself a glass of wine and leans against the counter.

"That sounds an awful lot like what happened to me, too. Josh…" Then she glances at me. "Cowboy and I were dating the summer between high school and college. I thought he was it. But then he left and enlisted. Broke my heart."

"But you two are together now," Lucy says.

"Years after he left, I was assigned an estate matter at a new firm I worked for. The matter involved Josh. Things weren't easy, but we managed to find our way back to each other."

Shaw glanced out the window. "It looks like the burgers will be done soon. CT wanted to get everyone fed right away so then we could all relax."

She grabbed a stack of plates from the cupboard and set them on the counter.

"What can I do?" I ask.

Shaw points to the fridge. "Can you grab the platter in there? It has the cheese, lettuce, and onions."

I open the fridge and sure enough, there is a platter with everything already prepared.

Peaches walks in from the back deck.

"What are you lovely ladies up to?" he asks.

"Lucy, this is Peaches. He's a huge flirt but he's harmless," Shaw says.

"Lucy? You must be here with Cody." He smiles. "He sure is a lucky man." Peaches then takes her hand and kisses the back of it.

"Don't even think of doing that shit with my woman," Donny says as he walks inside next.

Peaches turns to me. "He's just jealous because he doesn't have an ounce of my charm." Peaches winks but I'm certain it's more for Donny's benefit than mine. I can't help but smile.

Out of nowhere, a man with a twang sings from Peaches back pocket. Something about peach picking time.

Peaches grabs his phone out of his back pocket. "Damn it! Who did this?"

"What is that?" I ask.

"Sounds like Merle Haggard to me," Shaw says grinning.

Peaches' head shoots up. "This is country, isn't it? Damn it! I knew it. Cowboy did this, didn't he?"

Peaches storms out the back door toward Cowboy and Shaw laughs.

"I'm positive it isn't Cowboy but, man, whoever keeps changing his ring tone, thank you," Donny says laughing.

I walk up to Donny and whisper in his ear. "Is it you?"

He's still laughing. "No. I wish I could pull something like that off. The man always has his phone, so I don't know how they're doing it. But it's great."

"How do you know it isn't Josh?" Shaw asks.

"He's hardly ever in the office and that thing changes every couple of days."

Three small boys come running into the kitchen.

"Mommy, the movie's over. Can we watch another?"

Then one of the boys notices Donny.

"Maverick! Can you draw another picture for us?" the taller boy asks.

"Yes! Please!" the smaller one echoes.

"Boys, Maverick is busy," Shaw says.

"Actually, I don't mind. Let me find some paper," he says as he walks toward a drawer in the other end of the kitchen. He pulls out a paper and pencil and begins sketching.

Fox comes in next. "You guys should hear Peaches out there. He's convinced Cowboy has been messing with his phone." The man shakes his head. "CT will be in soon with the burgers."

The taller boy runs over to Shaw holding a picture. "Look Mommy!"

I catch a glimpse of a fluffy dog. It's quite good and I know Donny must've drawn it fast.

"Wow, that's good," I say.

He shrugs.

"Whatever. Just stay away from my phone," Peaches says as he walks back into the kitchen with Cowboy right behind him. A tall dark-haired man that I don't recognize follows and immediately goes to Lucy, wrapping an arm around her waist. I glance out the window and notice Trax standing near

CT but staring at his phone. Then he shakes his head, puts it in his pocket and says something to CT who is putting the last of the burgers onto a plate.

A song erupts from Peaches rear end again. This time it's different, but it's still about peaches.

Peaches reaches for the phone and stares at it. His face getting redder by the minute. He glances at Cowboy who is standing there, no way he could have touched the man's phone.

"I'll find out which one of you assholes is doing this and you'll pay."

"Daddy! Uncle Peaches swore!"

Peaches rolls his eyes. "Sorry. Here, for the curse jar." He takes his wallet out of his pocket and pulls a dollar out then hands it to the older boy.

"Keep this up and you'll put him through college," Cowboy says with a grin.

CHAPTER 34

SARINA

"WAS STORMY THERE?" Melanie asks me the moment I step off the elevator into the office Monday morning.

Melanie has been asking me about Stormy ever since she met him.

"He was. Briefly."

"Did you mention me?" she asks.

"And how would I have done that? 'Oh, by the way, my friend likes you.'"

Melanie clapped. "Yes, that. Exactly that."

I laugh. "Were you stalking the elevator just to ask me that?"

We turn into my office, and she closes the door.

"No, I was trying to catch you because Jim came in early in a shit mood, then left carrying a box saying he's taking the week off."

That's odd for Jim. But since Christmas is this weekend, it should be a slow week around here anyway.

"Thanks for the heads up. Hopefully nothing comes up. I have the Allen deadline tomorrow that I intend to make. I'm not working over the Christmas holiday this year."

Last year I didn't mind. But this year, I have plans with Donny that I don't want to miss.

"Okay, I'll make sure no one disturbs you then." Melanie leaves, closing the door behind her.

A few hours later, I'm wrapping up to head to lunch when Melanie opens my door.

"Sarina, I'm so sorry to bother you but Doug isn't here, and the front desk says they need a VP level to approve some visitors."

Doug is the CFO and he had mentioned he'd be entertaining some clients at lunch today. But visitors that need VP level approval. That's odd.

"Did Jim have something on his calendar he forgot about?"

"I asked his assistant and he said no."

I stand and follow Melanie down to the first floor where I'm confronted by several men and women all dressed in black. Most have on jackets that say CIA on the back.

"What's going on?"

"Sarina?" Agent Harding steps forward. "You may remember me."

It's the woman that took down Lee. "I do. Thank you for your help with Lee."

She nods. "We need to locate Jim Albright."

"Jim? I was told he left this morning stating he was taking the week off. He's probably at home."

She shakes her head. "He's not. But regardless, I have a warrant to search his office."

She hands me a piece of paper. "But you don't have Asher Vaughn clearance to go up there." I'm trying to read the paper but it's all jumbling together.

Why do they need to search Jim's office?

"Sarina, can I see that?"

I turn to find Evelyn, our General Counsel at my side. I hand her the paper and she scans it.

"Sarina, you will need to escort them to Jim's office. They have a right to search his office and only his office."

She hands the paper back to the agent.

"Thank you," Harding says to Evelyn.

"Follow me."

We all somehow manage to fit into an elevator. Once the doors open, I walk to Jim's office. They follow behind me in silence.

His door is closed, and his assistant is away from his desk.

I open the door and am surprised to see most of his belongings are gone. He didn't have much but there were some photos of him with some celebrities on his bookshelf.

"Sarina, can you please wait in your office?" Harding asks.

"Can you at least tell me what this is about?" I ask.

The woman shakes her head. "All I can tell you is that this is a matter of national security."

National security? Damn it, Jim. You better not have shared company secrets with one of your hookups.

I nod and turn. The other agents have filed into the office making it feel smaller and more cramped than usual.

Once I exit the room, they close the door. I walk to Melanie's desk where she's standing staring in my direction.

"Do you have any idea what is going on?" I ask.

Melanie shrugs.

Ten minutes later, Jim's office door opens. Agent Harding runs down the hall with her phone to her ear.

"Where'd you find him?" she asks. "Great. We'll be right there."

All of the agents follow her and pile back into the elevator. As soon as the doors close, the fourth floor is blanketed in silence.

I walk into Jim's office and every drawer is open. I realize his computer is missing. Did they take it? Had he?

I sent a text to Donny asking if he knows what is going on.

He responds right away that he doesn't but he'll find out.

* * *

Four hours later, I haven't heard from Donny. Our CFO, Doug, nor Evelyn have no idea what is going on. We're all on edge.

I work as much as I can because I'm serious when I say I have no intention of coming in here over the holiday weekend coming up.

My phone rings and I jump.

Donny.

"Hey, I hope you have news."

He sighs. "I do. It's not good."

I lean back in my chair bracing myself.

"Jim is being held on suspicion that he's the mastermind behind the stolen laser weapon system fiasco."

I laugh. "I'm sorry. But Jim? He's no mastermind."

"According to Harding, he is. Lee finally told them everything he knew in exchange for some deal. It was Jim that recruited Frank. Frank recruited Lee. According to Lee, both he and Frank thought Jim was an idiot."

I'm hearing the words, but I can't believe it. "But why would Jim do that? It doesn't make sense."

"Lee says that Jim kept bitching about Asher Vaughn not appreciating him and how he was going to get what he deserved."

What he deserved? Jim is a terrible CEO and apparently delusional too.

"And he thought he deserved how ever much money he thought he could get for this weapon?"

"I'm sure Harding is asking that question. There's more."

I brace myself. I'm not sure how much more I can take.

"The CIA believes Jim is responsible for Frank's death too."

I rub my temple. "I thought Frank had a heart attack."

Although Norah swore up and down Frank was murdered.

"The results from the autopsy came back. Frank was poisoned."

Damn. Norah was right.

Jim is a killer?

I reach for my bottle of water and take a sip.

"Do you think Norah was working with Jim?" he asks.

I nearly choke. Why the hell would she work with Jim? I'm about to ask him this when I remember her yelling at him. She had an affair with the man, and I wasn't any wiser until she basically told the office.

But Norah has been the one pushing for the autopsy. "You think Norah helped kill her father? That doesn't make sense. Why wouldn't she just accept it was a heart attack then?"

Donny sighs. "You're right. I'm just struggling with the idea that Norah was innocent in all of this."

"As angry as I am with her, I think she is. I think she was too focused on how to get my job."

"I'm sorry. Are you almost done for the day? Do you want me to come pick you up?"

I stare at my inbox. "No. I have a few more things I need to take care of. But thank you."

"If you change your mind, just call. I love you."

"I love you, too."

I set my phone down. I need to talk to Melanie to help process all of this. But when I open my door, I spot Norah at Melanie's desk crying.

Slowly I walk over.

"I feel so dumb," Norah says to Melanie.

"Norah, none of this is your fault."

Norah blows her nose. "But it is. I introduced Jim to my dad! Then he killed him. I was so stupid."

Melanie notices me approaching.

"You think Jim killed your father?" I ask.

Donny just told me this. How would Norah know already?

Norah nods. "I just got the autopsy results. My dad was poisoned." Norah sobs harder.

Melanie glances at me.

"I knew it had to be Jim. My dad was so happy when he was released on bail. He told me he thought he was going to rot in jail so he blackmailed Jim to hire him the best attorney he could. And Jim must have."

I lean against Melanie's desk. Jim really was the one behind it all. I still can't believe it.

"That morning I found my dad, he'd texted me an hour before asking me to stop by a little later than planned because he was meeting with Jim."

Melanie hugs Norah. I can't stop thinking about something she said.

"Why would you introduce Jim to your dad?" I ask.

Norah swallows. "Jim said he wanted to meet him, and I thought it was because he wanted to propose and you know, get my dad's blessing first. I know. I sound pathetic."

Melanie wraps an arm around her shoulder. "No, you don't sound pathetic. Jim lied to you. That isn't your fault."

"It is my fault. I fell for his lies!"

I cross my arms. "Did you know your dad was involved in the missing weapon?"

Norah pulls away from Melanie.

"No! I would have turned him in myself."

Norah grabs a tissue from the box on Melanie's desk and sobs into it.

Am I a bad person for wondering if Norah is really upset or if this is a performance? In the short time I've known Norah, I've never seen her show much emotion.

"I'm sorry," Norah says wiping her eyes. "I'll let you both get back to work. I'm going to head home."

Melanie gives her one last hug then Norah turns and leaves.

Once she's on the elevator, Melanie turns to me.

"So, do we believe her?"

"You don't?" Frankly, I'm shocked. Melanie was so consoling.

"I don't know what to believe anymore."

She crosses her arms and I realize that while Norah may have lied to me, Melanie has been through hell with what Noel did to her.

"Neither do I."

"Jim seemed like too big of an idiot to pull off something like this."

"Well, he didn't pull it off. Everyone was caught."

I stare at the elevator Norah just took. At least I hope so.

CHAPTER 35

Donny

"Thanks for meeting with me. I know it's Christmas Eve, but I thought you'd want to hear this," Cowboy says as CT and I enter the conference room. Rover is already sitting at the table.

"Cowboy, good to see you," I say. "Thank you again for helping out Sarina."

I'm grateful for what he and Shaw did.

"Anytime you guys need anything, I'm here."

CT glances around. "Yeah, what did you do to Stormy?"

Cowboy laughs. "He's having a rough day, so I told him I'd come in and talk to you guys."

"Rough day? Is he okay?" Rover asks.

Cowboy laughs. "He's fine. You'll see for yourself later."

"Should we call the rest of the guys in?" CT asks.

"No, this is about the Asher Vaughn case. According to Agent Harding, Lee said there was one thing he never understood."

"Just one?" CT asks. "Sorry, but he didn't seem like the brightest guy."

"He said when he met with Frank, Jim, and a couple of Frank's guys, Jim handed him a hoodie and said he needed to wear it when everything went down."

Fucking Jim. "He was the one that bought it with Sarina's credit card."

Cowboy nodded. "Looks like he set her up from the beginning."

"And he had access to her office and her purse at all times."

Why hadn't I thought of that?

"Please tell me they have Jim for Frank's murder. I want that fucker to rot in jail," I say.

Cowboy shakes his head. "Unfortunately, no. They searched Jim's place but didn't find the poison. While they are certain he did it, they don't have anything connecting Jim to Frank the morning he died, aside from Norah swearing Jim was the last person to see her dad. Jim swears that Norah wanted her dad dead so she could have his money. It turns out Norah was named on an account of Frank's."

"Suspects with no evidence," Rover says.

"According to Harding, they have plenty of evidence to connect Jim to the theft of the weapon. He's going away for a long time," Cowboy says.

I glance at CT who is frowning. "How could Norah come into money? Wasn't all of Frank's cash seized?"

"Apparently he'd set up a trust for her years ago. The CIA doesn't have any proof that it was set up with nefarious funds."

"How much are we talking?"

Cowboy leans back. "Five hundred dollars."

CT frowns. "That's it?"

"Apparently there had been more in it earlier this year but Frank withdrew it. But that money seemed to just vanish."

"How much was withdrawn?" CT asks.

"Just under ten million dollars."

"Ten million dollars is simply missing?" CT asks as he runs his hands through his hair. "There has to be a paper trail."

"Harding and her team are looking," Stormy says.

My mind is racing. Did Frank already get the money to Norah? Does she know more than she let on? Or is she really just an innocent, clueless cat lady?

"There's more," Cowboy says as he leans forward. "Lee gave up the name of the other two guys who they worked with on this job."

"Did you find them?" I ask.

Cowboy nods. "Their bodies were found buried on Frank's property off paradise road."

"Did Frank kill them?" CT asks.

"Lee claims Frank did. Harding isn't so sure so they're waiting on some more tests to come back to confirm. But they do have Lee for the deaths of the PV Transport employees."

I lean back in my chair. "It sounds like it's finally over. Jim and Lee will be in prison for a long time. The rest of the guys are dead. Sarina is finally safe."

Cowboy nods. "Yes, she's finally safe."

Relief washes over me.

"Hey, you guys going to be in there all day or are you ready to get your asses beat?" Peaches asks from the doorway. "We'll all waiting on you."

Cowboy shakes his head. "We're done. Go have fun."

"You're winning in your dreams, Peaches!" CT says as he runs out the door.

"Hey," I say turning back to Cowboy. "Did Harding ever

mention how Frank and Lee knew where the transport would be?"

Cowboy shook his head. "No. She didn't."

Rover and I walk out to the back patio where everyone else is geared up and waiting.

I glance over at Sarina who is all decked out in camouflage and laugh to myself. These guys don't know it, but she has several layers on and is ready for this.

"Where's Lucy?" Peaches asks Cody.

"Right here," she calls. Her outfit matches Sarina's.

Cody grins. "Wow. You look hot."

Peaches rolls his eyes. "Save it for the bedroom, Pig Pen."

"You know if Stormy doesn't get here soon, we should start without him," Trax says.

It isn't like him to be late, and I know we're all thinking that.

"Cowboy said he's having a rough day. Anyone know what's going on?" I ask.

Before anyone can answer, the back door opens, and out walks Stormy. Or at least I think it is Stormy. He looks different.

"Holy shit! He colored his hair," CT says.

He's right. The gray is gone. He looks younger.

"You dyed your hair?" Rover asks, his mouth hanging open in surprise.

"I don't want to hear a word about it. Now have you guys divided into teams?" Stormy asks.

"We have. I'm captain of the red team and we have Pig Pen, Lucy, Trax, Fox, and myself. CT is captain of the blue team, and he has Sarina, Maverick, Rover, and now Stormy," Peaches says.

"Okay, you all know the rules. The last person standing wins for their team," Stormy says. "We start in five minutes when the bell goes off."

Peaches sets the timer on the loud bell we use for this game.

"And it's set. Go!"

"What do we do?" Lucy asks.

"Hide. Because when that bell goes off, it will be a free-for-all," Cody says taking her hand and leading her off into the woods.

I turn to ask Sarina which way she wants to go but she's already gone. I chuckle to myself.

I lodge myself behind a tree just in time. The bell goes off and I slowly and quietly creep around the tree.

"Shit!" I hear Rover shout followed by someone giggling. It must be Lucy. That means she got Rover.

I creep toward where I heard Rover shout.

"I'm out!" Stormy announces.

What the hell? That was fast. I spot Lucy and take aim. Just as I fire, Cody shouts, "Get down!" and Lucy falls to the ground as my shot sails past her. Missed.

But that was a mistake on Cody's part because now I know where he is. I creep up behind him and take my shot.

He spins around to see me.

"Gotcha."

Fox storms past covered in blue paint. "I never even saw her."

"Neither did I," Peaches says following him.

Damn. My Sarina is good. But that's the last thought I have before I'm splattered in red paint. I glance up and see a huge smile on Lucy's face as she runs back into the woods.

I can hear Lucy running and know it is just a matter of time before she's taken out.

I make my way to the back deck of MTS and sit down.

"Damn it!" Lucy calls. Well, that was fast.

"Your woman got me," she says as she sits on the bench just down from me.

"Well, this ought to be good. Trax versus Sarina," Peaches says rubbing his hands together.

I glance around. "Don't forget CT."

Peaches glances around. "That sneaky SOB always flies under my radar."

CT comes walking out of the woods next shaking his head.

"Damn Trax. That man is stealthy!" CT sits down and looks around. "Who's left?"

"Trax and Sarina," Rover says.

"She took out both me and Peaches," Fox says shaking his head.

"Damn! Maverick, you're a lucky man," CT says.

"I know."

After ten minutes and no sounds, I figure both are trying to outwait the other. Then I hear a twig snap, the pop of the paint gun, and then and Sarina yells. "Damn it! I would have had you if it weren't for that damn twig!"

A deep laugh comes out from the same area.

"You have to learn to glide through these woods if you want to beat me," Trax says as they walk out of the woods together.

"Oh please. One twig the entire game. Admit it. You had no idea where I was," Sarina says.

Trax meets my eyes. "You're right. I didn't."

I give him a nod. I know damn well he knew exactly where she was at all times. Trax is our best tracker. And that's why he always wins this damn game. But I appreciate what he did. He made Sarina's day.

"Great game guys. I really appreciate you all coming here on Christmas Eve to celebrate with our annual paintball game. Now, go have a wonderful Christmas and I'll see you all after the new year," Stormy says.

"Before everyone goes, I have an announcement," CT says.

The man looks serious and has everyone's attention.

"From here on, my new call name is Dom."

The group bursts into laughter.

"No, hear me out. Dom as in Dominate! It's a great name."

Peaches shakes his head. "CT, you can't change your call sign. Give it up."

"Oh shit! No way!" Rover shouts.

"What's going on?" I ask.

Rover glances up from his phone. "Rocco and Caite are coming back for a few days to enjoy the holiday season up here."

"When?" CT asks.

"Day after Christmas. They're staying through New Year's and want to make sure we can all get together while they are here," Rover says.

"Of course," I say.

"Leave it to me. I'll set something up," CT says.

I turn to find Sarina grinning at me. "I won."

"Yes, you did."

A few hours later, we are both cleaned up and sitting on my couch.

"Are you ready for tomorrow?" she asks.

Tomorrow is Christmas. And she'll be meeting my family for the first time. She's clearly nervous.

"I'm ready."

I know they'll love her. It's just how much shit they might give me. I've never brought a woman home for Christmas.

I'll be meeting her dad and brother the morning after Christmas. She patched things up with her brother and well, apparently, she tolerates her father. I've been debating whether to let her dad and brother know I plan to marry her.

I already bought the ring. But I'm not going to give it to

her just yet. Our relationship has moved fast, and I want her to be certain before we take the next step.

"What are you thinking so hard about over there?" she asks.

"You. Our future." I lean over and kiss her.

"Let's just hope you still want one after you meet my brother and Dad. They are a handful."

"I'm not worried," I say and kiss her again.

After what we've been through, anything else will be a walk in the park.

"I love you and nothing about your family will change that."

She grins. "That's good to hear. I love you too, Donny."

EPILOGUE

Dax "Rover" Adams

"That dress is fine," I say to my sister.

"No, this is New Year's Eve and I'm not wearing a cotton summer dress."

I roll my eyes. "Why is it even here then?"

"If you recall when I agreed to come over here, I packed fast. I wasn't thinking."

She clasps her hands together and gives me those doe eyes. "Please Dax?"

"Fine, we'll stop at the house on our way. Are you ready to go or do you need another hour to do your hair?"

She rolls her eyes. "I'm ready."

I'm silent on the drive over. We haven't been by the house this week since she came to my place and I have a bad feeling. I'm hoping CT's talk with John was enough. Darla said she hasn't seen him since that day. But something doesn't feel right.

I pull into the driveway and glance around. Nothing seems out of place. No strange cars on the street.

Darla goes into the house and I collect the mail. While I'm sorting it on the counter, my phone buzzes. A text from CT.

Fox: *Just found out there's evidence connecting Jim to Frank's death. I don't know the details but I'm assured he'll be going away for it. Thought you might want to give Sarina the good news.*

Dax: *How did you hear that?*

Fox: *Friend at the police department.*

I shake my head. He won't admit it but I know Fox has a thing for Detective McNamara. Whenever we need to work with the Pine Valley police, she's our contact.

I pocket my phone as my sister comes down the stairs wearing a very revealing red gown and really high heels.

"You've got to be kidding me," I say.

Her hands go to her hips. "What?"

"You're going to wear that around my friends?"

"Is there a problem?"

I wave my hand toward her chest. "Yeah, those things look like they are about to fall out."

She swats my hand. "They're fine. And I wanted to dress up like CT asked us too. Now let's go."

She grabs the pie we promised to bring and walks out the door.

As we walk to my car, I'm too focused on my sister's dress because I don't notice John until it's too late.

"Darla, I was just coming to get you." He's grinning as he walks toward us.

"What's he talking about?" I ask her.

"I don't know," she says.

"Dax! I'm happy you're here," John says.

John doesn't look happy. The man is glaring at me.

"John, what are you doing?" she asks.

John stares at me. "We had a good thing, Darla. Until your brother stuck his nose into our business. What he told you are all lies. He doesn't want you with anyone else."

Shit. I need to find out what my sister told him.

"John, my brother was just looking out for me."

Darla tried to step closer to John, but I grabbed the back of her coat and kept her close to me.

John laughs. "No, see right there. He wants to control you. He always has. Think about all those stories you told me when you were growing up. You have to stop letting him control your life, Darla."

"I don't control her, asshole," I say.

John turns his attention to Darla. "It's New Year's Eve. We should be together. Come with me honey."

I stare at my sister who is crying now. I know she wants to say no but the man is holding a gun on me.

"She's not going with you," I say.

John glares at me then turns his stare to Darla.

"Is that true?"

She nods.

He lowers the gun and shakes his head.

"I'm sorry Darla, but that's the wrong answer."

Before I can charge the man, he's lifted the gun again and aimed it at me. I jump to my right as a shot rings out.

The pain pierces through my side as I go down.

"Dax!" Darla shouts.

"Get in the car Darla!" he shouts at her.

"I'm not leaving my brother," she says.

"Oh yeah? Well maybe I should shoot him again and finish off the job." John lifts his gun again.

"No!" Darla shouts. "I'll go with you."

I try to stand but I can't. I can't stop them. There is nothing I can do but lie on the ground and breathe trying my best not to black out.

I hear two car doors and then the car tires screech away.

I reach in my pocket and find my phone. I dial 911.

"What's your emergency," an operator answers.

I tell her I've been shot and give the address.

I close my eyes but soon after I hear sirens in the distance. All I can do is lie here and wait. And think.

You should have killed me, John. Because I'm coming for you. We all are.

WANT to know what happens to Dax? His story is coming soon. Sign up here to receive an email notifying you of release.

BOOKS BY DANIELLE PAYS

MORGAN THOMPSON SECURITY TEAM

Morgan Thompson Security Series

Defending Sarina

Shielding Connie - Early 2022, Add to your TBR now!

* * *

Dare to Surrender Series

Chasing Her Trust

Taking Her Chase

Saving Her Target

Trusting Her Hero

* * *

Dare to Risk Series

Deceived

Pursued

Played

Consumed

* * *

Other Works

Steamy - A Steamy Romance Anthology (Paperback only)

Conceal - A Salvation Society Novel

Love is Coming to Town - A Christmas Anthology

To learn more about her books, please visit her website at https://daniellepays.com

ACKNOWLEDGMENTS

I want to thank Susan Stoker for allowing me to write in her Operation Alpha world. I absolutely loved her characters Rocco, Ace, Phantom, and Tex from the SEAL of Protection: Legacy series and was so excited to be able to use them in my story too. I also want to thank everyone at Aces Press for answering my numerous questions.

I want to give a huge thank you for my readers. I really appreciate your support!

To my betas readers Kerry, Caroline, Melissa, and Tesh, thank you.

Thank you to Furious Fotog/Golden Czermak for the fantastic cover photography. And to Maria @ Steamy Designs for the cover design.

Thank you to April Bennett, The Editing Soprano for all your editing and to ReGina Raham for proofreading.

ABOUT THE AUTHOR

Danielle Pays writes steamy romantic suspense with twists you won't see coming. She enjoys romance as well as mystery and suspense and blends them both using her beloved Pacific Northwest for inspiration with its mix of small towns and cities.

When not trying to write her characters into some kind of trouble, she can be found wrestling her new giant puppy into a harness, guzzling coffee at her kids' soccer games, or binging Netflix shows.

Want to Connect with Danielle?

Sign up for her newsletter and get a free short story.

https://BookHip.com/VPMFMCW

Facebook Reader Group: https://www.facebook.com/groups/DaniellePaysReaderGroup

Website: https://www.daniellepays.com

Facebook: https://www.facebook.com/daniellepays/

Instagram: https://www.instagram.com/daniellepays/

Bookbub:https://www.bookbub.com/authors/danielle-pays

Goodreads: https://www.goodreads.com/author/show/19241197.Danielle_Pays

Twitter: https://twitter.com/DaniellePays

facebook.com/daniellepays
twitter.com/DaniellePays
instagram.com/daniellepays
bookbub.com/authors/danielle-pays

There are many more books in this fan fiction world than listed here, for an up-to-date list go to www.AcesPress.com

You can also visit our Amazon page at: http://www.amazon.com/author/operationalpha

Special Forces: Operation Alpha World

Christie Adams: Charity's Heart
Denise Agnew: Dangerous to Hold
Shauna Allen: Awakening Aubrey
Linzi Baxter: Unlocking Dreams
Jennifer Becker: Hiding Catherine
Alice Bello: Shadowing Milly
Heather Blair: Rescue Me
Misha Blake: Flash
Anna Blakely: Rescuing Gracelynn
Julia Bright: Saving Lorelei
Cara Carnes: Protecting Mari
Kendra Mei Chailyn: Beast
Melissa Kay Clarke: Rescuing Annabeth
Samantha A. Cole: Handling Haven
Lorelei Confer: Protecting Sara
Anne Conley: Redemption for Misty
KaLyn Cooper: Rescuing Melina
Janie Crouch: Storm
Sarah Curtis: Securing the Odds
Jordan Dane: Redemption for Avery
Tarina Deaton: Found in the Lost
Aspen Drake, Intense
KL Donn: Unraveling Love
Riley Edwards: Protecting Olivia
PJ Fiala: Defending Sophie
Nicole Flockton: Protecting Maria

Alexa Gregory: Backdraft
Michele Gwynn: Rescuing Emma
Casey Hagen: Shielding Nebraska
Desiree Holt: Protecting Maddie
Kathy Ivan: Saving Sarah
Kris Jacen, Be With Me
Jesse Jacobson: Protecting Honor
Silver James: Rescue Moon
Becca Jameson: Saving Sofia
Kate Kinsley: Protecting Ava
Rayne Lewis: Justice for Mary
Heather Long: Securing Arizona
Margaret Madigan: Bang for the Buck
Ellie Masters: Sybil's Protector
Trish McCallan: Hero Under Fire
Kimberly McGath: The Predecessor
Rachel McNeely: The SEAL's Surprise Baby
KD Michaels: Saving Laura
Lynn Michaels: Rescuing Kyle
Olivia Michaels: Protecting Harper
Wren Michaels: The Fox & The Hound
Annie Miller: Securing Willow
Kat Mizera: Protecting Bobbi
Keira Montclair: Wolf and the Wild Scots
LeTeisha Newton: Protecting Butterfly
Angela Nicole: Protecting the Donna
MJ Nightingale: Protecting Beauty
Victoria Paige: Reclaiming Izabel
Anne L. Parks: Mason
Debra Parmley: Protecting Pippa
Lainey Reese: Protecting New York
KeKe Renée: Protecting Bria
TL Reeve and Michele Ryan: Extracting Mateo
Elena M. Reyes: Keeping Ava

Deanna L. Rowley: Saving Veronica
Angela Rush: Charlotte
Rose Smith: Saving Satin
Lynne St. James: SEAL's Spitfire
Dee Stewart: Conner
Harley Stone: Rescuing Mercy
Sarah Stone: Shielding Grace
Jen Talty: Burning Desire
Reina Torres, Rescuing Hi'ilani
Savvi V: Loving Lex
Megan Vernon: Protecting Us
LJ Vickery: Circus Comes to Town
Rachel Young: Because of Marissa
R. C. Wynne: Shadows Renewed

Delta Team Three Series

Lori Ryan: Nori's Delta
Becca Jameson: Destiny's Delta
Lynne St James, Gwen's Delta
Elle James: Ivy's Delta
Riley Edwards: Hope's Delta

Police and Fire: Operation Alpha World

Freya Barker: Burning for Autumn
B.P. Beth: Scott
Jane Blythe: Salvaging Marigold
Julia Bright, Justice for Amber
Anna Brooks, Guarding Georgia
KaLyn Cooper: Justice for Gwen
Aspen Drake: Sheltering Emma
Emily Gray: Shelter for Allegra
Alexa Gregory: Backdraft
Deanndra Hall: Shelter for Sharla
EM Hayes: Gambling for Ashleigh

India Kells: Shadow Killer
CM Steele: Guarding Hope
Reina Torres: Justice for Sloane
Aubree Valentine, Justice for Danielle
Maddie Wade: Finding English
Laine Vess: Justice for Lauren

Tarpley VFD Series

Silver James, Fighting for Elena
Deanndra Hall, Fighting for Carly
Haven Rose, Fighting for Calliope
MJ Nightingale, Fighting for Jemma
TL Reeve, Fighting for Brittney
Nicole Flockton, Fighting for Nadia

As you know, this book included at least one character from Susan Stoker's books. To check out more, see below.

<u>SEAL Team Hawaii Series</u>

Finding Elodie
Finding Lexie
Finding Kenna
Finding Monica (May 2022)
Finding Carly (Oct 2022)
Finding Ashlyn (TBA)
Finding Jodelle (TBA)

<u>Eagle Point Search & Rescue</u>

Searching for Lilly (Mar 2022)
Searching for Elsie (Jun 2022)
Searching for Bristol (Nov 2022)
Searching for Caryn (TBA)
Searching for Finley (TBA)
Searching for Heather (TBA)
Searching for Khloe (TBA)

<u>The Refuge Series</u>

Deserving Alaska (Aug 2022)
Deserving Henley (Jan 2023)
Deserving Reese (TBA)
Deserving Cora (TBA)
Deserving Lara (TBA)
Deserving Maisy (TBA)
Deserving Ryleigh (TBA)

<u>Delta Team Two Series</u>

Shielding Gillian
Shielding Kinley

Shielding Aspen
Shielding Jayme (novella)
Shielding Riley
Shielding Devyn
Shielding Ember
Shielding Sierra (Jan 2022)

SEAL of Protection: Legacy Series

Securing Caite (FREE!)
Securing Brenae (novella)
Securing Sidney
Securing Piper
Securing Zoey
Securing Avery
Securing Kalee
Securing Jane

Delta Force Heroes Series

Rescuing Rayne (FREE!)
Rescuing Aimee (novella)
Rescuing Emily
Rescuing Harley
Marrying Emily (novella)
Rescuing Kassie
Rescuing Bryn
Rescuing Casey
Rescuing Sadie (novella)
Rescuing Wendy
Rescuing Mary
Rescuing Macie (novella)
Rescuing Annie (Feb 2022)

Badge of Honor: Texas Heroes Series

Justice for Mackenzie (FREE!)

Justice for Mickie
Justice for Corrie
Justice for Laine (novella)
Shelter for Elizabeth
Justice for Boone
Shelter for Adeline
Shelter for Sophie
Justice for Erin
Justice for Milena
Shelter for Blythe
Justice for Hope
Shelter for Quinn
Shelter for Koren
Shelter for Penelope

SEAL of Protection Series

Protecting Caroline (FREE!)
Protecting Alabama
Protecting Fiona
Marrying Caroline (novella)
Protecting Summer
Protecting Cheyenne
Protecting Jessyka
Protecting Julie (novella)
Protecting Melody
Protecting the Future
Protecting Kiera (novella)
Protecting Alabama's Kids (novella)
Protecting Dakota

New York Times, *USA Today* and *Wall Street Journal* Bestselling Author Susan Stoker has a heart as big as the state of Tennessee where she lives, but this all American girl has also spent the last fourteen years living in Missouri, California,

Colorado, Indiana, and Texas. She's married to a retired Army man who now gets to follow *her* around the country.

www.stokeraces.com
www.AcesPress.com
susan@stokeraces.com

Made in the USA
Columbia, SC
20 November 2021

49400146R00170